GIRL 43

MAREE GILES

For Jaime

First published in Great Britain as *Invisible Thread* by Virago Press in 2001

Published in Australia and New Zealand in 2014
by Hachette Australia
(an imprint of Hachette Australia Pty Limited)
Level 17, 207 Kent Street, Sydney NSW 2000
www.hachette.com.au

The author gratefully acknowledges permission to reprint copyright material from the following:
Untitled Osip Mandelstam from *The Third Voronezh Notebook* © 1937.
Reproduced by kind permission of the Writers and Readers Publishing Cooperative Society Ltd., London.
Bib and Bub by May Gibbs. Reproduced by kind permission of HarperCollins Publishers Australia.
Mikhail Bulgakov: The Master and Margarita. First published in Great Britain in 1967 by Harvill. Copyright in the English translation © The Harvill Press and Harper and Row Publishers, 1967. Reproduced by kind permission of the Harvill Press.
Courage: J.M. Barrie © 1922. Reproduced by kind permission of Samuel French Ltd., on behalf of the Estate of J.M. Barrie.
All other material quoted is either in the public domain or the copyright holder has not been found. Every effort has been made to contact remaining copyright holders and to clear reprint permissions. If notified the publisher will be happy to rectify any omission in future editions.

All characters in this publication are fictitious and any resemblance to real persons, living or dead, is purely coincidental.

10 9 8 7 6 5 4 3 2 1

Copyright © Maree Giles 2001, 2014

This book is copyright. Apart from any fair dealing for the purposes of private study, research, criticism or review permitted under the *Copyright Act 1968*, no part may be stored or reproduced by any process without prior written permission. Enquiries should be made to the publisher.

National Library of Australia
Cataloguing-in-Publication data

Giles, Maree, author.

Girl 43/Maree Giles.

ISBN 978 0 7336 3321 8 (paperback)

A823.4

Cover design by Christabella Designs
Cover photograph courtesy of Trevillion
Author photo courtesy of Gareth Brown
Digital production by Bookhouse, Sydney
Printed and bound in Australia by Griffin Press, Adelaide, an Accredited ISO AS/NZS 14001:2009 Environmental Management System printer

MIX
Paper from responsible sources
FSC® C009448
www.fsc.org

The paper this book is printed on is certified against the Forest Stewardship Council® Standards. Griffin Press holds FSC chain of custody certification SGS-COC-005088. FSC promotes environmentally responsible, socially beneficial and economically viable management of the world's forests.

Note from The Author

'Researchers have argued that Australia has the highest rate of institutionalisation of children in the world. So how, as a nation, do we respond to this?'

Dr Adele Chynoweth, Curator and Researcher,
The Australian National University

When this book was first published in 2001 in London, the true nature of Parramatta Girls' Home in Sydney was a neglected piece of Australian history. The general public were unaware of events at these institutions and the Australian government found this naivety convenient. Especially since the wilful brutality at Parramatta remained at the heart of its operation until it was closed in 1973. History is not so convenient when those who were there can still speak of it.

More than 30,000 girls under eighteen were sent to Parramatta Girls' Home between 1887 and 1974. Most were charged with 'offences' that were flimsy and archaic. The home's colonial and convict history passed on a legacy of brutality and ignorance. Once you walked through the gates of Parramatta Girls' Home, you became a number. Mine was 43.

The culture of aggression was evident from your first moment inside. Each girl was branded a delinquent. Today's social services are a far cry from the ethos of extreme forms of discipline and humiliation at Parramatta.

In the spring of 1970 I was a typical rebellious teenager enjoying the freedom of the Sixties. I was part of the revolution that contributed to radical cultural change. My parents were from another era, the conservative 1950s, an emotionally repressed time where conformity ruled. Victorian mores and rigid social conservatism were mindsets many people found hard to shed. My parents didn't understand my behaviour nor that of my peers. In January of 1970 I defied their rules and went to Pilgrimage for Pop, Australia's first outdoor rock-music festival, held at Ourimbah on the central coast of New South Wales. Looking back now, it seems a harmless and innocent event.

At the festival I met a boy. On our return to Sydney I moved in with him. We were happy and free. Then one morning, just five months after the music festival, there was a knock at our door. It was the police. They arrested me and a few weeks later I was sentenced to a nine-month stay at Parramatta Girls' Home by the Children's Court. My crime was being 'exposed to moral danger, uncontrollable and neglected.' I was sixteen. The age of consent.

Upon my release I left Australia for good. Thirty years later I was living in London and trying to make the transition from journalism to fiction. I submitted a short story to a competition and won. One of the judges, publisher Barbara Daniel of Little, Brown, invited me to submit a novel. I was aware at the time that I hadn't yet found my voice, style or genre. Her encouragement gave me the confidence and conviction to finally write the story about my experience at Parramatta.

It had been almost thirty years since my time there. The truth of what happened at Parramatta, Hay and similar institutions had not yet been made public. Although I felt compelled to write about it, I doubted its potential to arouse interest. Then I stumbled upon a small article in *The Times* that caught my attention. It was about young unmarried Australian mothers who had been forced into giving up their newborn baby for adoption. I knew immediately that their story and mine were a perfect match. I had witnessed girls inside Parramatta who 'disappeared' when their pregnancy was full-term. They were taken to hospital in the middle of the night to give birth. Further research confirmed that along with thousands of others, they had become the victims of forced adoption.

I now had the right ingredients for a dramatic story. But when I began to write, I wasn't sure I could resurrect the dark memories. And yet there they were in vivid, powerful and humiliating detail. It was a terrifying journey.

Part of my mission was to respect and protect the dignity of the Parramatta and Hay girls. It was a grim task because what was done to us was degrading. But it was vital to expose the raw vulnerability of our confinement and hold a mirror up to a culture of secrecy, lies and state-sanctioned criminality. In so doing I had to reveal emotionally stark and shocking situations.

While writing the novel I could not have imagined that Parramatta, along with other institutions and the forced adoption scandal, would be included in two Government Apologies and a Royal Commission Inquiry. In this sense my book was ahead of its time.

Although Parramatta and Hay were Australia's most notoriously inhumane reform schools for girls, there were more than 850 similar care homes for children at that time. Many are still being investigated.

The media attention fuelled by the Royal Commission public hearings in 2014 had a deeply upsetting effect on Parramatta girls, including me. The women who testified gave brave and exhaustive accounts of their experiences that stirred up memories of a dangerous place. The term sadist seems old-fashioned these days, but I can think of no better description for the people in charge of our 'welfare'. The irony of these institutions was that we were sent there for training and rehabilitation and our own protection.

I wrote *Girl 43* to try to make sense of what it meant to be a Parramatta girl. This history, the Apologies and Royal Commission Inquiry, challenge the spirit of a nation that prides itself on being civilised and lucky.

Maree Giles 2014
www.mareegiles.com

I say this as a sketch and in a whisper
for it is not yet time:
the game of unaccountable heaven
is achieved with experience and sweat.

And under purgatory's temporary sky
we often forget
that the happy repository of heaven
is a lifelong house that you can carry everywhere.

OSIP MANDELSTAM, 9 MARCH 1937

One

Sydney, Australia
May 1970

I know what democracy is. It means living in a fair society, where you have free thought, equality and the right to live however you want – so long as it's okay with everyone else, especially the law.

I know because I looked it up in a dictionary. This girl with sly eyes and sores on her face said it to me when I was put away.

'It's not democratic, this place,' she whispered, stabbing her porridge with her spoon.

I didn't have a clue what she was on about, but I didn't want to look like a dummy by asking. And I was frightened one of the officers might notice and punish me. Talking wasn't allowed in the dining hall.

I kept the word in my head for three days, till library session.

September 1970

There's a girl in the next bed crying.

She's got untidy blonde hair. I know she is crying, because her shoulders judder and now and then she whimpers. I'm used to seeing girls cry. We all do it, in here.

The room I am in shimmers like oil in a puddle, black and purple swirls. I rub my eyes, they are sandy and raw; this makes them even worse, sending tears across my temples to settle in pools in my ears.

I close my eyes to stop the stinging. My head is throbbing, my limbs ache, my memory is blank.

After a while I open my eyes again, blinking. I lift my head; it hurts, like it did that time when me and Louise drank some of Mum's whiskey. I drop my head on to the pillow. God, what's wrong with me?

I try to lift my head again. This time I am aware of something between my legs, and the pain in my tummy. When I move my legs a sharp pain tugs at my crotch. I reach down with my hand. There's a bulky rough pad stuffed between my legs.

I lift the sheets. My nightie has got HOSPITAL PROPERTY stamped all over it in blue. I pull up the nightie and feel my tummy. It feels funny, floppy, and the skin loose like Granny's elbows. It should be tight and swollen. It was like a drum-skin, last time I felt it. When? Today?

Nothing is familiar. This is not Sick Bay – the ceiling there is white; this one is blue. I glance around, but can only take in a forty-five degree sweep because I can't move. God, what's happened? It's not Sick Bay, and it's not my dormitory, or Jarrah Cottage, it's a ward, a hospital ward. My baby! Is my baby all right? Why is my tummy all soft and flabby? What's happened?

The girl next to me is sobbing softly into her pillow. I lie really still, listening to her. There is something about her voice that alerts me, something familiar. I lean up on my elbow, the pain between my legs is awful.

I can see her face now, one side of it. The other side is pushed into the pillow. Her blonde hair is matted and stringy across her cheek, and she is sucking a hanky. It is twisted, grey and soggy. She pushes her hair back a bit, and I can see who it is. *Mary!*

She seems completely unaware of me. Just stares into space. Must be frightened of having her baby. I lie back and stare at the ceiling, trying to figure out what has happened.

I glance along the ward; no sign of any nurses or doctors. The other beds, four on each side of the room, are empty. The door is shut; probably locked.

I move my legs apart a little and peer down in the gloom to see what is happening. My hand is shaking – will I see the top of my baby's head poking out? The pad is soaked in dark-red blood. My baby! It must be coming! I try to sit up again, but can't, because the pain cuts through me, right up to my back passage, like a razor blade.

I turn my head to search for a buzzer. Behind me on the wall there's a square metal plaque, with tubes and wires and red buttons. Under one of the buttons it says: PRESS ONCE FOR ATTENDANT. I reach my hand over my head, the pain makes me wince, but I can't reach it.

I fall back on to the pillow, breathless and dizzy. For a long time I just lie there. The ceiling is awash with hundreds of moving black spots.

Mary is quiet now, asleep, I think; her breathing is heavy.

After a while the ceiling becomes clear and the starkness of the paint seems livid. I close my eyes and try to remember.

Sister Dawson – where is she? She said I was going to the hospital to have my baby, but I wasn't in pain, there were no contraptions like she said there'd be, and when I asked her she said: Don't worry about a thing, you're in good hands – she gave me an injection, said I needed it for the journey to the hospital – that's right. She said I was going with another girl. Mary.

There is something about hospitals that makes you feel safe. The smell of medicine, that clean smell, like the cough medicine my grandmother gave me. It's a smell that makes you feel cared for. I close my eyes and try to relax, taking slow, deep breaths . . . but the pain in my tummy, and the pad, and the blood; what's happening to me? Am I in labour? Does this always happen, this pain, and the blood? Sister Dawson said the contraptions would come and go in bursts, and when they got closer together, the baby would come. If that's what the pain is, they are so close together they've merged. So my baby, it must be coming!

Suddenly, without warning, vomit slops from my lips on to the bed covers.

'You okay?' Mary says.

'Where am I?' I murmur, wiping my mouth with the back of my hand.

'Mars.'

There's a pool of yellow vomit on the sheet. *The nurses will kill me.*

'Got any tissues?'

'In the cupboard.'

I pull out a big handful and mop up the mess. There's no bin near my bed, so I drop them on to the floor. The effort exhausts me. I lie back and close my eyes.

'You had a shitty time, did ya?' Mary says.

'Eh?'

'You had a pretty rough time. With the birth.'

What? I close my eyes and try to remember. I have a baby? Mary says I had a *hard time*. How does *she* know? It can't be right. Can it? *When?* When did it happen?

I remember my feet being tied up with leather straps. My ankles were pressed into these cold, U-shaped metal stirrups and two nurses were holding my cracked heels, staring at my crotch and looking worried. I remember that much. Is that when it came?

I couldn't move at all, tipped up like that on my back, I was trapped. I tried to push myself up on my elbows to see what they were doing.

There were people everywhere, crowded near the door and outside it, too, the ones at the back craning their necks. *God!* There must've been about forty of them. When I tried to sit up the nurses ducked under my legs and pushed me down. They gripped my shoulders and pressed me into the bed. One put a pillow on my chest so I couldn't see.

'What's wrong, what's the matter?' I cried. '*What's wrong?*'

'You don't need to worry about it,' she said. She twisted her hand around my wrist till it burnt. 'It has nothing to do with you,' she hissed.

I remember . . . I remember now . . . I could feel my baby's head, in between my legs. Like a bowling ball wedged there; the pain was terrible, as if I was being split open, like a seedpod.

I remember moaning, '*Get . . . it . . . out . . . now!*' My voice didn't sound like mine. It was deep and growling, and it frightened me.

After that there was a kerfuffle, and suddenly everyone except the nurses disappeared.

The other nurse stood over me and slapped my face.

I remember her lips. They quivered.

'Shoosh!' she said. 'You lie still. We'll take care of everything. Just lie still and you'll be all right.' Her voice had a catch in it. I closed my eyes and was lost.

The taste of vomit and salt makes me long for a bath. I want to clean my teeth and pour a gallon of ice-cold water down my throat. How can I lie here thinking about my furry teeth when I've just had a baby?

Where is it? Where is my baby? Why isn't it by my bed? Won't it need feeding? They'll bring it soon, probably when I can sit up a bit. I can't wait to see it.

I'm lying on my left side, facing Mary. Her cheeks are

flushed pink. Her yellow hair has grown faster than mine. She is still staring at nothing. She hasn't moved an inch. Her blue eyes are like milky pools.

'It's dead,' Mary suddenly whispers, glancing at me. 'My baby's dead. *Stillborn.* That means dead.'

I'll wet myself if someone doesn't come. Any minute the wee is going to pour out into the blood-soaked pad and wash down my legs on to the mattress. *The nurses will kill me.*

I'm so hot and sticky; I'm dying for a shower. Where are the nurses? Why don't they bring my baby to me?

'Mary!'

'Don't panic. I'm not going anywhere.'

'Ring the bell, will you. I can't reach mine. My bum is killing me.'

'I've got them too. Not as many as you, though. Sister said you've got them right up inside.'

I frown. She sounds so cheerful. For someone whose baby is dead.

'Press the button, will you, I'm dying.'

'Don't steal the limelight,' she says, pressing the buzzer.

It's a weird thing to say, but I'm too worried about not wetting the bed to be bothered with jokes.

A few minutes later the double doors swing open and a large nurse waddles in. She has short bleached hair with an inch of black regrowth.

'What's the problem, Mary?' she says. She is standing by Mary's bed, peering through piggy blue eyes.

'Not me, nurse. Ellen. Needs a wee.'

'Hurry, *please*, nurse, I'm nearly wetting myself.'

She disappears through the double doors again, her mouth pressed into a red slash. I groan and reach down to press my fingers against my urethra (I've got the lingo now).

The nurse comes back carrying a large, shallow metal bowl with a piece of green paper towel over the top. It lifts at one corner, as though a ghost has slipped in.

She places the bowl on the bed, tilts it into the mattress and firmly wedges it under one cheek of my bum. Then she eases her arms behind me, one each under my armpits, as though she is about to drag a dead body off.

'When I get to three, lift yourself up and back,' she says.

'But . . . I can't, it *hurts*.'

'It's not that bad. You girls do exaggerate. Come on: one, two . . . *three*.'

I manage to move a few inches. The pain, like hot needles, makes me cry out. I can't bear to put any weight on my bum. I slump sideways, panting.

'*Straight back*,' she says, 'you can't use the bedpan lying on your side.'

'But it *hurts*—'

'Come on. Once again, one, two . . . *three*.'

I heave myself back. This time I do it. I'm sitting up, but oh God, it hurts. I feel sick again, and dizzy. The nurse is a white blur.

She forces the pan under me. I wriggle on to it breathless, like a stranded whale struggling over the sand back to the sea.

At last the cold metal is snug. She pulls my nightie up over my tummy, eases the pad away and deposits it in a bin at the end of the ward. The smell of old blood wafts up from my body.

It is awkward and embarrassing, perched on the bed weeing in a pan. At first it makes a loud noise, like a tap filling a metal bucket. Mary is watching the whole procedure, transfixed. I want to hit her. I try to control it so it trickles, but I can't. The relief is enormous. Pieces, like jelly, ooze out. My insides are coming out. I can't reach the tissues to wipe myself.

At the end of the bed the nurse is smoothing the sheets.

'Finished?' she inquires, looking past me.

'Thanks,' I sigh. 'Thank you, nurse.' I'm so grateful I could kiss her.

She removes the bedpan; it is full and I'm worried it might spill. But she manoeuvres it with a surgeon's steady hand, places it carefully on the locker and covers it with the green paper. From her pocket she takes a clean pad and stuffs it between my legs.

'Can I have a bath? Or a shower?'

'You have a lot of stitches. Wait until you feel better.'

'Did I have a boy or a girl?'

'A girl,' she says, flatly. As though it's no big deal. I don't suppose it is, to her.

She gathers up the sicky tissues and drops them into the bedpan, then walks to the end of the ward, balancing my wee, and disappears behind a door. I hear the sound of a toilet flushing. I close my eyes. The heavy aching returns, pinning me to the bed. It's not a physical pain, like the one between my legs and in my tummy; it's inside me, right through me. A girl. I had a girl. I can't believe it – I'm a mother. Just like that. I want to see my baby; I want to touch her, smell her, feed her. Will she have my big ears? I hope she's pretty, and smart, and brainy, not like me. I don't want her to be like me. My breasts are leaking. I want my baby. Oh, I do wish they'd hurry up and bring her.

'*Nurse! Nurse!*' I shout.

But it is too late. The slow swoosh of the door punctuates the air, and the room is quiet again. I hear footsteps fading along the corridor. I lie still, heart pounding, helpless, the urge to leap off the bed so powerful that my skin feels as if it will rupture.

I lean up on both elbows, ears pricked. Footsteps, I hear footsteps, coming this way, she's coming back. With my baby, I bet. The double doors swing open and she marches towards me, stomach first. She is holding a small silver dish.

'Be quiet!' she barks. 'You'll wake up the dead.'

'Where's my baby? Can I see her now, please?' I say eagerly. I smile at the nurse, but she hasn't noticed, her eyes avoid mine.

'Lie still,' she says. She turns her back to fiddle with something in the dish.

I crane my neck to see what she is up to: a thin fountain of water squirts out of a needle and sprinkles the lino.

'What's that?' I say.

'Time for your painkiller,' she says.

'I don't want it. It makes me feel sick.'

She clicks her tongue as if I'm a naughty kid.

I don't like nurses. I don't like hospitals.

'You'll do as you're told,' she snaps. 'You are still in custody. Sister Dawson will be here later. If she hears you've been playing up you'll be punished. You don't want to be sent to Myalla now, do you?'

Myalla is way out in the bloody back-blocks. It's an old prison they use for real bad girls. Anyone who plays up at Gunyah goes there. They make you build brick walls all day in the sun, then you have to knock them down and build them again the next day. I saw girls come back skin and bone. No one ever looked proud when they came back from Myalla. But I'm not scared of going there, I'm not scared of anything any more.

'But when can I see my baby?' I say. 'I'm all right. I can hold her here in bed with me. I won't be sick any more, I promise.'

Her eyes slide away from mine, but she is grinning, as if I'm stupid. I remember my plan, the one I put into action at Gunyah. I think: It's not getting me anywhere, being nice.

'You don't have to worry. Your baby is in good hands,' she says, matter-of-factly. 'The staff here are all well trained and she is being fed regularly.'

'But I want to see her. Give me my baby, you fucking bitch.'

'I beg your pardon?'

'You heard. It's my baby, and I want to see her. Bring her to me now, I want to hold her.'

'I don't think so, somehow,' she says. 'Not when you speak like that.' She reaches behind me and presses the red buzzer. Seconds later the doors swing open and three grim-faced nurses burst into the room.

'This girl is giving me problems,' she says to them. 'Give me a hand to hold her still, please.'

'Fuck off!' I shout. 'Don't you know anything about democracy?'

One positions herself at the foot of the bed and grabs my ankles. I struggle, but the pain is crippling.

Another scurries to grip my wrist, twisting the skin in a Chinese burn. The third one performs the same trick on the other arm. I hear something clatter on to the floor.

The fat, bleached nurse pulls up my nightie. Without turning a hair, she jabs the needle into the side of my thigh.

The room is black. My head hurts. I try to lift it, but can't. There's a smell of stale blood. My eyes are full of grit. My bottom hurts. *What's happened to me? Where am I? Where's Sister Dawson?* Vomit seeps into my mouth, like bitter milk, and spills on to the pillow. It settles beneath my cheek; I can feel the sticky warmth cooling against my skin. I close my eyes and sink.

My own groaning wakes me. My chest is aching; there is something around me, pulled tight. I reach under my nightie. There is material, rough bandages, wrapped around my chest, like a mummy, squashing my bosoms flat. Spasms of pain fire through them, and they throb. *Like a mummy*. I'm a mummy. My baby, I want to see it. I'll go and find it, in the nursery, with the others.

When I push back the sheet a sour smell wafts out: blood, sweat and vomit. I shuffle my legs to the edge of the bed, and let my feet drop to the floor. It is cold and gives me a jolt.

I rub my eyes. I can hear breathing in the next bed. The

darkness is swimming. My body sways like a reed. I bend over and drop my head between my knees, taking deep breaths.

I sit there for ages, crouching over myself, breathing in the stale smell of my own body, like a drunk.

After a long time, I lift my head and listen.

A baby is crying. The room is pressing down, I can't breathe, it's as if I have a plastic bag over my face. I am still swaying, and my head pounds. I try to steady myself and take deep breaths, but it's no use, there's no air, no air at all . . . Then suddenly I hear my own voice screaming in the darkness, and I stagger off the bed in search of the baby's cries.

There's a square of pale light in the distance. I stumble towards it, frantic, because beyond it the baby is there, somewhere, and it might be mine; it might be my little baby, crying for me.

At the block of light I stop. My heart beats hard inside the bandages. I peer through the glass panel at a long, softly lit corridor.

I push the door – it's open – and pad across the shiny floor towards the crying. It's cooler in the hallway, and the fresh air wakes me a bit. I can smell Dettol and other mediciny smells. The baby's crying is louder now; the sound of it makes my blood pump harder, my breathing comes in short gasps.

Halfway down the corridor there's a broad window overlooking a blue room. There are lights with blue bulbs hanging from the ceiling and, regimented beneath them, dozens of cots with tiny, tight bundles of white, like sleeping silkworms. I can see their heads poking out of the parcels, some with dark tufts of hair, others bald and wrinkled. Some look grey, as if bruised.

I stand there staring with my mouth open, as though I've just discovered gold. I can't count them – there are too many, thirty at least. Some of them are crying, but I can't tell which ones. I stumble further down the corridor.

At the end there's a door that I figure must lead into the nursery. I turn the handle, but it's locked. I limp further along, searching for another way in. There's another door. This one is open. Inside it's dark, but through the gloom I can make out a big chrome sink and buckets, and bedpans, and shelves stacked with towels. At the far end in the gloom are two cots.

For a moment I just stand there open-mouthed, too scared to move. Too scared to look. I take a deep breath.

My hands are squeezed into tight fists over my mouth. I hold my breath and move closer. In each cot lies a sleeping baby. I think of baby Jesus in holy swaddling. These babies are wrapped in regulation hospital sheets; I can see the blue printing: HOSPITAL PROPERTY.

Slowly, I put my face closer to one. Its pearly eyelids flicker. What do babies dream about, I wonder? They have no experience, nothing before their birth, no pain – or does it hurt them when they are born? Do they dream of their birth? Do they remember their mother's womb, the soft, warm interior, the gurgling of veins and blood?

I reach into the cot and gently place the back of two fingers against its cheek, my hand seems enormous; its skin is warm and silky. I am shaking, and a sudden urge to hold the baby close overwhelms me, a surge of something unfamiliar.

Two tiny hands are poking out at the top of the bundle, tucked just beneath its chin. Around one wrist there's a name tag. Carefully, I move the tiny hand so I can see what it says, but the room is too dark, so I put my head closer, squinting. It says: PERRY. Perry?

I turn to the other cot. My heart feels as though it might implode, the bandages are pulled so tight round me.

The baby's delicate profile is dark against the white sheet. I move my face closer, and my lips brush through its feathery hair. My warm breath against its cheek comes back at me. Its tiny, moist mouth releases short, sharp breaths.

I can't see the wrist band, as its hands are tucked tight inside the blanket, so I unravel the covers. It is so small, so small and helpless, I can't believe how tiny it is. Its hands are tucked amongst the tight folds of a cotton nightdress, fingers furled at the tips. I pull the tagged wrist away, straining in the dark to read the printing.

It says: RUSSELL. I clamp a hand over my mouth. I look at the baby's face. *My baby's face.* She is sound asleep. Her mouth is dewy and puckered, as though she wants to be kissed.

Suddenly my mummified chest feels as if it is filling with hot liquid. The pain makes me wince.

'Just what do you think you're up to?'

The voice cuts through the silence, like a mallet on my skull. I reel around. A nurse is silhouetted in the doorway. She has a resentful look on her face, the look that means: You worthless piece of shit.

'This baby,' I blurt, 'it's called Russell. That's my name, my last name. Is this my baby? Is it mine, nurse? Is this my baby? Why is she here, in this cold room? Why isn't she in the nursery? Why can't I have her next to me in the ward—'

'Be quiet and get back to your bed, you're not well enough to be wandering around.'

'No. No, I won't. Not until you tell me—'

'Get back to bed. I heard you're a troublemaker.'

She is blocking the doorway, hands on her hips like a bossy rooster. There's something familiar about her thin red mouth and pebbly eyes with their stubby eyelashes. Before I know it, she's on me, holding both wrists tight; she twists her fingers and the burning collapses me.

She quickly wrenches my arms behind my back and locks me in front of her. I push back against her, but she sticks her knee into the small of my back and shoves me towards the door. I try to fight her, but my limbs are floppy from all the injections.

She bulldozes me into the corridor, and I curve back into her, groaning. She shoves harder and wrenches my arms further up my back; my fingers are pressed just beneath my wing-bones.

I press harder and harder into her, moaning, 'Let me go, let me go.' But her grip tightens and she propels me past the nursery, then suddenly two nurses appear beside us. They crouch down and grip my ankles.

I try to kick them, but my body has turned to lead. As they lift me into the air blood trickles between my legs. They plonk me on a stretcher like a butcher's carcass.

'Hold her hands tight here, hurry, while I get these straps into place,' the fat nurse barks. The other two – thin and pale-faced – separate and scramble to each side of the trolley. They pinch their bony fingers around my wrists and squeeze hard.

I struggle as the fat one pulls the leather strap across my ankles; I try to kick her in the face, but she's too quick for me, she has it fastened in no time. She pulls another strap over my thighs, and two more across my stomach and arms. Now I can't move at all. I think: Is this a strait-jacket? Why are they putting me in one? I'm not mad. *Am I?*

The fat one disappears, mumbling, and the other two push the stretcher along the corridor in silence, with expressions that mean: *There*, that'll teach *you* a lesson! They put me in a small room. I stop struggling and take deep breaths, trying to gain some control, because it's like being trapped inside a glass box; my throat has seized up, and when I try to scream there is only the sound of husky gasps. Mum would call it Rothmans' Rumble.

The fat nurse rushes in carrying a silver dish with a syringe on a square of green paper.

'What's that? What are you giving me?' I gasp. 'I don't want any more medicine. I don't need painkillers, I'm all right. Why don't you tell me if that's my baby? Tell me. Please, tell me,' I sob. 'I want my baby, I want my baby.'

The needle stabs and twists into my skin. I close my eyes, groaning. Then blackness.

Two

March 1970

The magistrate reckoned I was in moral danger. Whatever that means.

The courtroom door opened and my mother walked in, looking nervous and pale. My heart began to pound; I hadn't seen her for three months, not since I left home because of my stepfather and Mum's nagging.

She criticised everything: my clothes, my hair, my weight, my table manners, my speech, nothing – *not one thing* – I ever did or said was right.

There was a big fight the day I left because I wanted to go to a pop festival with my friend Louise, and they wouldn't let me. We struggled on the front verandah, Jack and me, and he broke the gold bangle that Mum gave me for Christmas. I was more upset about that than the fight.

As I ran down the drive he shouted after me, 'If you

dare go, I'll get the police on to you.' I laughed. I laughed out loud because some of my friends were allowed to go. He couldn't stop me.

Mum shut the courtroom door, paused and looked at me as if to say: *Why*, Ellen? *Why?* That pained look, as though someone was dying.

I turned my head away from her and stared at the walls, pretending to study the paintings – grim scenes of Australia in the olden days: caged convicts and angry soldiers firing pistols at the sky; early settlers in stiff outfits rowing ashore from tall ships; sweaty sheep-shearers in outback sheds and greedy-eyed gold diggers living rough on their wits.

It went against the grain, turning my back, because Mum always said it was rude to turn your back on someone. But I couldn't help it. I was thinking: I'm not going to look at you, *I'm not*, because it's *your* fault, all this; if you and Jack hadn't told the police, I wouldn't be here now, I'd still be with Robbie. We weren't hurting anyone. We were happy. We were.

Mum tiptoed across the room and stood next to me in front of an empty chair. When she tried to grab my hand, her nails scratched at my skin. I pushed her hand away. She fiddled with her white gloves. I wished she'd go away. I didn't want to see her.

On my left was Miss Riley, a large, orange-haired policewoman, who seemed to hate my guts. She really had it in for me, but I don't know why.

By the door a dark-suited bloke with a peaked cap stood with his legs apart, his thick arms folded across his chest. He stared straight ahead, as though we weren't even there.

The room was small and stuffy, with no windows, just a bare light bulb inside a plain brown shade. Facing us was a large desk, inlaid with brown leather. Next to it sat a pinch-faced girl in a pink dress.

The door opened again and the magistrate walked in. My heart began to pound, because although he wasn't that scary-looking, the atmosphere in the room changed as he settled himself behind the desk. You could tell they were all nervous by the clearing of throats and the straightening of backs.

The girl handed him a black ring-binder. He nodded at everyone, gave me the once-over, as though I was a specimen, and sat down. Everyone else began to sit, so I did.

'Stand up,' he bellowed. He glared at me as I stood up again.

I didn't know where to put my hands. In the end I folded them, put my weight on one leg and tilted my head, but it felt wrong . . . awkward.

It struck me then that I was on trial, like in a movie, and I thought the whole thing was pretty stupid. I didn't hurt anyone, or steal anything. We were happy, me and Robbie, we were so happy. I thought: Soon as I tell the magistrate, and my mother says she doesn't mind me living away from home because of the fights with her and Jack, he'll be okay about it and let me go.

He read the papers in the ring-binder, then looked at Miss Riley over the top of his wire-rimmed glasses and said, 'Would you care to read your deposition, Miss Riley?'

She stood up, holding a piece of paper in front of her. As she rose the smell of stale sanitary pads lifted with her and settled around me and Mum. I noticed my mother's nostrils flare in and out.

'Yes, sir, Mr Callahan,' Miss Riley said. She clamped a fist over her mouth, cleared her throat and began to read her statement in a clear, loud voice.

'This deponent on oath states: My full name is Erica June Riley. I am a Constable of women police attached to Coolamon Police Station. At about 4 pm yesterday, the third of March 1970, I saw the young person now before the court at Coolamon Police Station, where she had been brought by myself and a Sergeant of police, from a room in Searles Court, East Esplanade, Manly.'

She paused to clear her throat again, then continued.

As she read her statement, an odd feeling swept through me, like you would imagine the warm earth must feel when a black, cold shadow creeps over it, blotting out the sun and the light.

'I said, "Ellen, you know me?" She said, "Yes, Miss Riley." I said, "What is your full name?" She said, "Ellen Jane Russell, I'm sixteen."

I gasped. 'I never said that!' I looked at the magistrate. 'I never said that to Miss Riley.'

Mr Callahan had one of those straight, thin mouths, like a bloodless knife-wound. He glared at me and the slash grew thinner. I couldn't imagine him ever kissing anyone.

Come to mention it, I couldn't imagine any of them kissing anyone, not even Mum. They all had smirks on their faces, as if I was a fool; I could tell that's what they were thinking.

I waited, expecting him to say, 'Well, what *did* you say to Miss Riley?' But he just gave me a long, hard stare.

I whispered, 'I never said that—'

'Be quiet,' he snapped, 'and let Miss Riley finish. You can have your say later.'

I chewed at the skin around my fingernails. A piece came off in my teeth and blood bubbled up. It streaked the rim of my cuticle. I sucked it hard to stem the flow, but it kept pouring out.

My heart was knocking against my long, flimsy dress – I could actually see the regular pulse of it. I had dressed in a hurry when the police came to get me yesterday, so it was crumpled from being on the floor of our room, and the bodice was egg-flecked from breakfast at the station: revolting cold scrambled eggs and soggy white toast.

My mother was ashamed of my appearance. I could tell by the angle of her mouth and the glaze of her eyes, when I glanced at her. She was moulding a nicer girl in her head. A girl in patent-leather shoes, frilly white blouse with lace and milkmaid sleeves and a tartan jerkin over the top, green pleated skirt, and a hanky tucked into her trainer bra.

Instead, she had a daughter she didn't know standing next to her. A girl who was turning into one of those hippy types. A girl she couldn't figure out.

Yesterday, after they took me to the police station the

jovial sergeant said to Miss Riley, 'Don't take this girl's prints, will you? She's only fourteen.'

But Riley had other plans. I knew by the look in her red-lashed eyes. I don't know why she didn't like me, but she didn't. Maybe because it took her so long to find me. But I wasn't hiding. Mum knew where I was, because I phoned her, and she sent me some money once. She said to me, 'So long as you're safe and you're behaving yourself. Just be careful. If you want to come home you know you always can.'

When the sergeant told Miss Riley not to take my fingerprints, she raised one ginger eyebrow at him, as if to say: *You softie.*

The sergeant went into a back room to collect his jacket and car keys, then signed off at the front desk. As he left the station through the front door he winked across the room at me. I smiled, and gave a small wave.

Miss Riley was standing behind the duty desk, shuffling papers.

I was seated in a corner on a gummy vinyl chair, locked in a wooden pen, lost in thought. I expected Mum to come through the door any minute to take me home. I imagined her face, full of shame for dobbing me in to the police.

As soon as the front door's swishing settled and the sergeant's unseen footsteps faded somewhere down the street, Miss Riley unlocked the gate and said, 'Get over here.'

At the desk she lifted her arms to grip my hand, and a strong whiff of BO travelled up my nostrils. I reeled. She tugged me closer and snapped, 'Stand here and keep still!'

Then she stared at my head and grinned. 'What do you call that?' She pointed at my hair and curled her top lip, 'Heinz 57 Varieties?'

'The sergeant, he said not to . . .'

'I'm in charge now,' she snapped. When she moved, her crisp blue shirt crackled.

On the desk was a shiny wedge of flat brass set into a wooden block, about nine inches long. With small, firm movements she pushed a small roller across the top of an ink pad that oozed black, then across the length of brass. I wondered how she managed to get things done with such long fingernails; fiddly things, like typing, and locking and unlocking handcuffs.

She took my hand and separated my first finger from the others, pressed the tip on the inky brass, then lifted my hand, as though it wasn't connected to me, and rolled the tip of my finger from side to side, just once, on a piece of paper, lifted it and took another clean finger and repeated the process. When Riley's skin touched mine it felt cold and clammy. The uneven freckles on her white arms gave me goose bumps.

I looked at my prints and thought: That's not me.

She said, '*There*. That'll fix *you*. Now go and sit down.'

Later, hours later, Robbie came through the front door of the station with my blue suitcase. He glanced at me, as if I was an embarrassment.

He had his good jeans on, which surprised me, because he only ever wore them for special occasions, like going to the disco or the doctor. He had on a clean short-sleeved Hawaiian shirt, too. It reminded me of my mother and her holidays. His long blond hair was combed and wet.

I rose up from the chair a bit, smiling. I was so pleased to see him, but I was disappointed and surprised at his reaction. I thought he'd come rushing over to me, all worried. He lowered his eyes and swaggered over to the reception desk.

He and Riley whispered for a few minutes with their backs to me; I strained to hear, but couldn't.

Then Robbie turned to leave, lifting a hand to wave at me as he walked across the room. When our eyes met he grinned sheepishly and looked at the floor.

At the door he paused. He propped it ajar a few inches with his knee, then swung it wide open, gave me a look that was full of pity, and disappeared. The door hissed as it closed.

I could have followed him. Although I was locked inside the pen, like a sheep, I could have hurdled over it and walked out on to the street. But I didn't. I just sat.

In the trapped air of the small courtroom, the magistrate was looking at Miss Riley with his chin pressed into his neck. His mouth curved down as though Miss Riley was reading something that would change the course of history. His eyeballs were raised in the upper sockets, leaving an expanse of veiny white below. I wondered if it came naturally, this gruff image. Or if he went home at night with a smile and a lighter mood, to cuddle a loving wife and play with his kids . . .

'. . . I said to the young person, "Ellen Jane Russell, you were reported missing at Coolamon Police Station on the twenty-ninth of January 1970. Where have you been since then?" She said, "I went up to the Ourimbah Pop Festival and I met a boy, Robert Clarke, and I've been with him ever since." I said, "Were you sharing a room with Robert at the boarding house in Manly?" She said, "Yes".'

Miss Riley's voice would curdle milk, I thought, hating her.

I looked at the floor and shifted my weight to the other foot. She shot me a glance, as if she could read my thoughts. I lifted one hand to my mouth and chewed at my thumbnail; my chest was getting tight, as though I was in a snare.

'I said, "Have you been there all the time?" She said, "Yes." I said, "Have you been working since you left home?" She said, "Yes. For the first week after I left I stayed on at my old job, but then I left and I haven't had any work since then."'

The way she said it: as though I was a derro living in an alley.

'I said, "What money have you been living off?" She said, "I drew eighty-five dollars out of the bank and I got sixty dollars when I left my job. I've just run out of money and I got a job today and I'm starting on Monday." I said, "Where?" She said, "Amber Motors, Balgowlah."'

Miss Riley paused again, and her elbow went in and out, as though she was a bird building up courage to take off from a height. The movement released another wave of BO that made my eyes water. Slowly, I shifted to my other foot and turned my face the other way. By now the whole room seemed thick with her odour.

She drew in her breath sharply and went on: I said, "Have you been having intercourse with Robert Clarke while you've been living with him?" She said, "Yes."'

I'm nothing if not honest. What did she want me to say? No, we played with dolls?

I went bright red. It was one thing to tell someone that in privacy, another in a room full of strangers.

'I said, "You will be appearing at the Metropolitan Children's Court tomorrow regarding being neglected and exposed to moral danger."'

She looked at me in that way that meant: That'll fix you. Her mouth was puckered, as if she was pretty pleased with herself. She sat down heavily.

It struck me, then, that everyone in the room knew all about my personal life, and they all seemed to hate me. And I thought it wasn't fair, because I didn't know a *thing* about them, except my mother of course; but the others, they had no history apart from the few minutes in this hot room.

And I thought: There'll come a day when no one will be able to tell me what to do. There'll come a day when I can be myself. My mother always said that, when I complained about not having many friends, or feeling ugly because of my big ears or my pimples; *Be yourself*, she'd say.

But she was always criticising. She didn't even have to speak; I could tell by her looks, even when she was standing behind me looking at the length of my skirts, or the tightness of my jeans across my bum. Being myself was impossible around Mum.

The magistrate looked fed up. He let out a long sigh. He shuffled some papers and studied them carefully.

I was bored. The same boredom I felt at school, sitting for hours listening to some ugly teacher go on and on about trigonometry and algebra. I just wanted to get it over with so that I could go home to Robbie. My feet ached and I wanted a bath and something to eat.

The March humidity sapped the air and made everyone in the room sigh, like those short blasts of wind that come suddenly, fitfully, on a stifling hot day, whipping up dust bowls and rubbish.

He stopped reading and stared at me as though I'd committed a murder. A flush of heat singed my cheeks. I wasn't sure if I was allowed to sit down, or what. So I just stood there, sighing and folding and unfolding my arms, waiting for instructions.

'Can I hear the District Officer's report, thank you, Miss Riley?'

Miss Riley jumped. 'Yes, sir, Mr Callahan, of course,' she said. She flicked through some papers and cleared her throat.

Suddenly I yawned. I couldn't help it; the heat in the room was terrible.

'Are we keeping you up, Miss Russell?' Mr Callahan gave me a deadly look. I stared at the floor. 'Please begin, Miss Riley. I can see we have before the court a rude, as well as uncontrollable, young person.'

'Yes, sir, that's right.' Miss Riley turned her freckled face to glare at me. My heart quaked. Even her eyes were freckled, the gold iris around the black pupils flecked with dark ginger.

Riley began to read the report: 'The court will hear that the girl's behaviour has been unsatisfactory for the past year at home. She stays out late, some nights not returning to the family home until 1.30 am. She is still in bed every morning when her mother leaves for work, and Mrs Russell does not know when or if she leaves for work, and does not know when to expect her daughter home. Girl says she does not go home for the evening meal because her mother nags her and her stepfather hates her. Mr Russell, girl's stepfather, has now left the home—'

Gone?

I looked at my mother. I hadn't noticed before, because I was busy pretending to study the paintings, but her brown eyes were red-rimmed and bloodshot. A wave of guilt and sadness swept through me. I wanted to put my arms round her and say I was sorry, but I was too scared to move.

'Mrs Russell considers it impossible to modify the girl's attitude, says girl resents all authority. However, she does not want the girl committed to an institution, as she threatened to "go bad" if this happens to her.'

Girl. Christ, can't they even say my name? I chewed my nails and read the report Miss Riley was holding, over her shoulder, stuff about me and Jack and Mum. I looked at the man in blue by the door. He looked like a shop dummy. I wondered whether he would budge if someone tickled his chin with a feather. If it wasn't for the swell of his chest when he breathed, I'd swear he was a dummy. He didn't even blink.

'Are you listening, young lady?' Mr Callahan boomed. I jumped.

'Yes,' I said. I bit my lip.

He looked at Miss Riley. 'What does the District Officer recommend?' he said.

'Placement away from home is suggested,' she replied triumphantly.

I clamped a hand over my mouth and chewed at the palm.

'What do you mean?' I moaned. My voice was muffled. 'I'm going home, aren't I? I haven't done anything wrong. My mum, she knew I was okay, I phoned her, I've got a new job starting Monday. I want to go home.'

'Be quiet and come forward,' Callahan barked.

I stepped to the front of his desk, trembling. I put my hands behind my back, because I imagined he had a long cane under his desk that he would produce at any tick of the clock to whack across my knuckles.

'It appears your poor mother is at the end of her tether with your behaviour,' he said. 'Not only has your attitude been unsatisfactory at home, but you have been exposed to moral danger by living with a boy for the past few months.'

Up close, the whites of his eyes were nicotine-yellow. His grey hair was thinning, greasy strands were plastered across his sweaty pink dome. He had large, strong-looking hands. He gave me a hateful look. I felt as though his eyes had speared me on to the thick air. I wanted to crawl under the table and die. I couldn't say so – he would get even more angry – but I hated him too.

On the desk, resting in a round, flat bowl, was a small wooden hammer. Would he bang it and say I could go home? I wanted to go home to Robbie. We were so happy. We were.

'You have been charged with being neglected and exposed to moral danger under the terms of the Children's Act,' Mr Callahan said. 'Do you understand the implications of that?'

Moisture had gathered at the corners of his mouth.

'*Do you understand?*'

I stared at the floor and shook my head. I didn't have a clue what he was on about.

He tapped the desk with the tips of his fingers.

'You are considered by this court to be uncontrollable. I am therefore sentencing you to six to nine months' detention at the Gunyah Training School for Girls. You will be taken there this afternoon. Is there anything you wish to say?'

Suddenly my whole body began to feel hot. It started at my toes and whooshed to the top of my head. My heart beat like the wings of a trapped bird. I began to scream, like someone in a Hitchcock movie. I never screamed, ever, so it was a shock, it sounded shocking.

I grabbed the edge of the desk and held on with a sudden, awesome strength.

'You can't do this, I haven't done anything, don't send me away, please. Please! I haven't done anything,' I pleaded.

The back of my throat was parched and raw. The sounds seemed to come from my stomach. It was as if someone had split me in two with an axe.

'Officer!' Callahan shouted.

A scuffle broke out behind me, then two beefy arms

squeezed my waist. I gripped the heavy desk. The arms wrenched me backwards. The desk came too.

Miss Riley got in on the act and grabbed my right arm. She tried to prise my fingers off, her red claws scratching at my skin, but I pressed harder into the wood till the tips of my fingers turned purple. The desk scraped across the floor. Behind us some chairs toppled.

'Ellen, oh Ellen, *don't*,' my mother cried. But I didn't see her, my eyes were full of biting tears, my face burning with rage.

'I haven't done anything,' I sobbed. 'I haven't done anything, I want to go home.'

The last thing I saw when the officer dragged me away was Mr Callahan, hunched on his chair like a shy child. It gave me a lot of satisfaction, that, seeing him stranded on his chair without his big desk to protect him. It was like he was naked.

I was put into a small room. The dummy banged the door shut. I heard the clunk of keys, the sharp scrape as a key turned in the lock. Except for a bench, the room was empty. I sat down.

When I moved I could feel my stomach lurch inside me, like a hot-water bottle. I bent my head into the skirt of my dress and sobbed. The ink on my fingers came off and stained the paisley cotton.

A few minutes later I heard the door being unlocked.

My mother rushed in and draped her arms around my neck. Her face was full of anguish, as if they were putting *her* away.

'*Don't*,' I said, 'don't touch me.'

I pushed her away. She twisted her gloves. 'Why are you pushing me away like this?' she said.

'You've done this to me!' I snapped.

'I haven't! It was Jack, *he* told them. We were so worried about you. *He* rang the police, not me. We didn't know they'd do this, we didn't know they'd put you away. You shouldn't have gone off with that boy, Ellen.'

'Tell them. Tell them you want me to go home, please, Mum,' I pleaded. 'I don't want to go to that place. I've heard about it, you can't – don't let them send me there, *please*, Mum. *Please*, go and tell them.'

I tried to stop crying but I couldn't, the sobs came in heavy waves, as if someone was banging a rug against my back.

'I *have* tried, Ellen. I've been trying all my life to help you,' she was saying. 'I have tried.'

'But I haven't done anything, I haven't done anything,' I sobbed.

'Now, now, Ellen dear. The magistrate is a busy man. He doesn't just drop everything to see people. I've already asked Miss Riley and she said it's too late, once the sentence has been passed.'

I looked into her eyes: they were waterlogged paint, swirling and oily. I buried my head in her lap and wept. She stroked my hair, her hand felt warm on my scalp. She rocked me to and fro, as though I was a baby.

'There, there,' she whispered, 'it'll be all right, dear. I'll come and see you. You're better off away from that boy.'

I cried and cried into my mother's lap, then suddenly she was leaving because the officer, a blue blur at the doorway rattling his keys, said it was time. She left the room slowly, one arm stretched out towards me, as though an invisible thread linked us. Her face was full of pain.

The dummy locked me in and I stared at the white walls. My eyes were red and swollen, and the tears kept streaming, endlessly. An itchy rash appeared on my arms; hundreds of tiny blistery bubbles full of clear stuff. I scratched and scratched, till they burst.

When I moved I could smell Robbie between my legs. Just before the police picked me up at our room at the boarding house, we had sex. I didn't let him do it much, I didn't like it, it hurt. And he had his mates sleeping on the floor some nights, so I was too embarrassed.

But he was pushy yesterday morning, aggressive, like my stepfather seemed to get with Mum sometimes. I caught Jack on top of Mum once, when they forgot to lock the bedroom door. Instead of the familiar flatness of the bed, I opened the door to find an elephant under the covers. I could hear my mother's urgent whispers escape beneath the heaving mass: 'Jack! Ssshh! It's Ellen, stop!' but he rasped, 'I can't' and carried on pumping and groaning. I ran outside into the back yard, disgusted. I'd never seen my Mum that close to a man. Here was this man, a fat, red-faced stranger in *our* home, on top of my mother!

I was glad he'd gone, he didn't have a clue how to act with me. He tried to teach me how to waterski once, in the deep, brown water up the Hawkesbury River, where the sharks come in. 'You'll be all right,' he kept saying,

'I've been skiing these waters for years and no sharks ever got me.' He had a stupid grin on his face all day because I couldn't get up on the skis. I was glad he'd gone. But I felt sorry for Mum.

Anyway, Robbie went off to work and not long after, my friend Lizzie, whose room was just down the corridor, bashed on the door.

'There's two coppers downstairs at reception looking for you – *quick, hide*!' she panted.

But there was nowhere to go. The room had only a bed and a chest of drawers. Our clothes were draped around the walls on the picture rail, like a St Vincent de Paul charity stop. I stood there, waving my arms up and down saying, 'What'll I do, what'll I do?'

Then they knocked on the door and it was too late.

I could have climbed out the window on to the corrugated-iron awning and made my getaway. But part of me said: No, you haven't done anything, what are you worried about? Just tell them it's all right, my mother knows where I am, and they'll go away. But Lizzie, she got me all worked up, she was scared of the cops.

Sitting in the courthouse, locked in the tiny white room, I scratched my arms and went over it in my head, thinking it was all a mistake, that my mother was out there right now talking the magistrate into letting me go home with her. I was sure she would come back any minute and say he'd changed his mind, then me and Mum could drive home as though nothing had happened. I pictured myself down at the lake swimming by four at the latest, and phoning Robbie after he finished work to let him know I was home again.

There was some writing on the wall in the holding room, rude words that Robbie's friends used a lot. Fuck and cunt. It made me embarrassed to look at them. I remember the first time I saw the word fuck. Someone wrote it in chalk on the footpath near Mum's gift shop. I asked her what it meant and she went purple with anger. She said it was a word used by people who didn't know how to express themselves properly, and I must never, ever say it.

Up the other end of the room was some scrawly writing on the wall that I couldn't read. I walked across to get a closer look. It said: *Gunyah is hell on earth.*

Three

Her feet go down to death; her steps take hold on hell.
PROVERBS 5:3

The ride to Gunyah along Parramatta Road was a blur of traffic and car salesyards strung with coloured flags and huge neon signs.

When the street narrowed here and there and the car slowed down through busy shopping areas, I was able to focus on people's faces as they bustled along with their bags. It suddenly struck me then: I was a prisoner. The blood drained from my face.

'I feel sick,' I said. Miss Riley just sniffed.

Soon the car had to stop under a railway bridge to let a lorry pass. The black, dusty walls were plastered with torn posters and dented, old-fashioned tin billboards: Ford Pills: *the gentle, tasteless, painless laxative for all the family . . .*; Aeroplane Jelly: *I like it for dinner, I like it for tea . . .*; Dettol: *used in our great hospitals, the chosen antiseptic of modern surgery.*

There was a picture of a smiling nurse next to the Dettol

bottle. She had dark hair pinned under her veil, ruby-red lips and thick eyebrows. I thought of my cousin Pam, a nurse at Bedowrie Hospital. She has a nice smile like that. Except that Cousin Pam is hard as nails.

Miss Riley stared ahead and didn't say one word. Her jaw was set hard like a gangster's, now and then her ears moved up and down. There were large flakes of wax nestling in the curves of the ear facing me. I kept wanting to tell her, as I would a close friend: *You've got gunk in your ears, didn't you shower this morning?*

It was hot and stuffy in the car. I couldn't open the window, because there was no handle. The stink from Miss Riley made me feel sick. I tried to ignore her, but I couldn't help examining her, because she was so repulsive. There was a wart on the inside of her right index finger, stained black. I hoped she wouldn't hold my hand, in case I caught it.

I wanted to go home to Mum, have a shower, put on some clean clothes and lie on the carpet in front of *Gidget* or the *Three Stooges*, or some cartoons. I wondered what my stepfather was up to now he'd left Mum. Probably down the yacht club sucking back schooners of lager. Celebrating. I imagined Mum in the empty house after work, getting herself dolled up to go out. She wouldn't let any of this spoil her fun. There were plenty more fish in the sea, that's what she'd be thinking, and she'd soon catch another one.

The driver pulled off the main highway into a wide shopping street crowded with people. It was like a movie, jumbled up: fast, then slow; blurry, then clear.

A few people stared at the car, but they couldn't see us, because the windows were tinted in the back. It was as though I didn't exist.

Everything on the street looked normal and pleasant. The sun was shining out of a brilliant sky, the shoppers were friendly-faced and fresh.

We drove past a boutique called Zip. Only last week I was in the city branch, and Robbie paid. I chose a green maxi-coat that I wore out to the Spinning Top, a disco in Manly. It was the daringest thing I ever owned, but Robbie didn't take his eyes off me that night, so after a while I didn't care about people looking. Of course, *Mum* wouldn't like it. She'd say it was bad taste, especially over jeans. She always reckoned jeans looked like a uniform, because *everyone* wore them. I thought of my clothes in the suitcase Robbie brought to the station, and I wondered if they were in the boot of the police car.

All the way to Gunyah I thought it wasn't right: I hadn't done anything, it was a mistake and my mother would come and get me later, or tomorrow.

'Take a good look, Ellen,' Miss Riley said, tightening her jaw. 'It'll be a long time till you're in the land of the free again.' I thought: God, she thinks she's in a HumphreybloodyBogart movie.

The car pulled into a side street, where old sandstone buildings replaced the bright, modern shop fronts. The street became narrow, just how I imagined the streets in London might look: cobblestoned and shadowy. From the top of a long, high wall that rose straight up from the road, leaving no room for a footpath, a mass of dark-green ivy spilled down and fingered the crumbling bricks.

We stopped in front of a solid, black timber gate set in the middle of the wall. Above the gate was a sign that said GUNYAH TRAINING SCHOOL FOR GIRLS. Underneath, in fancy gold lettering, it said: *Est. 1887.* I thought, Christ, it's older than Granny.

The driver got out, stretched his legs and strode to one side of the gates. He pressed a bell set into the wall. Then he leant against the bonnet of the car and lit a cigarette. I watched the smoke leave his lips and rise into the still blue sky, like a distress signal.

After a while, a door in the middle of one of the gates creaked open. A tall, wide-shouldered older man in a dark suit stepped out and shook the driver's hand. Dangling from the man's trouser belt was a large bunch of keys. When he moved they clanged against his hip.

Riley stared straight ahead, not moving a muscle.

'Who's he?' I said. She ignored me and worked her jaw.

The man disappeared back through the door, and a few seconds later the gates slowly opened.

The driver brushed the grey ash off his uniform, straightened his hat and slid into the car. He revved up the engine and nosed the car into a big open courtyard.

The grey-haired man was standing by the gates. He had big, bushy eyebrows that stuck out untidily, like a hawk's. Lizzie would try to make a joke of them. I imagined her giggling and nudging me – not obviously like she does when she's feeling confident, but sneakily, like she is around people in uniforms.

The driver flicked a switch on the dashboard and got out to open the back doors.

'This is it,' Riley said, 'get out stand still and *be quiet!*'

I got out and did as I was told. My legs wobbled. All the way from Sydney I had chewed my nails, and now the skin was torn and bleeding. My palms were sweaty.

I looked up. The sky was so vivid it hurt. It seemed smaller. A brick wall about twenty feet high surrounded the courtyard. It was joined to the side of a two-storey Victorian building with a green wrought-iron railing on an upstairs balcony. Like the houses in Paddington that Mum always said were nothing but slums, even if they were being done up. But the windows on this place had bars across them.

The tall man in the grey suit was talking to Miss Riley and the driver. Miss Riley smiled and smirked as if there was some private joke between them. She handed him some papers. When they moved, their polished black shoes crunched on the gravel. After a few minutes they all shook hands and Miss Riley and the driver got into the front of the car.

The man opened the gate.

From where I was standing I could see the road. Some cars whizzed past. I could have run through the gates and sprinted off in the opposite direction, as they couldn't chase me up a one-way street. But I didn't. I just stood there, gawping.

As much as I hated Miss Riley, I didn't want her to leave me. I was used to her, in a weird sort of way. At least she didn't hit me or anything.

Mr Bushy Eyes saluted the driver as the car went under the archway. I lifted a hand to wave to Riley. I hated myself for crawling, but she didn't notice anyway. The wheels spun in the gravel, then they were gone. I had a dry lump in my throat. He locked the gates and stared at me.

I gulped and looked at my feet. My sandals were covered in a film of grey dust.

He marched towards me.

When he was a few feet away, when I could see his ice-blue eyes under the thick sprouts of grey, when I could see the blond and black hairs sticking out of his flared nostrils, a hot torrent of wee wound its way down my legs. It filled my sandals and seeped out from under the soles of my feet into the gravel. He glared at the foam and arched an eyebrow. I was dying to step out of the puddle, but I was set like plaster to the spot. My face went bright red.

'I'm Mr Hewitt,' he boomed, 'I'm Supervisor here at the Training School. Been up to no good, have you, young lady?'

I tried to speak, but nothing came out. I managed to mumble 'No, sir,' but it was the worst thing I could've said, because he shouted, 'I beg your pardon?'

There was a long pause, mainly because I couldn't get my voice to work.

'I *said*, you have been up to no good, haven't you? Well? I'm waiting.'

'Yes, sir,' I said, surprising myself, because I managed a faint snarl.

'Being facetious won't get you anywhere,' he said.

I gulped and lowered my eyes. I was shaking all over, as though I was being electrocuted.

'Right, let's get you registered and cleaned up,' he said.

He went up the steps to the front door. I followed quickly. My sandals squelched. I stuck each foot out behind me a few times and shook away some of the wee, like a puppy.

He unlocked the door. He seemed to know every key off by heart. I expected to see lots of girls inside, on their way to classes, but the wide, dark hall was empty.

Except for the deep ticking of a grandfather clock, it was quiet. Brown paintings of ugly people from another era – from England by the looks of their stuffy expressions and high collars – lined the shiny white walls. The polished floor was tiled in a mosaic of geometric shapes in muted red, green and yellow. As I stepped through the door, my foot slipped and left a wet skid mark. The hall smelt of lemons and rotting leaves.

He closed the door and turned the key in a big, square copper block. It grated noisily and echoed along the hall.

'Come on, come on, get moving,' he said.

I trotted behind him. He unlocked another door and ushered me into a cool, shadowy room. I shivered. He flicked on a round, brass light switch near the door and the room sprang into life. It was full of dark, sombre furniture. Deep-green velvet curtains covered two high windows, and the walls were covered with more brown paintings and heavy, red flocked wallpaper. Above a huge fireplace was a big carriage clock and two marble statues. Another wall was covered in bookshelves, locked behind glass doors.

'Stand here,' he said. He pointed at the floor. I stood right on the spot.

He sat behind a leather-topped desk in a chair as large and ornate as a throne, studied the papers Riley had given him, then stretched across to drag a clipboard towards him. It had a sheet of paper attached with columns of names and ticks. He put a tick next to my name and signed his initials in another column.

'Right, Ellen, now that you are registered, let's get you over to Matron, and she and Officer Griffiths will sort you out.'

All sorts of questions whizzed through my brain. Who was Officer Griffiths? Why was she called *Officer* Griffiths? Was she a police lady? What was she going to do? I only needed a shower or a bath, and some clean clothes. Maybe my Mum had dropped some clean stuff off for me, after leaving the court.

And Matron, what was she going to do? What exactly is a Matron, anyway? Isn't that someone who's in charge in a hospital? Or is that a Sister? What about lessons? And where would I sleep? Were they going to put me in a cell, like they do in prisons? It wasn't fair. I didn't hurt anyone.

I wanted to go home to Robbie, curl up in front of the TV or listen to some music on his stereo, or maybe muck about on the upstairs verandah at the boarding house. It was great fun last weekend. We spent Sunday afternoon dangling a fishing line on to the pavement with a wallet attached. When passers-by tried to pick it up we were in fits.

What would he be up to now? He must know what has happened to me. I bet he went back to the police station to get me. The sergeant would have told him I was put away.

He probably argued about it, stuck up for me, then visited my mother to tell her it was all a mistake. I remembered his face when he left the station. That look. It made me think I might never see him again.

Blue Eyes shoved the folder into a drawer, then strode over to the door where I stood and flicked off the light. He gripped my arm and pulled me into the hall. He smelt of pipe tobacco. He locked the door, then took me down the hall to another door.

He unlocked it and we stepped out on to a wide verandah with a corrugated awning. A set of broad, tiled steps led down to a long path with a roof and open sides. Purple flowers dangled from the roof like jewellery.

To our right there was a large area of bitumen and beyond it, about thirty feet away, was a long wooden fence, about twelve feet high. Behind the fence someone shouted orders, but what she said wasn't clear. In a gap at the bottom of the fence I could see two pairs of feet in flat black shoes. One pair paced up and down at one end of the fence; the other at the opposite end.

My arm was hurting. Mr Hewitt had strong, meaty hands. Between the joints of his fingers, stiff grey hairs grew out of magnified black roots. I tried to loosen his grip and pull away, but he squeezed me tighter.

At the bottom of the steps he turned right and followed a footpath along the edge of the verandah to a windowless brown shed that smelt of creosote. A door was fastened open against the wall with a hook. Inside it was brightly lit and stuffy.

Mr Hewitt yanked me through the door. On the far

side of the room were wooden lockers with painted numbers on the doors. A pile of folded brown clothes was stacked on a table. On another scrubbed table were four black sewing machines, like my grandmother's old Singer. Next to them were open baskets stuffed with cotton reels and packets of needles and pins, a wooden box with tins of Nugget and Kiwi shoe polish, and an old Arnott's biscuit tin full of buttons.

At one of the machines sat a small, chubby woman wearing a short-sleeved white shirt. Her black hair curled stiffly on to a broad, oily forehead. She was hand-sewing one of the brown garments. She looked up. Her eyes were black as dull marbles. She nodded at Mr Hewitt, but ignored me.

'This is the new girl, Ellen Russell. I'll leave her with you, Miss Griffiths.'

'Thank you, sir,' she said briskly.

Without a word, or a look, Mr Hewitt left.

I waited. And waited.

Miss Griffiths carried on sewing as though I wasn't even there. I began to think about coughing, to remind her that I was, when she pushed her chair back from the table with a loud scrape.

'Over here,' she said. She went to the numbered cupboards and opened number forty-three. She pulled out a bundle of clothes: two long, brown short-sleeved dresses and some itchy-looking navy bloomers. Four pairs of white socks, and a pair of thin, blue flanelette pyjamas and a threadbare blue chenille dressing gown, plus some singlets.

She handed them to me. They smelt of camphor. She

shut the locker and sat down at the table to write in a black book, like the accounts book Mum uses for stock-taking at work.

'Call out what you've got, one at a time, and check to make sure your number, forty-three, is sewn inside each garment,' she said.

I did as she said, and she scribbled in her book.

When everything was counted, she went to another cupboard with two big doors and opened it. Inside, stacked on shelves, were dozens of brown leather lace-up shoes, tied together in pairs with string. Each shelf had numbers from one to nine written in white along the front edge.

'What size are you?' she asked.

'I'm not sure,' I said. 'I *think* I'm a six, but it depends on what make they are. My Mum and I always get mixed up about shoe sizes when we go into town—'

'*Be quiet!*' she snapped.

I bit my bottom lip.

'Just tell me in one word your shoe size,' she said.

'Seven,' I muttered.

She pulled out a pair of size sevens and placed them on the table, then wrote it in her book and ticked it.

'Right,' she said, and closed the book. She pushed the pencil behind one ear and said, 'Come with me.'

I followed her through a door to one side of the shoe cupboard, into a smaller room. There was a chair and a wooden table in the middle of the room, with a bright light bulb glaring down. On the table was a green cloth and a pair of scissors.

'Sit,' she said, gripping the back of the chair.

I sat down and she swung the green cloth over me and fastened it at the back with a press-stud. I looked down at the timber floor. Splinters of hair filled the cracks in the floorboards.

She stood behind me, slid her thumb under my hair and gathered it into a tight bunch. The skin stretched and made my eyes water.

She reached for the scissors and began to cut through the bunch. Each time the blades came together my hair made a crunching sound. I could feel the cold steel against my neck, and once or twice the points went into my skin and I flinched.

'*Sit still*,' she said.

When she finished with the back, she positioned herself near my right shoulder. Her stomach was hot against my arm. She smelt of Vaseline. I leant away, but she gripped the sleeve of my dress and pulled me back. A few slivers of hair sneaked into my mouth. I spat them out.

'I said, sit still!' she snapped. 'You'll be punished for insubordination if you're not careful. Here five minutes and already you're in trouble.'

'Please don't cut it too short over my ears, they stick out. *Please* can you leave it a bit longer over them?' I pleaded.

'*I . . . beg . . . your . . . pardon?*' she said. She leant forward and slammed the scissors on the table, and folded her arms over her stomach. '*I . . . beg . . . your . . . pardon?*' she said again, only much louder.

She glared down, her eyes boring into me. I lowered my eyes. My hair, what was left of it, swept across my cheeks, like a dog's floppy ears. Some of the cut hair fluttered on to my sandals and prickled my toes. The back of my neck itched.

'Are you telling me what to do?' she said.

I glanced up. Her mouth was pinched and wrinkled, like a monkey's bottom.

I didn't answer. My heart hammered. I closed my eyes to fight the biting tears that were beginning to well, and I clenched my teeth and ground the back ones hard. My cheeks were screwed into balls. I didn't want this woman to see me cry, I didn't want her to be angry, in case she hurt me.

She picked up the scissors.

'Look up,' she said.

I unscrunched my face and lifted my head.

She slid the scissors between the tops of my ears and the side of my scalp and cut the hair in one smooth movement. It landed on the floorboards like the feathers of a plucked duck, and all at once I understood Riley's comment about Heinz 57 Varieties: it was gloomy in the bathroom at Searles Court and I didn't realise what a hotchpotch of colour my hair was, after Lizzie tried to bleach it a few weeks ago. Now, under the glare of the bald light bulb, I could see that it was a jumble of dark brown (my own colour), blonde, copper, yellow and mouse. Miss Griffiths cut the other side. Tears spilled from my eyes and dampened the hairs on the cloth.

Only my fringe remained, covering my forehead. It, too, had its uses. Mum was *always* telling me to pin it back so that the pimples underneath could 'get the air to them'.

Officer Griffiths poked one half of the scissors underneath, the sharp point scraping on my spots. With one clean slice, she lopped it off a quarter of an inch from my skull.

It seemed like hours before she came back. My bum was numb. I lifted one cheek to rub it, then the other. I paced up and down a few times, keeping a sharp ear out for footsteps, because she had told me not to move an inch till she came back. It was hot and close in the room. The smell of some stuff she had put on my hacked hair was vile.

I heard the click-clack of footsteps, like soldiers, and someone shouting. Apart from that, it was quiet.

I touched my hair. It was ragged and sticky. The smell made my nose curl, it caught in my throat. I ran my fingers along the edge of my ears. They felt huge and sticky-outy. I couldn't cry any more, I was exhausted. I'd lost track of time.

I wanted to have a shower – a long, luxurious one, with lots of soap and shampoo – then rub some nice body lotion into my skin and slide between soft, clean sheets to read a book. *Seven Little Australians* is my favourite, and I like Enid Blyton.

Just before I left school my English teacher loaned me a book of poems by an Irish poet called Yeats. I loved his poetry. It seemed a big step up from Dorothea McKellar's *A Sunburnt Country*. It made me feel hopeful. Like there was another way of saying things. I thought I might do that one day: keep a diary, or try writing some poems. I remember once being asked in an English lesson to write down how I felt about my best friend. The teacher said I had *potential* after she read it. I wasn't sure what she meant, so I looked it up in a dictionary. I thought she had insulted me, in a roundabout way, because the dictionary said it meant *possible* – anything is possible. I wondered: Did she mean there was hope, even for a dummy like me?

I was thinking all this in the hot room, remembering lots of things about Mum, too. How she works hard to buy me nice clothes, and how happy she was about marrying Jack. I couldn't think about her for long, it made me restless; I didn't believe it was Jack on his own who told the police I ran away. She said, 'We were worried.' *We.* They *must* have been in cahoots.

I thought of my grandmother Alice, how she died in some hospital I'd never heard of and I didn't get to say goodbye, but my thoughts returned to Jack and Mum, and me not being allowed to go to their wedding, because *he* said it wasn't the right environment for a young girl at the reception: a club, somewhere in the city.

And I thought about them having sex, him drinking beer all the time, burping at the table, snoring in the lounge, with his pink, hairy balls poking out from his shorts. And then I thought again about them telling the police.

The rash on my arms itched. I scratched it hard till it bled.

The day they got married they left me with my godparents. An English couple called Janice and Doug, with three pale kids who were always sick and never ate fruit, and were terrified of the redbacks that lived in clusters under the back verandah.

I sat in their back yard on the swing seat the day of the wedding, hating my stepfather. The next day they came for me, and his chest was puffed out like a pigeon's, his face red from beer, his breath reeked; Mum looked washed-out and coy. She handed me a piece of wedding cake wrapped in a paper serviette and looked at me as if she'd just handed me her life.

At home I went out into the back yard and climbed up the jacaranda tree to eat it. The paper was stuck to the cake. I peeled it off and took a bite. It tasted bitter, like turps. I spat it out and threw the rest to the chooks. They wolfed it down.

My thoughts were interrupted by footsteps.

'Stand up!' Officer Griffiths bellowed. I leapt to my feet. 'Come with me,' she said. I followed her through the clothing room, into the dimly lit courtyard.

At the other end of the covered way I could see rectangles of white shining from a big building. Inside the windows, I could just make out the tops of lots of heads. Old Mother Hubbard marched in front of me to a low sandstone building with a corrugated tin roof.

We walked up the sloping concrete pathway. The door was open. I could hear running water.

She stopped in the doorway to speak to a tall, thin woman with short brown hair and pock-marked skin. They stood, silhouetted in the doorway like two blackbirds, whispering. I waited outside and stood on tiptoe to look at the people in the distant building. I could hear the faint clatter of crockery. My cottonwool tongue scraped at dry gums. When I moved, my stomach lurched as if half-filled with water.

'I'll leave her for you to sort out, Miss Wyndham,' Miss Griffiths finally said loudly, for my benefit. 'Send her over to Sister when you've finished with her.'

Griffiths was looking me up and down, as if I was weird.

'Any more insolence from you and you'll be put into isolation,' she said, her thin lips pursed. Then she walked off towards the dining hall, leaving a strong whiff of cheap perfume in her wake.

Inside the shower block, Stickpin ordered me to strip off. She pointed at a narrow cubicle. It smelt of Pine-o-cleen. There was a wooden seat across it with a thin, scratchy blue-and-white towel with the initials GTSG printed on it. Next to it was a plastic soap dish cradling a bar of Sunlight soap. I put the bundle of clothes that Griffiths gave me on the seat. I hesitated, expecting Stickpin to walk off and leave me to undress, because there was no door on the cubicle. But she just stood there.

'Time's up,' I heard a woman shout from the other room.

I reached my hand over one shoulder and fumbled to push down the zip, then stretched up backwards with my other hand to pull it down the rest of the way. Miss Wyndham stared at me.

'Get on with it,' she said.

I pulled my dress up over my head.

'Hurry up,' she said.

I tucked my dress under my chin, pressed it against my neck to hold it in place, and reached around to undo my bra. I shook the straps down my arms and it landed on the concrete floor in a puddle.

'I said, *hurry up*!' she snapped. 'Give me your things.'

I bent down to pick up my bra, with my dress still pinned under my jaw.

'And your dress and underpants,' she added.

I handed her my bra, and as she snatched it she tugged my dress away. I doubled over to cover my breasts.

'Come on, come on, get a move on, get those underpants off.'

I turned my back to her and pulled down my pants. The crotch was stained yellow. When both feet were free I scrunched the pants into a bundle. She took them and stuffed everything into a dark-blue bag hanging on a hook.

'Wrap the towel around yourself,' she said, 'and follow me. Bring the soap.'

I did as she said.

In the shower room my mouth fell open. I could feel myself staring. My mother always told me it was rude to stare, but I couldn't help it. Under the showers, in full view of five uniformed women, about twenty young girls with cherubic faces were frantically washing their bodies, as if they were in a race. They looked younger than me, some only eleven or twelve. They all hung their heads.

One of the women looked at her watch and shouted: 'Time's up!'

The girls hurried to a row of open cubicles at the far

end of the room, a few still with soap in their hair. Huddled in cubicles on our left stood about twenty other naked girls clutching bars of soap. They stared at their feet, shivering.

'Put your eyes to the floor, Ellen Russell,' Miss Wyndham said.

I bent my head. Pubic hairs curled like question marks in a puddle near my feet.

'Go and put your towel in that cubicle,' she said, pointing. 'Then soap your hair.'

Soap my hair? Did she mean what I thought she meant? Rub my hair with dry soap? My grandmother once used Sunlight to wash my hair, said shampoo was too expensive and soap did just as good a job. My hair went stiff as a board afterwards and stuck out like straw.

I rubbed on the soap; it tugged at my dry hair. Miss Wyndham stood in front of me with her feet apart and her hands clasped behind her back.

'You were told to look at the floor,' she said. Her voice sounded gravelly, like a man's. Her skin was puffy and dull and pitted, like a damaged mushroom.

'I . . . I can't get the soap to lather,' I said. I curled one corner of my top lip and shook my head, because it seemed so silly, rubbing dry soap on to dry hair. I had the soap in one hand, palm upwards, and shrugged my shoulders, as if to say: *How dumb.*

She dropped her arms by her sides. In one hand was a length of black rubber hose about two feet long. I thought: What's she going to do with that, unblock a drain or what?

Suddenly, she lunged at me, like a sword fighter,

grabbed one of my arms and belted me across the thigh with the hose.

I doubled up, squealing. A huge, throbbing red welt appeared on my leg. Tears swamped my cheeks.

'Time's up,' someone shouted.

The girls rushed across the wet floor to their cubicles.

'Don't speak out of turn,' Miss Wyndham said sternly. 'Now get in the shower.'

I hobbled across the cold concrete, rubbing my leg, and stood under a shower. The water stung the welt and I winced again, but it felt warm and soothing on my back. Your best feature, Mum always said. Smooth-skinned and straight-shouldered. Good posture is *so* important, especially for a girl.

Except for Miss Wyndham and another officer, the room was empty now. They watched me silently, Miss Wyndham kept glancing at her watch. It seemed I was only under the water half a minute when she said, 'Time's up.' I didn't even get a chance to wash my bottom. And my hair was still soapy. The lemony scent of the soap made me think of Granny, the soft folds of her bosom cradling my head.

'But, I haven't—'

'You heard!' she cracked. 'Get out and dry yourself, then go to the other recess in there and put your dressing gown on. And *don't* speak out of turn. You will be told when you may speak.'

I did as she said, fast. I could tell she meant it. I didn't want her to hit me again.

Four

She caught him and beat him, until he was red.
Oh never get out the wrong side of the bed.
May Gibbs

In my dressing gown and brown shoes, which were too big after all, Miss Wyndham led me along the covered way towards the dining hall.

We turned a dark corner and followed a wide path past a building as big as a factory. My hair was stiff and sticky, but I felt better than I had done all day.

Eventually we arrived at a low sandstone building with lights shining inside. Above the green panelled front door, the name Bethel House was chiselled into the stone.

'This is Sick Bay,' Miss Wyndham said.

'What's that place next door?' I said, looking at the house with bars on the windows.

'*Don't* speak out of turn!' she spat. 'That means: *wait until you are told to speak*. Otherwise, *be quiet*!'

I clamped my mouth shut. It was an effort, because I was dying to ask her all sorts of things.

A wide, timber verandah stretched along the full length

of the clinic. From a clump of shrubs in the front garden came the loud roar of cicadas.

I looked up. The sky, smaller somehow, was flecked with silver stars. The crescent moon looked ready to drop from the sky. I remember nights – nothing like this one, that's for sure – down by the lake, where the sky seemed forever promising. Nights that were black and still. Nights that crackled with cold; nights that throbbed with the leftover heat of day. Nights when the days were – when I was free. Nights when I'd spent the whole day doing nothing but diving into the salty lake off a rusty drum, half a mile from the shore. At the time I didn't know that all that was – happiness.

Inside Bethel House, a table lamp glowed yellow through the window. The warm, trapped air along the verandah smelt of frangipani and jasmine. Sister would help me, I just *knew* she would.

Miss Wyndham rapped the brass knocker twice and we waited in silence. After a few minutes the door opened.

Before us stood a short, thin woman. She was wearing a blue-and-white nun's veil that just skimmed her shoulders, and a nurse's uniform. On her chest a blue-and-white badge said Sister Iris Dawson. Above it was a gold stopwatch. The top of her head was level with my shoulders. Her grey hair was tucked neatly under her cap, and behind a thick pair of grey-rimmed glasses her bright blue eyes twinkled. She smiled, revealing a row of perfect white teeth, like Granny's false ones. Her skin looked soft and smooth. Compared to the other old bags she looked harmless, and straight away I felt better.

I thought about what I would tell her: about court, and Miss Riley taking my fingerprints, and how I wanted to see Robbie. I'd tell her it was all a big mistake, that I didn't belong here, that I didn't do anything wrong and I should be sent home. I imagined she would hold my hand and take me back to the office to tell Mr Hewitt, and then my mother would arrive to collect me.

'Come in, come in,' she said. Her voice was soft.

'This is the other new girl, Sister. Ellen Russell,' said Miss Wyndham.

'More grist for the mill,' said Sister, smiling.

'Good luck,' said Stickpin, clicking her heels together. She turned and disappeared into the dark.

Sister Dawson closed the door, turned a key and slipped it into her pocket.

'Come with me, young lady,' she said.

I followed her down the long white hall, which had the same geometric floor tiles as the main building. There must have been a glut when they built the joint, I thought, they're everywhere.

Inside a brightly lit white room was a narrow stretcher. A sheet was tucked tightly over it and at one end a square of stiff, green paper towel. At the foot of the bed there was a light on a tall, thin metal stand. On a small trolley silver dishes were stuffed with cottonwool balls, bottles and jars grouped together in order of height. There was a roundish silver thing that looked like a headless duck. Next to it were some sanitary napkins and a box of Kleenex. In one corner of the room was a large sink and a foot-pedal bin overflowing with scrunched tissues. The room smelt of Dettol. The whole place smelt of Dettol. I could taste it.

A large poster was pinned on one wall: FOR YOUR PROTECTION, it said in bold black print. Underneath was a human silhouette with a skeleton painted over it in white, and numbers in small circles, like the pictures we studied in Science at school. I was going to read the rest of the writing, but Sister pointed to a chair.

'Sit down, dear, and put your things on the table,' she said. 'I need to ask you some questions first.'

I dumped my clothes on the table and sat down. I peered at her. *First?* What did she plan to do after the questions? Put me to bed? Give me something to eat? She sat on another chair and took a large notebook from the trolley, then pulled a pen from her top pocket.

The questions were all about my health. Did I drink alcohol?

'Not much,' I said, 'I don't like the taste.'

Did I take drugs?

'No,' I said. 'My boyfriend smoked some stuff, but I didn't.'

She gave me a strange look, as if she didn't believe me for one minute, then she asked me about my diet.

'I eat lots of fruit,' I said.

Did I take regular exercise?

'Yes, I love swimming.'

Was I taking any medication?

'No,' I said, thinking: What a nice woman.

When did I last have a check-up with my doctor? Was there a history of heart disease or cancer in my family?

'My grandmother had a heart attack and died,' I said. Parkinson's Disease?

'Never even heard of it.'

Had I had my tetanus shots, and diphtheria?

'Yes.' Had I had measles? 'No.' Mumps? 'No.' Did I have any brothers or sisters? 'No.' Did I have any allergies? To medicine?

'Yes,' I said. 'No, I mean, not to medicine, but to something – there's this rash, on my hands and my arms, and I used to get hives, terrible they were, all over my legs; the hospital at Bedowrie took my tonsils out because they said that would stop the hives, but it didn't, I still got them, so maybe this rash is connected to the hives, I don't know, but apart from that I'm very healthy, I do a lot of swimming.'

She said, 'But not to medicine? You are quite certain you are not allergic to any medicines?'

'No,' I said, 'I don't think so.'

'Good,' she said. 'And when did you last menstruate?'

'I don't know exactly,' I said, blushing, 'about four weeks ago, I think. I don't know the exact dates or anything.'

My red face was fading to its normal shade when Sister said, 'Have you been having intercourse with anyone?'

I went bright red again.

'How many boys have you slept with?' she asked.

'Only Robbie.'

'You must tell me the truth, Ellen.' She narrowed her eyes, but they still looked like blue saucers.

'I am telling the truth,' I said.

'All the girls in here have been promiscuous,' she went on. She gave me a long, penetrating stare. I looked down at my lap.

'I can soon tell what you've been up to,' she said softly. She smiled.

'I shouldn't be here,' I blurted, 'it's all a mistake. I haven't done anything . . .'

Suddenly she laughed, as if I was an idiot, and said, 'That's what all the girls say. You are here for your own protection.'

She sighed, long and hard, and clicked her tongue as though I was a five-year-old.

She closed the book and pushed the pen back into her pocket, then stood up, shaking her head and tut-tutting. 'What are we going to do with you, eh?' She smiled again.

I looked at her, searching her face for some sign that it was all over, that she understood and would phone my mum.

'Now lie on the bed and pull your dressing gown up over your tummy, please, Ellen,' she said.

'Huh?'

'Come along, come along, we haven't got all night. I'd like my supper before midnight. I want you off my hands for the evening.'

I lay down with my knees bent up. I folded my arms over my chest. I shivered. I had a good view of the poster now.

There was some other stuff, but I couldn't even pronounce it, and an address in Sydney for information and advice. I didn't have a clue what number five meant, or

> **FOR YOUR PROTECTION**
> **Learn these facts**
>
> *Syphilis causes:*
> 1 INSANITY
> 2 PARALYSIS
> 3 BLINDNESS
> 4 HEART DISEASE
> 5 ANEURYSM
>
> also:
> PREMATURE SENILITY
> ABORTIONS
> BIRTH OF BLIND AND DEFORMED CHILDREN
>
> *Gonorrhoea causes:*
> 3 BLINDNESS
> 6 ARTHRITIS
>
> also:
> MUTILATING OPERATIONS IN WOMEN
> STERILITY
>
> **ONLY CHASTITY GUARANTEES SAFETY.**

sterility or mutilating operations, but I didn't like the sound of any of it. How did you get these things, anyway? Was this the plague the kids at school used to rave on about? They were always giggling about it, but when I asked Mum she said I didn't need to know about such disgusting things.

Sister bent down to rummage on the lower shelf of the trolley. I was too scared to ask her about the poster in case she thought I was ignorant.

She straightened. She was holding a pair of white rubber gloves. She pulled one on to each hand. I was watching her every move. What was she going to do? Did she think she would catch something if she touched me? I expected her to pick up the stethoscope that was curled up on the trolley like a snake, but she picked up a tube of cream, unscrewed the top and squeezed out some clear liquid.

She held her elbows together, hands up in the air, with the jelly on one finger, rested the points of her elbows on my bent knees and tried to prise them apart. She looked very solemn.

'What are you doing?' I said. I clamped my knees together.

'We need to do some tests,' she said. 'Just relax, it won't hurt, let your knees fall to the bed.'

I kept them tight, like a vice.

'Just relax, dear,' she said in a soothing voice, 'it won't hurt, there's a good girl now, take some deep breaths, you'll just feel it cold on your skin, nothing more, that's it, just relax.'

I gazed up at her. She looked important in her veil: efficient, clean, caring. I slowly let my knees drop and closed my eyes tight.

*

I sat in the hallway, shivering. Sister was in another room doing tests.

I was *starving*, and tired, and the silver duck had hurt so much I was bleeding. She said it wouldn't hurt, but it did, it *did*. I'd never, ever been examined down there before. I was terrified. Embarrassed.

And now I was frightened to move in case I leaked on to my dressing gown, because Sister stuffed a pad between my legs without a sanitary belt, and the undies Miss Griffiths gave me were too baggy to hold it in place. I wanted to pull on my pyjama bottoms, but was afraid of getting blood on them. So I just sat there, crying.

After a long time a door opened and Sister came out with a grim look on her face. She sat on the other chair next to me.

'I'm afraid I have some bad news for you,' she said.

I looked at her. I thought she was going to say I had one of those diseases from the poster. I thought she was going to tell me I would go insane, or blind, or have a heart attack. Her eyes searched my face and she shook her head slowly, as though the end of the world was coming. This is it, I thought, I'm for it.

'*What?*' I said. 'What is it?'

'I'm afraid, young lady, you are pregnant,' she said.

All sorts of things ran through my head. Pregnant! It sounded to me as bad as the diseases. Pregnant.

I thought of Robbie. And Mum. A sort of frozen fear ran through my veins; it made me shake and go hot. I thought: *Fourteen*. You are only fourteen, you idiot, how can you be pregnant? What will you do?

Robbie will marry me. I can wear white and have the wedding at my old church, where I was christened, and my godparents can come, and my friends, and I'll meet Robbie's family.

Then I thought: No, I can't, I'm too young, you have to be eighteen, don't you? I thought of the baby, tiny and pink.

I thought: They'll let me go home now. Being pregnant is like being sick, isn't it? I didn't know anyone who'd been pregnant, except a girl at my school. She disappeared off the face of the earth, no one from school ever saw her again. I thought: I can go home now, to be with Mum, she'll know what to do, I'll be all right now, it's all been an awful mistake.

'Come on, Ellen. Let's get you into Dormitory Four with the other girls,' Sister said.

'I want my mother,' I said.

She took my hand and led me down the hall. I clenched my legs together to hold the pad in place, it made me walk funny, like a geisha. Inside another room, sitting under a bare light bulb, was a girl my own age with chopped blond hair. I could smell the hair lotion again, it made my eyes smart.

She was wearing a tartan dressing gown and brown shoes like mine. Her nose was long with a turned-up point, and she had small green eyes under thin, plucked eyebrows. She was short, with a tiny waist. Above it bulged the biggest bosom I ever saw. And where the dressing gown crossed at the front, there was a deep cleavage with clusters of angry pimples. She leapt to her feet and leered at Sister Dawson.

'You bitch!' she said through clenched teeth. 'You fucking bitch, you left me here for hours! I wanna go home. You bedda get the boss and tell 'im I wanna go home, or I'll punch your teeth in.'

Sister Dawson tutted, then said calmly, 'Come along now, Mary, that's enough of your nonsense. You'll be put into isolation if you carry on like that.'

'You can't put me in there, I'm pregnant.'

'Dear, oh dear, whatever will we do with you, eh? You girls get yourselves into trouble so easily these days. It's terrible, *terrible*. God have mercy on you.'

Mary gave me a dirty look.

'Come along now, let's get you both across to the dining room for supper, then Matron can get you up to your dormitories,' she said.

She flicked off the light and ushered us into the hall with small, swift hand movements, as though she was directing traffic.

'So,' Mary said, 'how'd you end up in here? Been cruising, have you?'

'Sorry?' I said.

'Aw, forget it,' she said, rolling her eyes.

'Be quiet!' Sister snapped. 'You are not permitted to speak to one another. You will not be allowed to speak to one another at any time, not even at recreation. *Do you understand?*'

Mary pulled a face and crossed her arms.

'Wouldn't wanna talk to *her*, anyway,' she spat, 'she's too up herself.'

I decided right there and then that I didn't like Mary. Whatever happened, I wouldn't be making friends with *her*. She was rude and raucous. Besides, she looked as if she'd hit me at the drop of a hat. Once was enough for me, with that hose in the showers.

Iris Dawson was sad.

During the past year thirty-two pregnant girls had passed through Jarrah Cottage. It was rare to get two together like this, however, and it made Iris worry about the state of the world beyond the walls of Gunyah.

They were morally beyond reproach, every one of them. Still, she thought, in an effort to console herself, at least *some* went on to serve others in an effort to make amends. Why, only last month a former inmate, Lynette Reece, had come back to visit with her new baby and thanked her. Lynette had trained as a nurse in the very same hospital where she gave birth. All my girls will see sense in the end, Iris thought. If Lynette can turn her life around, they all can.

Half-past nine at night, much later than usual. Miss Griffiths had delivered her supper to the cottage earlier; it was under a tin dish in the oven, going dry. The girls were tucked up in bed. It was quiet, peaceful, in the kitchen at Jarrah. Iris liked her own company. She liked to sit still and reflect.

She sat at the kitchen table and lifted the lid to reveal a plate of lamb's fry, bacon, mashed potato and peas. From her basket she pulled out a copy of the *Sydney Morning Herald*. She liked to keep abreast of the news. The world was changing so rapidly these days, she felt it her duty to stay informed.

After all, the girls were also victims of social change, and they needed guidance as well as protection while in custodial care, to better equip them for the pressures of modern society.

It was Iris's wish to improve the girls in every area, to encourage them to be models in everything that is good and noble. In God's eyes they were sinners, but sinners could be forgiven and learn from their offences. She most certainly did not agree with Mr Greaves, one of the Medical Officers who visited the school every few weeks, who considered the girls neurotic.

'They are not innocent, I agree,' she said to him once at afternoon tea in the Superintendent's office. She was quite certain he would be critical of the notion of inherent wickedness, and did not wish to incite a dispute.

'You may be of the opinion, Sister, that religious instruction and training in the domestic arts will provide these girls with the knowledge required to instil self-discipline, but I'm afraid the root of the problem lies in their upbringing. Their individual personal circumstances make them neurotic and this is a fact that is difficult to cure. I still hold with the more modern theory that it is environmental background, as well as the family situation, which determines an individual's behaviour. Not providence or fate.'

Iris sipped her tea politely, for she was not the type to

argue the point, particularly not in the company of men.

Mr Hewitt shifted uncomfortably in his leather armchair, puffing his pipe, one thorny eyebrow arched anxiously.

Matron sipped her tea and stared at her lap.

Iris thought Mr Greaves was a bigot and a know-all – with his pin-striped suit, why, he looked more like a spiv who might sell cars along Parramatta Road or vacuum cleaners door-to-door in Kingswood or Penrith.

Iris knew, because she read her Bible, that people *are* born wicked, but that fate could play a major role in influencing one's life.

From her own experience as a young girl, much younger than some of these hussies, one's background did not necessarily dictate one's future. One could tempt, and also mould, fate. If *she* could survive the brutality of being transported 12,000 miles to a harsh new life learning domestic duties on a country farm, anyone could turn their life around and change. One's personal history did not necessarily have to hinder improvement. Girls such as Lynette Reece were evidence of this. Through prayer and obedience and careful training, all was not necessarily lost.

Of course, there *were* girls, like that lazy drug fiend Mary Perry, for instance (in and out of Gunyah since the age of ten, and prior to that she was a state ward, shunted around from one home to another until fate and depravity got her pregnant, poor mite), for whom there was no hope. Perhaps, like Lynette, pregnancy would be Mary's salvation.

She began to eat her supper. Slow, thoughtful chewing.

Now and then she stopped to wipe the corners of her mouth with a white serviette rolled in a silver ring lying on the red formica table, and to read a few more paragraphs in the *Herald*.

It pained her considerably to see that Nixon was still sending in troops to Vietnam, and there was now talk of the war spreading to Cambodia. When will it ever end, this madness?

There was a story on the Overseas pages about more student protests. They should be at home with their families, Iris thought glumly.

Mayor Lindsay of New York said in an article that American society was on the point of spiritual, and possibly even physical, breakdown. Thank goodness our own politicians are just as concerned about the future of our young people, she thought. It made depressing reading. Confined within the grounds of the institution, as it were, except for the occasional Saturday morning when she took leave to shop in Penrith for toiletries and stockings, reading the news was essential if one was to keep up with life outside.

Pudding tonight was stewed apples from the school's own orchard, with baked custard. Iris tucked in heartily. When she was finished, she folded her newspaper and pushed it safely into her basket.

Then she washed her plates, dried them and put them away, deep in thought about a piece explaining the new divorce reforms in Britain.

The new legislation was theoretically emptied of the concepts of guilt and innocence, the very idea of which horrified Iris. Marriage was for good, as far as she was concerned, and anybody entering into it, taking their vows before God, was *obliged* – both spiritually and morally – to uphold those vows till death intervened. She tutted. Thank the Lord I do not have the burden of that particular social ill, she thought.

There was another piece that caught her eye tonight, the one about the 'acid way of life'. Didn't that new girl, Ellen, mention something about a pop festival?

Accompanying the story was a photograph of a half-naked girl at a pop festival near Melbourne. She was caked in thick, slimy mud, surrounded by a crowd of larrikins. The men had long hair and wore headbands, like American natives. The girls wore long skirts and an array of beads and bangles and make-up that made them appear quite mad. Dangling from a branch behind the mud-slung girl were her undergarments.

The reporter inquired what the girl's mother might say if she could see her now, and the hussy told him, 'She would probably say, "I wouldn't be surprised what my daughter got up to!"'

An inner frustration filled Iris. The very image of a mother so resigned to such behaviour was something beyond her comprehension. The girl's actions were apparently due to the effects of LSD, a powerful consciousness-expanding drug that hippies took in a glass of iced orange juice. It felt, the girl admitted, 'like an orgasm behind her eyeballs'.

Iris was mortified at such revelations, but thankful the newspapers saw fit to report these things. Without the knowledge supplied by news-gatherers, how could she possibly hope to influence her girls?

She was thorough in her clearing up. The kitchen needed to be left tidy for breakfast. She did a rapid visual check of the room before switching off the light and locking the door again. Now there was just one more chore she must do before going to bed. She had several telephone calls to make.

On her knees in her bedroom, Iris prayed hard for the two new girls. She prayed for their forgiveness. She prayed they would recognise their own ills, repent and realise they must do everything in their power to do the right thing in future. She asked God to give her the strength to challenge the girls, and to uphold the moral fortitude entrusted to her by the Church.

In bed, she sighed. She suddenly felt a little old. A little tired. It had been a busy year. Every year the same, but not long now until retirement.

There were plans afoot to phase out the present structure of school life and reopen with more modern methods of rehabilitation in mind. Her presence within the new regime would not be required. The school was to be divided into two sections, apparently, one for emotionally disturbed girls, the other for junior boys on remand.

But her work would not be wasted. She had managed to save a tidy sum and planned to move to Queensland, where properties were cheaper than in New South Wales. She dreamt of a small unit overlooking one of the canals surrounding Brisbane, with its own water frontage and a small boat with an outboard motor so that she could indulge in a little fishing. That much, she felt, she more than deserved for all her efforts.

She turned over on to her back. She removed her glasses and placed them carefully in their brown leather case on the small bedside table. She switched off the lamp and closed her eyes.

After a while she turned on the light again and lay quite still. Her limbs were rigid on the hard mattress. Something was troubling her, something one of those new girls had said, what was it? '*What if the family who want to adopt my baby change their minds? I don't want my baby to be orphaned,*' she had said, with the emphasis firmly on *orphan,* as though it was a disease.

Trollops, Iris thought angrily. She switched off the light and turned over stiffly, seething at the prospect of a restless night because of those tiresome teenagers.

Five

'This is Dormitory Four; anyone who is unwell or pregnant sleeps in Dormitory Four,' Matron shouted. Her crisp voice echoed around the high ceiling.

I thought: Why's she shouting when I'm the only one here? After stopping en route from the Clinic to go the toilet, Mary had disappeared. There was a kerfuffle behind the wooden fence between her and an officer, and then Matron, who was escorting us from the Clinic to the dormitory, suddenly ran to the officer's aid, leaving me alone in the dark yard. I could see three pairs of shoes through the gap at the bottom of the fence, and Mary's pants in a bunch round her ankles. She was kicking and skidding all over the place. The two women grappled with her, Mary screaming and cursing. Mum would say they all had St Vitus's dance, but I couldn't see the joke right now.

After a few minutes I heard a loud slap and the scuffling

stopped. Looking ruffled and red-faced, Matron came out from behind the fence. She said, 'Come along without young Mary Perry,' and marched ahead of me angrily.

Much as I didn't like Mary, I couldn't help wondering where she'd got to.

'You can work your way up, *if you behave*,' Matron continued, 'and eventually be sent to Jarrah Cottage. All the pregnant girls go there. There is a points system here at Gunyah, and you will be expected to work hard and be thoroughly punctilious to achieve high points. Girls who continually misbehave sleep in Dormitory Three, and work in the laundry or the clothing store with Officer Griffiths. If you misbehave in Dormitory Three you will be sent to Myalla. Girls in Dormitory Four are *not* considered exempt from their daily duties. Do you understand?'

'Yes, Matron,' I said, staring. I tried not to, but she was staring at me as though she expected me to look at her, *willing* me to, almost. Besides, I couldn't help examining her face: the long, pointy nose, the thin mouth that furled stiffly outwards and upwards, almost touching the top of her nose as she spoke. Her greasy grey hair was combed flat on her head, the left-hand parting so wide it revealed half an inch of white, flaking scalp. I was amazed, when she first turned around, to see she had long hair, scraped into a plait pinned flat on the back of her head with bobby pins.

'*Everyone* must work and do their share,' she said. Her voice made me think of an axe on metal. 'If you wish to attend school you may ask permission; otherwise you will work in the sewing room or the laundry, although laundry work is usually left for girls who misbehave. I suggest you behave yourself. Do you have any questions, Ellen?'

'No.'

'No *what*?'

'No, thank you, Matron,' I said, thinking: I've never seen anyone so *grey*. Even her eyes were grey, and her crêpy skin, and although she wore a beige twinset and a brown tweed skirt, the combination of all those dull colours looked . . . *grey*.

'There is a small locker for your things next to your bed. Put them away neatly. Then you may go to the television room.'

I did have a question, but Matron scared me. I wanted to know if I'd have to work in the laundry even though I was pregnant. It was right on the tip of my tongue, but Matron looked so fierce I chickened out.

My shoes click-clacked and sucked on the shiny brown lino as I followed her across the room. Click-clack, suck. She stopped by the end of a bed, and turned to face me, one hand resting lightly on the iron bed-end, as though she was showing me a luxury hotel suite.

'This is your bed. You will be expected to make it every morning and to keep your locker tidy,' she said. On each iron bedhead was a number. Mine was number forty-three, the same as the one sewn into my clothes.

I glanced around the room. There were plain green curtains on the high, many-paned windows. The windows had bars across them. The beds were perfectly made, their thin green cotton covers mitred and tucked in tight. Every bed sagged in the middle, as though a giant hand had punched them. At one end of the room was another small room, like an aquarium, all thick glass. Inside I could see a desk, a chair and telephone.

There were no teddy bears or dolls on any of the dormitory beds, no framed photos on the bedside cabinets, no pictures on the walls or posters. It was the plainest, coldest room I'd ever seen. I wanted to drop on the bed and cry. I wanted my mother.

I stuffed my things into the wooden locker by my bed, sniffling.

'Follow me,' Matron said, ignoring my tears.

We went out on to the landing, down the flight of grey-painted concrete steps and out into the dark quadrangle.

I hurried behind her down the covered way and we went through a door into a narrow, dimly lit corridor to climb a wooden spiral staircase with steep, shiny grey walls.

It was spooky, and quiet. Her brown leather shoes scraped on the worn timber and a couple of times I had to lean back when her heel nearly cracked me in the chin.

The light on the stairs was gloomy, but I could see the hairs on her muscly calves pressed flat beneath a pair of sheer, seamed stockings. Knotted blue veins meandered this way and that down to thick ankles.

The low-ceilinged room at the top of the stairs was dark and hot. It smelt of Sunlight soap and BO. At one end, up high near the ceiling, a black-and-white image flickered on an ancient mahogany television. The sound was turned up loud.

About twenty or thirty girls in dressing gowns and pyjamas sat on wooden chairs in rows, staring at the screen.

As we walked in they all turned round to stare. All eyes were on me. They all had short, butchered hair. They were thin and pale. No one smiled. No one spoke.

'Sit down here,' Matron said, pointing to an empty chair.

Then she went to the other side of the room to speak to an officer.

It was then that I noticed a girl underneath the television, facing everyone, with her arms outstretched to the side, like Jesus. She was obviously there as a punishment. Her face had a strained, embarrassed look. Whenever her arms drooped, she jerked them up sharply and shifted her weight.

I sat, rigid. Some girls still stared, others turned round to watch the TV. It was a Judy Garland movie. Her voice made my blood run cold. I wanted to go home. To my own bed. To my mother. To my own clothes and my own things, to my pretty bedroom, to my books: home, *home*.

We sat there for ages, staring at the screen in silence. Tears trickled down my cheeks. I wiped them with the back of my hand, but they kept coming, endlessly.

Before the film finished, the officer switched on a light and turned off the TV. I could see she had a smirk on her face, as though she was really gratified about switching it off seconds before the film's punchline.

Everyone stood. So I did.

'Line up,' the officer said.

We filed silently down the stairs along the covered way to the dormitory block. Upstairs, everyone stood at the foot of their beds with their eyes to the floor, waiting. So I did.

'One at a time, starting with number twenty, clean your teeth and go to the toilet,' she said.

It was then that I realised Officer Griffiths forgot to give me a toothbrush or toothpaste.

My heart flapped against my ribs. I tried to speak. My voice sounded thin and cracked, as though someone else had stepped inside me and was now talking on my behalf.

'Excuse me, but I haven't got anything to clean my teeth with,' I squeaked.

Till that moment, her eyes were constantly moving. She turned to look at me, her eyes still and dark. I swallowed. She was a tall, thin, blonde woman with black eyebrows and crooked teeth.

'Don't speak out of turn,' she said, narrowing her eyes. 'Come with me,' she added.

I followed her to the observation room.

'Here,' she said. She unlocked the door and from a drawer in the desk took an old tube of toothpaste and a dirty-looking tooth brush.

'Thank you,' I said.

When everyone finished, they stood at the foot of their beds again, eyes down, hands clasped behind their backs. So I did.

The officer ordered two girls to pull all the curtains across.

'Into bed. No turning over, no talking and *no moving*,' she shouted.

Everyone quickly slipped off their dressing gowns,

spread them on their beds and began to fold them neatly, like a shop assistant folds things, in stages. So I did, all the time watching the girl next to me, copying her. When she'd finished she put it into her bedside cupboard with her shoes. So I did.

I pulled the covers back and pushed my feet to the bottom of the bed. The sheets were starched and rough. The blue blanket smelt of camphor. The mattress was hard and lumpy and when I moved it squeaked loudly.

The light went out. I lay stiff as a corpse in the hollow, wide awake, all night.

I just about managed to keep out of trouble.

It was pretty easy, really. You just had to keep quiet. Not talk out of turn. Stand straight with your eyes to the ground. Work hard.

The girls who were always in trouble looked terrible. Worn out and thin. Some were bruised. Some of the Dormitory Three girls cut themselves on purpose. Anything sharp did the trick: stones, sticks they sharpened on the concrete, their fingernails. Or they gouged their flesh with pens or pencils, if they got hold of any. They always seemed to find a way. They cut one another's names in their skin. If they were caught they were put into isolation and made to scrub the walls for days on end. They were given only bread and jam to eat. They seemed proud of it. The other girls thought they were brave and exciting. I thought they were dumb.

Every day started before it got light. The officer on night watch ordered us out of bed. We stood by our beds blinking at the harsh light bulbs dangling from four brown shades in the centre of the dorm, till she told us to go to the bathroom one at a time.

I didn't know who else was pregnant – you couldn't tell because our dresses were so shapeless. I had to stop myself from staring, trying to work out who was. No one ever talked about it, and we weren't allowed to talk at all in the dormitories. Apart from the twenty minutes at morning and afternoon break time, talking wasn't *ever* allowed. If you got caught whispering you'd be punished.

Sometimes in the morning I noticed another bed was empty, but I could never remember who slept in it because I didn't even know half their names, and then someone new would arrive and I'd forget the bed's previous occupant completely.

I noticed the changes to my body – my tummy was swelling, as though I'd eaten too much; the singlet I wore tightened across my breasts, which felt tender and swollen, and the veins were bigger and had gone a deep blue. And my nipples seemed inflated and hard, and big lumps came up all around them, like goose-bumps. I felt sick all the time, too, and often vomited violently till my ribs ached. I thought it was because of the shock and my bad nerves, but one day Matron said it would soon stop, when I got past the four-month mark, and then I knew it was because I was pregnant.

Every morning, after using the bathroom, we all got dressed. After that, we cleaned the dormitory and made our beds. We took turns sweeping the floor and polished it with a stiff cloth on our hands and knees. We weren't allowed to kneel on a cushion; my knees were cracked and sore.

We cleaned the toilets and sinks with our bare hands and a smelly old cloth. We polished the windows, dusted the furniture. We were given points for good cleaning, good behaviour, good bed-making, good everything.

After morning duties we ate breakfast in the echo-filled dining hall. We weren't allowed to scrape our chairs on the polished timber floor. Everyone made a great effort to lift their chair up slowly and put it down gently. Scraping your chair was a terrible crime, and anyone who did it was punished. Some of the Dormitory Three girls did it on purpose. I began to think they liked being in trouble, for the attention. Every morning we ate porridge, lumpy and cold, with a teaspoon of sugar, a slice of white bread and butter, and a small glass of water. I couldn't stop thinking about hot buttered toast and fresh fruit.

After breakfast it was muster in the quadrangle. We filed out of the dining room and lined up, eyes down.

When Mr Hewitt shouted our number we called out 'Here' in turn. If it was a Saturday we were given chores to do all morning. Sometimes, after lunch, we played rounders or cricket in a small yard with the high stone walls pressing in around us. I hated games, so I hung round the edges.

I was getting fat. I didn't want to run because it hurt my back. And my bosoms were swollen, sore and itchy. They ached and stung, as if there were blades inside them. We weren't allowed to talk unless it was about the game. We stood there for hours. I shifted from one foot to the other over and over again, to try and stop my legs throbbing.

'What are you so fucking miserable about?' someone said to me once.

'What are you so happy about?' I said back. I looked at the other girls and thought, yeah, they like it here, because they don't know any better. This place is probably better than what they had outside. It was then that I started to think about home and how lucky I was to live in a nice house; even though it was only a small timber place, it was the setting that made it special, surrounded by bush with the lake out front. I made up my mind never to come back to Gunyah. Some of the girls had been in and out for years, probably on purpose – at least you got a bed and food, and if you were careful you didn't get punished. But I didn't want to come back, not ever.

On weekdays I went to school, one classroom with twenty-five girls. I was studying for the Nurse's Entrance Exam. The teacher, Mrs McGrath, was a short, tubby woman with a grey bun and a Scottish accent. She said I should try and make up for my bad ways by putting something back into the community.

'It is our duty to try and mould you girls into suitable citizens,' she said. Becoming a nurse was a good way, she reckoned. 'Part of *your* problem was you didn't have a proper job,' she said.

I said, 'I don't know what I want to be. I haven't figured it out yet.'

She said, 'Be a nurse.'

Mrs McGrath liked me. She always asked me to read

out loud to the class. She said I had good diction, whatever that is. She liked my compositions. She got me to write poetry. Soon I was writing lots of it. I smuggled some of my best ones out of class in my undies and gave them to Robyn, a girl in Dormitory Three who liked me. She was a bigwig. The girls all looked up to her. She had mouse-coloured curly hair and big poppy eyes. The others all said she was sexy, but I couldn't see it myself.

One day she cornered me at the bottom of the spiral stairwell after Library.

'Come on, Ellie, let Robyn kiss you, she wants to be your lover, come on,' her friend Shelley whispered. She forced me against the wall, then pushed Robyn in front of me. I could feel Robyn's breath on my face, we were so close. Officer Wyndham was still upstairs locking the library door. I was the librarian by then; Mrs McGrath recommended me because I was good at English. Miss Wyndham sent me to the bottom of the stairs in front of the others, because I was trusted to keep an eye on them till she came down.

All the girls were perched on the stairs like seagulls on a cliff, staring down at us. Robyn pressed herself against me. Her thin body was warm and rigid.

I slid sideways along the wall till I was against the locked door, but she moved with me. Shelley was holding her dress up high to shield us. Robyn looked into my eyes, her lips were moist and trembling. She held my hands tight, she was shaking stiffly. Then she leant her face into mine and kissed me on the lips with her mouth open. I crushed myself against the door, moaning. I wished I could float through the door like a spook. Just as she tried to part my lips with her tongue, Miss Wyndham appeared round the bend in the stairs. Shelley let go of her dress. Robyn turned away from me abruptly. My lips were wet with her saliva. She tossed her head and smiled up at Miss Wyndham. Everyone giggled. Vomit crawled up the back of my mouth, but I swallowed it. I wiped my mouth with the back of my hand and stared at the floor.

'What's going on down here?' Miss Wyndham bellowed.

Silence. Everyone looked at me. My face was burning. Miss Wyndham came down the stairs and gave me a filthy look, as though I was shit, then she said, 'I thought as much,' in a satisfied tone. She unlocked the door and ushered us outside.

All the officers looked at me differently after the kissing incident. Then one day Matron came up to me in the yard where I was sweeping leaves. She reached into her pocket and pulled out some small pieces of paper.

'What do you think this is, young lady?' she said. She looked as if she hated me. I glanced at the papers in her hand and shrugged.

'I don't know, Matron.'

'I'll tell you, then. You have been writing things, haven't you? About Gunyah. About the officers.'

I swallowed and looked at my shoes. My poems. She had my poems. About Gunyah, and being homesick, about it all being unfair, about freedom, about how cruel the officers were.

I thought she was going to punish me. But she narrowed her eyes and stared at me for ages.

'I have to admit, Ellen Russell, that a lot of what you say in this poetry is quite accurate,' she said. 'You are quite the clever one, aren't you? In normal circumstances, anyone caught smuggling paper or pens out of the classroom would be severely punished. But as you have not written any of the usual filth that most girls write, I will let you off this time. Just don't let it happen again, do you understand? Confine your ramblings to the schoolroom.'

I thought that was the end of it, so I carried on sweeping. The heat in my face cooled. But she stood there, fingering the poems.

'Thought you got off, did you? *Did you?*' she hissed.

'N . . . no, Matron. I . . . I'm s . . . sorry—'

'Smart aleck,' she snapped. Then she held my poetry under my nose and tore it into little pieces. It fell like snow at my feet.

'Sweep up that rubbish and place it in the incinerator,' she said and marched off.

I looked down at the paper. I could see the words *wander* and *skies* on a little triangle. On another piece, *be close to your dreams* and *caged*. On another, *I couldn't sleep at all last night, the wind outside was moaning like a wounded dog*. I stared at the words for a few minutes, then swept them up like she ordered.

After that the officers got at me any way they could. Sometimes I'd sit down for a meal and there'd be no utensils to eat with, so I went hungry. And if I left a mouthful or two on my plate at the end of a meal, they'd dish it up again at the next meal, and the next, till I ate it, gagging.

Another time, when I was getting dressed one morning, my shoes were gone so I had to go barefoot all day. And once I was made to sew up my pockets so that I couldn't put my hands in them. Even Mrs McGrath got in on the act and wouldn't let me have any paper or pens for two weeks. Every lesson I was made to sit in a corner with my back to the class, reading the Bible.

I didn't think much about being pregnant. It was like a dream. I didn't really believe it. I wrote about it in my poems, but even Mrs McGrath didn't realise. She said it was abstract poetry. I just couldn't imagine a baby inside me, growing. It was scary. No one ever talked about it, but sometimes at breaktime, when we were allowed to talk for twenty minutes along the covered way, or to sit on the hard benches around the quadrangle, the girls asked me what it was like, to have a baby. I said I didn't have a clue, I'd never had one before. They wanted to touch my stomach, which was big now, rounder. I wouldn't let them in case one of the officers saw.

There was an empty bed in our dormitory for months. Then one night Matron came to the dormitory after lights out. She had a girl in a dressing gown with her. It was that girl I had met the first night. Mary. She looked different. Beneath her enormous bosom her tummy had swollen. Matron watched by the door as Mary shuffled across to her bed and climbed in.

'You and Ellen Russell are not permitted to communicate with one another, do you both understand?' Matron shouted.

The next day at breaktime I tried to get near Mary to hear what she was saying to the others. She was surrounded by lots of girls, all eager to hear where she'd been and why.

I stood nearby, listening, pretending to look up at the branches of a gnarled old Moreton Bay fig tree. I kept stealing glances at her, when I was sure the officers weren't looking; there were a dozen or so of them all around the yard, some holding lengths of hose.

Along Mary's arms were pale, pearly scars. Her cheeks were pink, but her eyes were sunken, with dark circles underneath. Her legs and arms seemed thinner; when she stood up she looked like a beer barrel on stilts.

'Why'd Matron keep you in isolation so long?' a girl asked her.

'For my own good,' she said, patting her tummy.

'Did you try and get rid of the baby?' someone else said.

'Only 'cause Sister said things, y'know? She's a fuckin' cunt. Matron took the razor blade off me. When I got in lock-up I changed my mind anyway. I started to think about the baby. It's mine, all mine. I can feel it in there. Like a butterfly. It feels beautiful, y'know? Like a miracle. I couldn't hurt it. And I have to look after meself now, so I can take care of my baby. No fuckin' bastard is gonna push me around with my baby.'

'You're lucky,' someone said, 'I wish I had a baby. I wish I was pregnant.'

They raved on about a layette, whatever that is, and breastfeeding.

'Could you do it?' said one.

'I'd use a bottle,' someone said.

'What about the father?' asked one.

'Oh, he's fucked off,' Mary said, 'good riddance to bad fuckin' rubbish I reckon.'

'Who'll pay for the baby?' someone said. 'Who'll pay to feed it and buy its clothes?'

Mary looked at her. She frowned. 'I'll look after it,' she said.

'Yeah,' the girl said, 'but who'll look after it when you work?'

'It's my baby,' Mary said, smiling

'Are you gonna go to Jarrah Cottage?'

'You get your own room.'

'But what about Sister?' someone said. 'Aren't you scared of her? Sleeping in the same building.'

Mary glanced over her shoulder, then in a low voice she said, 'It's not her fault she has to give us medicine and stuff. Skinny old bag.' Everyone laughed.

The whistle went for mid-morning muster. We rushed to line up.

Mary was in front of me, a little to my right. All heads were bowed. I could see her from the corners of my eyes.

Mr Hewitt stood on a raised platform ticking the register. Behind him, a sudden gust of wind rattled the dry branches of a gum tree. When I looked across at Mary again a few minutes later, her face was white.

April 1970

The stone chapel reminded me of a cave I discovered near our house, cold and clammy, and smelling of wet leaves and possum shit.

We'd been given cardigans, but I was still freezing.

The chaplain was raving on about loaves and fishes, about the miracle of God's love through his Son. He had a monotonous voice that made me sleepy.

I'd been vomiting all night into a bucket next to my bed. The night watch was furious because she couldn't nod off in the observation room. My bones ached. I heaved so hard I thought my baby would come out and land in the bucket, screaming.

I was sitting at the end of a row against the sandstone wall, under a stained-glass window that depicted one of the disciples. I rested my shoulder against the wall; I felt sick again, and weak, so I leant my head on the rough stone. I dared not close my eyes because I knew I'd nod off and be punished. I haven't been punished once. Not since that first night when I was belted on the leg. And the next morning some woman made me scrub part of the brick wall for hours. It wasn't a punishment, really, she just made me do it, for something to do. I didn't do it right, she said when I finished, *Do it again*! I scrubbed for four hours, till my back felt like it would crack in two.

I tried to imagine Jesus dividing up the bread, but I kept thinking about Robbie at Ourimbah, swimming with me, the band music wafting across the fields, the mist on the hills around the valley, the smell of camp fires, the strange people. A lot of the blokes there looked like Jesus.

I remember being amazed when people took off their clothes to slop in a mud-hole. I thought I'd landed on another planet. People were weird, but friendly. The only thing I didn't enjoy was the communal toilet in a dome-shaped tent. When I walked past I could see in through the perspex door. Girls were sitting there doing their business, as if it was the most natural thing in the world to sit next to someone, shitting. I sneaked off into the bushes and found some furry leaves. I crouched behind a tree, stiff with fear in case someone caught me – there were people everywhere, up trees, inside tents, under blankets, inside sleeping bags – and the wee splashed against my legs and made a loud noise as it drilled a shaft in the dirt. I felt sure someone had heard it.

Robbie has a sinewy body, like Jesus.

The chaplain seemed to be talking to the thin air somewhere above our heads. I shivered. A girl in front of me stifled a giggle. Someone coughed. A long, dust-filled shaft of blue light shone right through St Peter's robes.

Robbie's hair is blond, not brown, and his eyes are light blue. He is good on a surf board. I suppose the closest Jesus ever got to surfing was taking a dip in the Red Sea.

I used to watch Robbie for hours at Manly beach. He cut his foot on a broken bottle once and I wrapped it up in my beach towel. He stumbled up the concrete steps, then kicked it off angrily. All the way back to our room blood dribbled along the footpath and I worried about the germs getting in and poisoning him. He lay on the bed with some tissues pressed to the cut and when I tried to put a Band-aid on he pushed me away and swore.

I'd know now what to do. Bodily functions. Bodily fluids. Poor Jesus didn't have a nurse standing by to stop the flow.

One day I was sitting on a toilet in the outside block being watched by Officer Wyndham. I had terrible pains in my tummy. I was straining so hard I thought my baby would pop out into the toilet bowl. Officer Wyndham noticed and told me to pull up my pants and follow her to the Clinic to see Sister.

'Good luck,' someone said as we walked away.

Sister didn't say a thing about my baby. Not a thing.

She poured Dettol and liquid soap – Phisohex, I think – into a bottle. She shook it vigorously, then fed it into a funnel connected to a long tube that she pushed inside me. It felt like a snake sliding in.

The solution swilled inside me like the ocean. She said, 'Lie still until it does the trick,' then she left the room. My insides burnt and slurped and gurgled. I was crying and in pain. When it was over I dashed to the toilet and sat there for ages like a rag doll, until I was hollow.

Sunday was my best day. After lunch, we were allowed to write a letter if we wanted. We were taken into the dining hall. As we filed in, an officer at a small table gave us one pencil and one sheet of paper each – the pencils were all counted and had to be handed in later, because of the bad girls who used them for tattooing.

We were only allowed to write to our families. I always wrote to my mother. I didn't know what to say to her sometimes, and I couldn't get too personal because the officers read all the letters. I tried to tell her how I felt. I said I was homesick.

She wrote back and asked if I wanted her to come once a month on a Sunday, but I said no, my hair was a mess and I didn't want her to see me till it grew a bit.

But that wasn't the only reason. I didn't want her to know I was pregnant. And I blamed her for being in Gunyah, for dobbing me to the police in the first place.

I told her I was behaving myself, that I had lots of points and soon I would go to Jarrah Cottage. All the best girls go there, I said. As I wrote the words I could feel the heat rise in my face.

One Sunday, halfway through letter writing, Officer Wyndham called out my name.

I looked up.

'You have a visitor,' she said. As I walked across the room the blood drained from my body. It must be my mother, I thought. But I told her not to come. I told her not to.

She was sitting on the long bench outside, under the covered way, with the other mothers and fathers. They all had pained expressions, as though they were ashamed to be there.

'Mum!' I said, and threw my arms around her neck. We clung there for ages, holding one another.

She was wearing a pale-pink woollen suit, with little bobbly bits all over it. A cream blouse frothed at her tanned neck. Pearl earrings glowed on her soft lobes. I looked into her crisp brown eyes, I could see myself in them. I looked awful, as though rats had chewn my hair in the night, and my eyes looked as though I'd had a fright.

Mum's hair was freshly permed and set in neat brown waves off her face. She seemed so clean and smart and stylish. I felt like a blob in a sack next to her.

'I've brought you some things,' she said. 'Oh, darling, it's so good to see you. But what have they done to your hair?'

I sat down and folded my arms across my swollen belly in the hope she wouldn't notice.

'I can't help it,' I said, touching it. 'They do it to everyone.'

She fidgeted with the clasp on her patent-leather handbag, as if she wanted to get going.

'I brought you some goodies, Jaffas and Minties, but the Superintendent took them. He said you can have them later.'

I said 'Thank you,' but I knew I would never see the lollies – no one ever got the treats visitors brought. The officers kept them to eat in the staffroom.

'I've got good points,' I said.

'It seems very clean, very well kept,' she said. 'You look well.' She unclasped her handbag, took out one of Granny's lace handkerchiefs and twisted it between her fingers.

'Did you get my letters?' I said.

'Are you studying hard?' she said.

'I want to go home,' I said. 'I hate it here. It's not . . .' I hesitated, because the word I wanted to say made me uncomfortable, I wasn't used to it. I held my breath, then said it in a rush: 'it's not democratic.'

Mum looked at me sadly. She put her hand on my forehead, pushed my hair back and slicked it down with her fingers. I pulled away.

'Don't,' I said.

'I'll *never* understand why you did this,' she said softly.

'I want to go home,' I said. 'They've got no right to keep me here. I'm not a criminal.' There was a long pause. Then I said: 'How's the shop?'

She looked at her hands. She turned them over and admired her pink nails.

'I'm going on holiday, as a matter of fact,' she said. 'With a friend.'

There was another long pause. I could smell her perfume and feel the warmth of her leg against mine.

'To Hawaii. On the *Oriana*. It should be lovely. I'm really looking forward to it.'

'Where's Jack? Have you seen him?' I asked. My chest felt as though it was caving in.

'I'll be away for six weeks. I just hope Berenice looks after the shop properly for me.' Berenice is my mother's employee. I always tried to avoid her if I could, she was nasty to me when Mum's back was turned.

'Is Jack coming home?' I said, but she looked away as though she hadn't heard.

I wanted to tell her about being pregnant. About how frightened I was. But I didn't want to spoil her holiday. And I was afraid to tell her in case she got angry. I didn't want her to get angry. I was sick of people being angry.

'Ellen?'

'What?'

'I had a phone call from Sister Dawson the other day. She is going to help you sort things out.'

'Can I come home after your holiday?' I said. I looked at her.

'About what to do. You know,' she said. She gave me a look that meant: I know *just* what you're going through. 'About this,' she said, and patted my stomach.

That night I gave a lot of thought to being pregnant. Not about what it was doing to me, the physical changes, the feelings – I hated all that, feeling fat. Being *pregnant* . . . that sounds like a disease. I was sick of hearing about diseases. Lots of the girls had diseases. They seemed proud of it. Sister gave them special medicine for it, injections. They called it the clap. For some reason it made me think of foot-and-mouth disease. Some girls in my dormitory said it was God's punishment for being a slut. Anyway, that night I started to think of myself as *having* a *baby*. That sounded much better than *being pregnant*.

I remembered the look on Mary's face in the quadrangle that day and what she said about it being a miracle. She looked so happy, as if she had something that was hers, all hers. I tried to feel happy, too. But my head was in a jumble most of the time and the rash on my arms was driving me nuts. I couldn't stop biting my nails. Most nights I fell asleep trembling like a divining rod.

After Mum said it out loud, it seemed more out in the open, like it wasn't that shameful. I lay on my back that night and dared to touch my tummy. I wanted to feel it move inside me. I tried to imagine what it looked like in there, curled up, naked. It was hard to believe. A *baby*, inside me. Would Sister tell me about breastfeeding? I didn't want to do that. It sounded unnatural. Would she show me how to change a nappy? Where would I have the baby? In Jarrah Cottage? Or in Sick Bay? That's it, Sick Bay. With *Sister* helping. I shuddered. I didn't want her to touch me ever again, not ever.

I will love you, I whispered. *I'll look after you.*

'Ellen Russell. Get out of bed and come with me.' Matron's voice sliced the dark.

The light came on. My eyes popped open. My heart thumped. *What have I done?* I racked my brains to try and remember what had happened today. Did I speak out of turn? Did I look up at muster? Did I do a rotten job of cleaning the dormitory floor? What? My bed? Didn't I do the corners straight? My locker, did I leave it untidy?

'And Carol Routledge, Marion Reeves, Kaye Sutton and Mary Perry. Get out of bed and get dressed.' We all jumped. 'Get back to sleep and mind your own business,' Matron snarled at the other crumpled heads rising from their pillows.

Dressed, we stood at attention by our beds, eyes down.

Matron scanned her clipboard. 'Carol Routledge, you were overheard swearing today at breaktime,' she said. She gave Carol, a skinny kid with terrible scars in the crook of each arm, a look that made my knees buckle.

'Marion Reeves, you did not clean the sinks properly in the main toilet block. Kaye Sutton, you had your eyes closed during chapel.' Marion and Kaye were best friends from Canberra. They were caught shoplifting scented soaps and bath salts in the runup to Christmas. They stood close together, and I saw that Marion had her hand behind Kaye and they were holding hands.

'Mary,' Matron said, 'you have been told not to turn over in bed—'

'But, Matron! It's me back, it's killing me 'cos of being—'

'Ellen Russell! You have been pushing your luck lately with your carrying on. You were seen leaning on the wall in chapel today. All of you, outside, *now*!'

We filed downstairs into the quadrangle. Matron led us down the dimly lit covered way. Halfway along, two girls were on their hands and knees face-to-face, scrubbing the path, so close their faces almost touched. An officer stood over them wielding a hose.

'Big, long strokes, come on, harder, that's it, put your backs into it,' she said.

'Must've been caught doing *you know what*,' Mary hissed in my ear as we passed them.

'What was that, Mary?' Matron said. She stopped walking, turned round and put her face right up close to Mary's. You could see her white breath in the still night air. Mary leant back, repulsed.

Then Matron looked at me. I gulped.

'Don't you think you're in enough trouble, eh? *Eh?*' she said. She poked the hollow in my shoulder with a podgy finger.

'Yes Matron,' I said.

'You can have a further two hours in lock-up for that.'

Lock-up!

'But . . . Matron . . . *please* . . .' I begged, 'please don't put me in there, I don't want to go in there, please—'

'You should learn to show some respect in a place of worship. You know the rules about conduct. You've had this coming a long time.'

I bowed my head. Tears dropped on to the tiles. The *ssh . . . ssh . . . ssshh . . . ssshh* of the brushes sounded like a steam engine. The smell of disinfectant killed every other smell – the stand of eucalyptus in the yard, the freshly turned earth along the flower borders surrounding the quadrangle, the fading embers in the garden incinerator. I thought: When I get out I never want to smell Dettol again in my whole life.

'You girls go one at a time to the sluiceroom and collect a bucket of cold water and a brush each,' she said. 'Mary, you first.'

We had reached the far end of the covered way. Mary disappeared across the quadrangle to fetch a bucket and brush. Just then Officer Wyndham appeared.

'Right, Miss Wyndham, can you supervise this lot while I take care of Ellen?' said matron.

'With pleasure,' Miss Wyndham grinned.

'Come with me, Ellen,' Matron said.

I followed her to the main building. We weren't allowed near it usually.

At the bottom of the steps she turned right and led me along a dark path. There was a steel door in the sandstone wall with a tiny window in the middle of it. Thick vines tumbled from the roof and snarled at my hair. As I brushed them away I could feel things dropping on to me, unseen.

She switched on an outside light and unlocked the door. It squeaked as she pushed it. She flicked another switch and a bare bulb in the middle of the room came on.

'Take these,' she said. She pointed to a bucket filled with water and a scrubbing brush. 'Get in and start scrubbing.'

I looked at the bucket. I peered round the door at the room. There were no windows, just grey concrete walls and an air vent in one corner, up high. On the floor was a stained mattress and a grey blanket, no sheets, no pillow.

I had a big, hard lump in my throat. I was shaking.

'But, Matron, I'm *pregnant*.'

She laughed. She threw her head back and laughed. I could see the silver fillings in her teeth. I imagined my Minties melting in her mouth.

'You're nothing special,' she said. 'In fact, quite the opposite. You are a silly little brat. How do you think you're going to manage? Stupid little slut. You need to do some growing up, girl. You've been *selfish*. Sister will soon put you right. You've been nothing but a dirty little slut. You girls don't deserve any help. You are lucky, *lucky*, do you hear, that someone like Sister Dawson cares enough to try and help you. Now get in there and be quiet. Another officer will be along shortly to supervise.'

I stood stock-still. Her nose shone under the cobwebby light. Beads of oily sweat covered her forehead. Her body smelt stale, like old rags. Her thin, dry lips were parted, and the air that came out smelt of mince meat.

I narrowed my eyes. '*I hate you*,' I said, 'I fucking hate you.' I couldn't believe it was me, saying that word. But it sounded all right. It sounded *right*.

She straightened. A look of shock crossed her face.

'Come with me,' she said. She wrenched me by the arm to the toilet block.

At the row of concrete sinks she twisted my arm behind my back and leant down heavily on me, so that I had to bend forward with my face in the sink. With her free hand she pushed a square of Sunlight soap into my mouth. I retched and spluttered into the Dettolled bowl.

'That'll teach you to swear,' she said. She pulled my head up by the hair.

Back at the cell, she pushed me through the door with a look on her face that said: *You should be terrified, you're in for it now.* I rubbed my arm briskly where her fingernails had made shallow U-shapes.

'Lucky for you you *are* pregnant, or you'd be off to Myalla before long,' she shouted. 'Now scrub.' She picked up the bucket and brush and dumped them at my feet. The door slammed. She turned the key. I stood under the light, listening to the boom-boom, boom-boom of my own heart. I thought my skin might tear open from the pressure underneath it.

I looked at the bucket, then I kicked it hard. It hit the wall with a crash and bounced off. Water slurped across the floor and licked the edge of the mattress. I kicked it again, and again, and again.

The noise was loud and harsh. It echoed around the room. Metal on stone.

After a while, after kicking it twenty times – maybe more – my toes began to hurt. I sat on the mattress, puffing. I bent my knees, folded my arms and rested the side of my head on them, listening to my heart: *thump, thump,* and my breath: *in, out, in, out.* On the floor near the wall there were rat droppings. I stared at them and a dry terror clamped my throat. Slowly, the sounds of my anger grew fainter, till the room was quiet.

I picked up the brush and began to scrub. I scrubbed for hours, till my knees were raw craters. I was wide awake. Then I lay down and thought about Matron calling me a stupid slut. My eyes were completely dry.

Six

What is the use of a newborn child?
BENJAMIN FRANKLIN

It was the first time in ages that I slept without shaking.

I dreamt of going home, of swimming in the sea. Waves crashed against my legs, kids laughed, people splashed and dived.

I stirred and felt the baby move inside me, *my* baby. Like waves lapping the sand, a soft shifting.

The light came on every hour and burnt my eyes.

I put my hands on my tummy. It felt warm and comforting. The skin was stretched tight. I could feel the baby's elbow, or knee, sticking out.

I will take you far away, to my island. We'll live in a tree-house. I can dive for fish: I did that in the lake near our house. You can reach down and feel for them with your hand. They were always dopey because the water was half seawater, half freshwater, and they didn't like the mud, so they were easy to catch. There are big crabs, and prawns, in the clear sea around my island. I'll find birds' eggs high in the forest canopy for us to eat. Catch lizards and roast them over a fire. I'll rub sticks together to make the fire – if the Abos can do it, I can.

Mum went away to Hawaii; I'll go away, too. But not without my baby. I won't go without it, not anywhere.

If it's a girl, I'll call it Jody. If it's a boy, I don't know, Richard, or David. What was my father's name? Maybe I'll find out one day, ask Mum again.

We'll make a good team, you and me. I'll make a grass-skirt, like the hula dancers'.

She'll be there soon, my mother, dancing the hula. Drinking from a coconut with a straw stuck in a hole. Or a pineapple with a paper umbrella on top. She showed me the photographs of her last trip there. She was sitting at a cane table with two men and a woman. The men wore flowery shirts. My mother wore a tight flocked dress, off the shoulders, and silk stilettos. Her lips were thick with dark-red lipstick. Her nails were long and red. It was a black-and-white photo, but I could still tell the colours.

I stroked my tummy. *We'll build a canoe on my island. I'll sharpen sticks and stones, carve our names on the hull. I'll weave hats to keep off the sun. Find one of those big clam shells, line the pearly inside of it with soft leaves and petals for you. You will sleep in the shade. I will feed you fruit, berries, crab meat. You'll be rosy-cheeked and happy.*

I know! Your bassinett can go in my room. That's a good place. At the foot of my bed. Mum will look after you while I'm at work. My Granny looked after me when my mother worked. She made lots of yummy *things, biscuits and cakes, but I wasn't allowed in the house much, not till tea-time. I went off to play in the bush with a pocketful of biscuits, or down to the lake for a swim. My mother will look after you. Or I will. Yeah, we can live with my mother. She'll help us. I'll get a job. I'll find something. I will.*

Old Ma Riley said I'd end up being a vagrant.

'What's that?' I asked.

'Hah!' she laughed, 'don't you know *anything*? It means *no job*, fool.'

It'll be all right. I'm not a dummy. I won't let these fucking cunts push me around.

Those words. Fucking cunt. Fucking . . . cunt.

You won't like those words. When you come I won't say them. Ever.

I want to be good. I want to be a good person. If I pass my exam I'll be a nurse. I'm a good person. God made me good. He did.

Mum gave me a book when I turned thirteen, *A Guide to Womanhood*. I remember the cover had a girl with a wide, white smile and clear skin, like someone in a Doris Day movie. Inside it had stuff about keeping healthy, and things I wasn't sure about at the time, and still aren't:

> Girls who expect to do well in school and in recreational activities, and to accomplish good and useful work in the world, cannot permit themselves to yield to every mood of self-indulgence. Nor can they let themselves develop a habit of retreating from the outside world into useless daydreaming and sexual

reveries. The mind and body must be kept under reasonable discipline and directed into sound activities.

I mean, what's a reverie when it's at home? Or as Mary might put it: What's a fuckin' reverie?

Mum gave me a packet of Kotex, too, and a funny-looking elastic contraption. I know now what it is, but at the time I thought it was some new device for keeping up my stockings.

'It's time you read this now you are thirteen,' she said, giving me the book, 'and don't stain the sheets.' She made me feel filthy.

We'll make up poetry. I'll tell you stories from the Bible, from my old books. Heidi. A Bush Christmas. *The kids in that, they lived in the bush, they survived. We'll have lots of Bush Christmases. We can make decorations from feathers and shells, dangle them from a tree near the beach. We'll take some things to my island in a rucksack.*

I'll call it Secret Island, because no one will ever know we're there. I learnt survival at Brownies. We made damper on a fire, it tasted like salty chalk. The sea will give us what we need. I know how to open oysters without a knife. You put them on a fire and the heat opens them. I'll tickle your tummy and kiss it. I'll lift you up and carry you on my back. We'll sit on the beach and watch the sea. We'll drink rainwater from empty shells. We'll eat pineapples and mangoes and pawpaws.

There's a rock that hangs like a canopy on my island – you can sit under it in the rain and stay dry. There's some drawings some Abos did. Lizards and snakes. We can draw our own. You can see where they made their fires. Dark patches on the yellow rock. Sharpened stones they left behind. If they can do it, I can. Our geography teacher called them uncivilised savages. You don't see them in Coolamon.

Robbie will come to the hospital. He'll bring a big bunch of flowers, and chocolates. And some little clothes for you. I want to dress you in black and white, and green. Not pink or blue. Something different.

You'll have blond hair, like his. He'll hold you and kiss the top of your head. He will look at me with love in his eyes. He'll take care of us, at his room. He will. There's a corner for your cot, just big enough.

Robbie will work hard, he'll get a better job. Mum said there's no future in making surfboards. He will cut his hair if I ask him. He'll be respectable and kind. I'll meet his parents. They've got lots of money. They live in a big house overlooking the water at Newport, where lots of rich people live. They'll tell him to do the right thing, to look after us. We'll get married in my old church. We will. They'll all be there. They'll all look at you.

He did this. Robbie started this, at Ourimbah. Behind the bushes, he pushed it in. It hurt, God it hurt. I told him to stop, but he just kept pounding away, like a madman.

I heard footsteps and voices.

I told him again: 'Stop, someone's coming.'

He said, 'Yeah, me,' and he kept ramming into me.

His jeans were around his ankles, he had my dress up, scrunched between us, and it dug into my skin. He held my arms above my head, I could feel the dusty earth on my moist skin. His mouth was hard, his whiskers scraped my chin. He pushed his tongue in and out of my mouth – it felt stiff, and his teeth ground on mine.

Then he made a groaning noise, like something hurt him, and he flopped on to me like a stuffed dummy, breathing heavily.

When his breathing slowed he backed away; his thingy was still stiff, he stuffed it into his underpants, rearranged it, then pulled up his jeans. He acted as if nothing had happened, like he'd just got out of bed and was getting dressed for work.

I lay on the ground, looking up at his lean body. Ants ran all over my feet and flies buzzed around my legs. I shooed them away and brushed off the ants. I looked up at Robbie. His muscly brown body was silhouetted against the bright-blue sky.

'I love you,' I said.

He grinned. 'Yeah, I love you too, babe,' he said. 'Come on, get dressed and let's go dance.'

My father lives in Seven Hills, Mum told me. In those dreadful western suburbs, she said. He *knows* where you are, she said. He *knows* we live in Coolamon. He came to our street one day and drove slowly next to my mother and Granny. I was in a big pram. 'He wound his window down and told me he wanted a divorce,' she said. 'He said if I wouldn't give him one he'd have me committed.'

My father was a mounted policeman. Mum called him the Philandering Ranger. After I was born, he put her in an old house with rats in the roof, way out in the bloody back blocks, because he was 'carrying on' with some woman in town. He didn't want my mother to find out, but she knew because he came in late, four in the morning sometimes. She could smell the other woman on his clothes. One day she found a brooch in the front of his car. He wasn't interested in me, Mum said. He never cared about me. Couldn't care less.

'Ellen Russell, get on with your scrubbing!' Behind the heavy door the voice was muffled.

Who's that? Not Matron. Some other fucking cunt.

'Fuck off!'

'I'll open the door if you don't scrub.'

'I hate you all.'

Silence.

The key turned. Miss Wyndham came in holding a length of hose.

'Go on, hit me,' I said. I sat on the mattress hugging my knees, looking up at her.

She struck my arm first. I winced and clamped a hand over the welt. My face scrunched and tears welled, but I didn't budge. She hit me again, near the first mark.

'You're all fucking cunts!' I screamed. 'Leave me alone! *leave . . . me . . . alone!*' My voice sounded strange.

She hit me again, and again. I rolled on the mattress screaming. She hit me all over my back. I could feel the blood, hot and prickly against the hairy hessian.

Then suddenly she stopped.

I was curled in a tight ball, whimpering.

She stared down at me, as if I was a dog. She was panting. Her eyes were popping, the irises dilated and black.

'You won't speak like that again in a hurry, wi. girl? Keep your big mouth shut and you might – mi₂ get out.'

She slammed the door and turned the key. The ligh. went out. I held myself and cried. I'm alive, I thought. I'm alive.

But something was different inside me.

All night long someone outside the door turned the light on every hour and I woke with a jolt. My eyes burnt with tiredness. My mind was a confusion of thoughts and images, dreams and voices.

I could tell it was morning by the light streaming through the air-vent. I could hear voices in the distance and wondered if it was a dream. Then I heard marching feet and shouting.

I took off my dress and it dropped to the floor. The blood on my back had dried into black crusty welts. I stood there in the dim light and craned my neck to look at them over my shoulder.

I caressed my tummy. *You'll be all right*, I whispered. *I won't let anyone hurt you. I'll look after you. One day I'll find my father and take you to see him. When he sees you, tiny and sweet, he'll let us in. He'll put his arms around my shoulders when I'm holding you, and we'll gaze at your face. He'll give me money to buy you things. He'll invite us back. His wife will be friendly. She'll like us, she will. There'll be cakes and drinks, and she'll knit cardigans and bootees for you. But don't worry, if they don't want us we'll go to my island, where it's safe. I'll take care of you.*

I remembered Mary's words, about not being pushed around, and the look on the other girls' faces. Like she was something special. I thought: I'll be like that. I won't let them push me around. This is the last time any of them hurt me. My plan was simple, it couldn't fail. I lay down again and shut my eyes. My mind and body were still.

Late August 1970

Sister pressed firmly with her palms on my bulge. They felt cool and smooth. Her nails were neat and trimmed. I pushed my hands under the small of my back to hide my own bitten nails.

'Everything seems to be in order,' she said. 'You may put your pants on again and sit on that chair.'

She washed her hands, then sat down on the other chair and clasped her hands together on her lap.

'Well, young lady. I am pleased you have settled into your room at Jarrah Cottage. It is much more comfortable than the dormitory, isn't it?'

'Why do I have to stay in my room all day? Why can't I still go to school?'

'Now, now, Ellen, you know the rules of conduct here. You must not speak out of turn. You need to rest. You have got your Entrance Certificate, so you no longer really need to attend school lessons.'

That's right, I know all about bodies and bandages and mouth-to-mouth. I could easily bind Robbie's cut foot now.

She reached for her black book on the trolley, and wrote in it.

'I have some good news for you, Ellen,' she said, smiling.

I looked at her. 'Can I go home? Can I go home before I have it?' I asked, feeling faintly excited.

'You know, Ellen, I have found a very nice family. They have waited a long time. Very good country people. They will be very happy.' She smiled. Her eyes seemed as big as saucers. I wondered what they might be like without the glasses. Small, probably, like blue peas.

'A family. A couple. A *married* couple. They will be very good parents.'

I went cold. I remembered what Mary said.

'No bastard is taking my baby,' I said and glared at Sister.

'Now, now, Ellen, don't be so silly. You are only fourteen. Illegitimacy is a terrible burden for a child to carry. To keep it would be selfish.'

'It's *my* baby. It's inside *my* body. No one else's. *Mine.*'

Her eyes widened. 'Do you love your baby, Ellen?'

'Course I do. It's mine.'

'And you want the very best possible life for your baby, don't you?'

'I want to go home.'

'Did you have a job before you came to Gunyah, Ellen?'

'They put me in here before I could even start there. But I'll get another one. Mum will help me.'

She shook her head and tutted. 'Your mother has her own life to lead.'

'I bet,' I muttered.

'What was that you said?'

'Why can't I go home now, to be with my mother, and the baby's father? I want to find Robbie.'

She moved her chair closer to me and leant forward with her arms on her thighs and her hands clasped on her knees. The knuckles were white.

'Look at me, Ellen. Do you think you are capable of looking after a baby? Have you got any money?'

'My room's got white curtains; my grandmother made them. And I've still got all my teddies and dolls, the baby can—'

'This couple have a lot of money. They will give the baby everything it needs. Just think of the happiness it will bring them to have a baby.'

There was a long pause. She gazed at me.

'But it's mine. I'm not giving it to anyone,' I said.

'Ellen, you would be a very bad and wicked girl indeed if you tried to keep it. You must not be selfish about this. The social worker, Mrs Gannon, will come and see you at the hostel. You must be a good girl.'

'I want to keep my baby.'

'Come, come now, Ellen. Aren't you ashamed of yourself for being so depraved? For getting yourself pregnant in the *first* place?'

I looked at the floor.

'Look at me, Ellen.' She leant forward a little further, so that her face was below mine, close – so close I wanted to push my chair back. Her breath came out cool against my face. It smelt of mint.

'Can you afford to educate this child?' she said, searching my face as if she were examining a disease.

I shook my head.

'Can you give this child all the things a two-parent family could?'

I shook my head.

'Can you feed and educate this child as well as a married couple could?'

I shook my head.

'Where is the child's father?'

I shrugged. 'He goes surfing in Manly, I can easily find him.'

'He could be anywhere, Ellen. These young larrikins don't care about getting girls like you into trouble. The sooner you realise that, the better.' She straightened and sat bolt upright in her chair and sighed. 'So, you don't know where he is, and even if you did, do you think he would be willing to bring up a child? I don't think so, Ellen. Can you offer this child the security of having a father?'

I shook my head.

'Did *you* grow up with a father, Ellen?'

I looked at her.

'That's right, Ellen. Your mother told me. He left when you were only six months old. So although you are not illegitimate, you still know what it is like to grow up without a father, don't you?'

'My grandmother died when I was twelve.'

'Would you want the same thing for this child? To grow up without a father?'

I shook my head.

'You have seen how hard your mother has to work to keep you, haven't you?'

'It's my baby.'

'Ellen, if you truly love the baby and care about it you will give it to this couple, who will care for it. They will give it a good and loving home. You cannot offer it that. You cannot offer it a father, or security. You are just a child. It is totally selfish and unacceptable to keep the baby,' she said. Her voice sounded thin. She smiled stiffly, briefly, and took a deep breath.

'All the other girls who have got themselves into trouble have seen sense. You have committed a wicked crime, Ellen. But you can make up for it by doing the right thing now.'

I rested my hands on the top part of my bulge, turned my fingers into my palms to examine my nails. They were chewed into ragged stubs.

I hung my head and sat on my hands. What if Mum wouldn't help me, how could I look after my baby? Where would I go? But she would – she *would* help.

'When will I have it?' I said. My voice sounded hoarse.

'You will get some pains in your tummy. Contractions. At first they are a long time apart, then they get closer. When they get closer together the baby will come.'

'Can I go home after that?'

'It's not quite that simple, but, yes, after you have the baby, you can go home. It is the baby we should be concerned about. Without a proper mother and father it will die. I know you will do the right thing, Ellen.'

'I want to go home,' I said.

*

I liked my room. Even though it was locked. The bed was comfortable, I had a bookshelf with some Enid Blyton books, a copy of *The Swiss Family Robinson* and *The Secret Garden* and a pile of comics: Superman, Phantom, Mandrake, Flying Doctor and Mickey Mouse. I read them over and over.

Jarrah Cottage wasn't like I thought it would be. I thought we'd be allowed to use the kitchen. And I thought there would be a lounge-room with a telly and a record player, or a transistor radio. I thought we'd all sit around talking about our babies, knitting bootees.

I could hear Sister locking and unlocking doors sometimes, and low voices. Late at night I could hear her heels clip the edge of the staircase as she went up to bed in the attic. Twice, I heard a real kerfuffle in the night, a girl moaning, then the footsteps of two, maybe three, people.

Sister said it was near to the time and I must rest and stay quiet in my room. I didn't speak to anyone except her for weeks. I still dreamt of my island; then sometimes I imagined my baby laughing in the garden with my mother and me. I thought of its voice. I thought of it crying. I will hug it and kiss it until the hurt goes away. It won't die, I'll feed it. Mum and me, we'll take care of it. Sometimes I dreamt we were with Robbie in a beautiful house with a swimming pool and a view over the water, and we went fishing in a white cruiser around Pittwater. His family do that. We'll be part of their family, we will. I'll be their daughter-in-law. Robbie told me all about them. But then, maybe my island is the best place for us.

One night when I was in the middle of a dream, Sister unlocked my door and switched on the light. I sat up, blinking.

She clapped her hands twice and said, 'Come along, Ellen, get dressed. You are going to the hospital to have your baby.'

Seven

The cruellest lies are often told in silence.
Robert Louis Stevenson

Early October 1970

Lavender. It reminds me of my grandmother. She grew it in our garden. A long, mauve cloud skirting the path. She sat on the steps and watched me pick a bunch. I handed it to her, she smiled and hugged me.

I put the rake between my legs and ran up and down the path, like a horseback rider, then I turned, sharply, like a cartoon character, and galloped back to her. When she laughed she sounded like a seal, and I could see the silver clips that held her teeth in place. Her laugh was contagious, we doubled over in hysterics.

A few days later she gave me a small white sachet with my name embroidered on it – *Ellen Jane*, all fancy – above a clump of embroidered lavender.

'Smell it,' she said. It smelt of lavender and soap. 'I

dried the lavender in the oven and sewed it inside the muslin,' she said.

I keep it here, under my pillow. There are lacy doilies everywhere in our house, dainty crocheted mats and runners, embroidered pillows and hankies, my grandmother, she makes all these lovely things; she grows lavender, and lemons, and keeps chickens and bakes biscuits; she's got soft curly white hair with bobby pins in it, to keep the curls in place. She fell over once, in the back yard. I heard her cry my name: Ellen! *Ellen!* I rushed out the kitchen door, and she was on her back on the grass with her legs in the air, like a fallen horse. The tops of her stockings were wrinkled, her legs thin and bony – I was shocked at how thin they were. Her baggy bloomers had rolled up, revealing the gap between her stockings and her flesh-coloured corset, the skin on her thighs was white and crêpy, not like her arms, which were brown and crinkly, with grey sunspots. She lay there, rocking on her rounded spine with a look on her face that said: I'm dying. I stood there, gawping. I didn't know what to do. After a while I reached down and held out my hand and she winched herself up, panting. I remember feeling so relieved when she brushed the grass off her dress and went back into the kitchen as if nothing had happened. A while later she called me in to dinner.

'You'll be sorry when I'm dead and buried,' she said, putting my lamb's fry in front of me.

What time is it? Where's my mother? Is it time for work? I *love* the scent of lavender.

My job, my new job, at Amber Motors. I don't want to go today. I don't feel well.

Has Mum gone to work already?

Where's my doll, the big one? My head, oh, my head, it *aches*.

Where am I? What's happened? This isn't my room. Or the dormitory. Or my room at Jarrah. I'm so dizzy. Am I drunk? My head is throbbing. Am I sick?

Hospital, I am in hospital, that's right. I had a baby. I had my baby. The nurses, they took it and put it in a room. Why don't they bring it to me? It must be hungry, mustn't it? It must need feeding.

There is someone on my bed, I heard the mattress squeak.

'Nurse,' I groan, 'nurse! My baby, can I see my baby?'

'Ssshh.' A girl's voice. 'You're at the hostel. Ssshh, it's all right. You've been asleep, you're okay, ssshhh.'

She is sitting on the edge of my bed. She has short blond hair, but it's not Mary. This girl is pretty, she has a perfect red mouth, blue eyes like huge almonds. There is make-up on them, black eyeliner, thick brown on the lids, pale lipstick. She is wearing a pink mini-dress, and platform shoes. Her nails are long and pink. Where did she get it all? Why is she allowed to dress like that?

I blink at her. The nurses, that fat one – I remember she gave me an injection. They held me down.

'Why are these bandages around my chest?' I say to the girl on my bed.

'To stop the milk,' she says.

'Why? What about my baby?'

'They feed them with bottles.'

'But my baby, I want to see her. I told them, I want to see her. I want to try and feed her myself.'

'You've got thirty days,' she says.

'What?'

'Get better first. I'm going. I signed the papers and everything, but it doesn't matter. When I've got myself sorted out, got a job and a place, I'm going back.'

I don't have a clue what she is on about. I moan and hold my head. I want a shower. I want something to eat. I smell of sweat and dried blood.

'Where's my baby?'

'At King Street. This is Nardoo. A hostel. For unmarried mothers.'

I look at her. 'You mean, I've been moved somewhere else? And I'm free now? I can go home?'

'Sort of. But you can't go far like that,' she says, glancing at my crotch. 'The nurse said you had a rough time. But it won't take long. A few salt baths and you'll be right as rain. You'll like it here. You and that other girl, Mary: she's in a bad way. You've come from Gunyah, haven't you? What's it like in there?'

'I just want to see my baby. Why won't they let me see it? Where is it? Have they brought it here? Where's yours? Where's Mary?'

'She's gone a bit funny. Her baby died. Stillborn it was. Isn't that bloody awful? Imagine, having it inside you like that, *dead*.' She pulls a face.

The room is bright and painted yellow. My eyelids are heavy, everything's blurry and my arms and legs feel hardened, I can barely move.

The room swirls and spins. I see Matron's face and Sister's, and a strange man in the back of a van, and traffic lights. I smell Dettol and vomit. My tongue feels like an old lizard in my mouth. A woman in grey pleats is standing next to my bed, her knees against the mattress. She is clasping a clipboard, tapping it gently with a pen. She speaks, but her voice is muffled and echoey, as though she is inside a well.

'Be a good girl ,' she says coarsely.

I strain to recognise her voice, to focus on her face, but all I see is a set of white teeth and dark hair. I can smell cheap perfume.

There's a mirror on the wall. I haven't seen myself in a mirror for weeks. At first I used to look at my reflection in the window in my room. I looked hideous. The view beyond my own reflection wasn't much better: it overlooked the laundry, a big, factory-like building with four massive chimneys where all the bad girls wash the linen from the loony-bin next door. Miss Wyndham took me there once, as a warning. It stank of wee and shit and bleach, and the steam made it unbearably hot. The girls looked hard-eyed and sick.

One day I got tired of the view, tired of my fat belly, so I pulled down the blind and stopped looking.

Where am I?

The girl, she's still on my bed.

'Are we allowed to have a bath, or a shower?' I whisper.

'You can borrow my shampoo if you like,' she says eagerly. She pushes a hand inside a pink flowery bath-bag and pulls out a plastic bottle, as though she was waiting for me to ask, as though she *knew* I would. 'Here,' she says, handing it to me, 'and you can have this. Lavender hand-lotion.' She has a look on her face that says: I know exactly what you're going through, I'm an *expert*.

'Where'd you get it?'

'I bought it before I went to hospital. I was working as a housekeeper.'

'Whereabouts?'

'For a rich family in Bankstown. He's a hot-shot in the police. They wanted me to give my baby to a friend of theirs, someone real important, they said. The social worker sent—'

'Where's your mother?'

Her face is serious. 'She dumped me. Ages ago. When I was a baby.'

'Why?'

'She adopted me out. Didn't want me, I s'pose,' she shrugs. 'But they didn't like me, my new family, not really, and he was a bastard. He used to *do things*, you know?' She pulls a face. 'I've been in and out of different homes ever since I ran away from them. But I don't care. I've got Yvonne now. I'll get myself sorted out, then I'll go back for her. She's beautiful. They let me hold her and I bottle-fed her. She's got dark hair. Don't listen to any of the nurses or social workers. I'm getting her back.'

'How come you didn't get sent to Gunyah?'

'Just lucky, I s'pose,' she shrugs. 'You've got thirty days, you know. This girl told me. She's had two babies. She's keeping this one. She's seventeen.'

I close my eyes and touch my ugly, floppy stomach. The bandages around my chest smell sour.

She is still sitting on my bed; I feel her move. I open my eyes, blinking. Yes, she is still there, smiling. She has a lovely heart-shaped face.

'How long have I been here?'

'Three days.'

'Christ!' I close my eyes and gradually, in fragments, I remember things: the fat stubby-lashed nurse at the hospital, my screams, my baby's profile on the white sheet, the needles in my legs, loud voices, the pain and the smell of sick and medicine.

I open my eyes again. The room is bright and sunny. Yellow curtains tumble at the high, unbarred windows. The heart-shaped girl is sitting on my bed. I smell lavender.

'Where is this place, anyway?'

'Clovelly. Near Bondi.'

'My name's Ellen. Call me Ellie. What's yours?'

'Kerry. Kerry Carter.' She looks pleased with herself. I can see her more clearly now. Her teeth are grey.

'Are you sure,' I ask sleepily, 'are you sure my baby's all right?' I try to lift my head, but it drops on to the pillow again like granite.

'You look bloody awful,' she says.

I close my eyes again and float.

I can hear a bus, or a truck, pulling up outside, the hiss as a door opens, footsteps crunching on gravel, girls chattering. I ease off the bed. My bottom is still sore, but the salt baths are healing the wounds.

I pad across to the window in the new pink slippers Mum sent. She sent new dresses, too; big baggy tents with swirly patterns in bright colours. And a pair of step-ins, though why they're called that I'll never know, because I can't even drag them over my hips, let alone step into them. They are made of the strongest elastic known to man, and when I put them on the floor they stand up on their own.

The dress I'm wearing today is the only one I like, navy blue with a sailor's collar and a small bow at the neckline. It's not my taste, it's Mum's, but it's luxury compared to hessian.

'What's going on?' I say to Kerry. She is lying on her bed reading *The Woman's Day* magazine.

'They've been to the hospital for their check-ups.'

I stand at the window and stare down. We are on the second floor, with a sweeping view over the neat tropical gardens.

Spilling out of the bus are about twenty-five girls, between my age and about twenty. Every one of them is pregnant. Or very fat.

'How come we don't see them?'

'They're in another block. They look awful, don't they? I hated being fat. It looks ugly. I couldn't wait to get back into my jeans and short skirts.'

She is standing next to me now, looking at the girls.

They waddle slowly across the gravel drive towards a two-storey Victorian building. There are two nuns with them. I recognise one, Sister Benedictine. She stood by my bed when I first arrived and curled her hairy top lip as if I was poisonous. Her green eyes seemed to drill my skin. She said I was an empty vessel. And when I asked her about my baby she said I had abused God's temple, so I got what I deserved. She said I was the scum of the earth.

At the end of the long drive, with its trimmed lawns and palm trees, a nun is busy locking the iron gates.

'We're prisoners,' I say flatly to Kerry.

'You can't sleep on the streets.'

'I slept on the beach once.'

'You're game.'

'Because of my stepfather. I ran away. But I went home the next day. It was freezing.' I don't tell her the real reason I went home: that I was hungry.

'I'd be too scared,' she says. She looks at me as if I am a bigwig.

There is a long silence, punctuated by the crunching of footsteps on the stones. They filter into the building like a troop of sullen, plump ants. The last one disappears, and a nun slams the door.

'Your tummy's gone flat,' Kerry says, glancing at my belly. 'Even in that tent you look skinny.'

I smooth my hand over the folds of my dress.

'How old are you, anyway?' she says, looking me straight in the eye.

'Seventeen,' I say.

It is a week since I arrived. I worked it out from what Kerry told me. Three days, she said, you've been here three days. That was four days ago.

I thought I'd never sit down again. I am having three salt baths a day. At first it stings like crazy, then I can't feel it. I fill the bath right to the top so that I can float. I think of my baby, how she floated inside me. I wonder how she is – if she's crying, if she misses me, if she is hungry.

Sister Agnes took the bandages off today. There's no milk left, I have deflated like an old balloon. They still hurt, but not nearly as much.

As she leant over to unpin the bandages behind my back, I was conscious of an atmosphere, light and airy. Kerry was in the bath. The sun was already hot in a sapphire sky.

Sister Agnes is younger than the other old bats. Kerry calls her Gidget, after the fresh-faced actress Sally Field, because of her rosy cheeks and straight, white teeth. Except Sister Agnes isn't wacky. She is serious. She is deep in thought most of the time, as if she is really worried about something. Maybe she's praying all the time, I said to Kerry once. 'Thinking about sex more likely,' Kerry said flatly.

I was dying to know what made Sister Agnes become a nun. Before all this, I thought about becoming a nun. My friend Louise did, too. We used to talk about it sometimes on the bus to primary school. I thought it would be a good thing to do mainly because of the company – I figured you'd never get lonely with so many friends, and I was pretty attracted to the idea of goodness and God and life ever after. You are at that age. But the nuns put me off. Because something's not right when you can be religious and cruel, both at the same time. I always thought religion meant being kind and fair, loving and generous. I didn't want to be cruel.

A tingling, feathery sensation swept through me as Sister Agnes unravelled the bandages. My eyes drooped, my head and shoulders went loose. Her touch was so gentle. She placed her neat, warm fingers on my chest, carefully avoiding my nipples, and pressed them as if she was checking to make sure the milk had gone. Her breath was warm on my skin.

'This looks fine,' she said, nodding as though it was all thanks to her.

'What made you become a nun?' I said, coming straight out with it.

She gave me a sharp look that I took to mean she was surprised and flattered by the question.

'You don't mind me asking, do you?' I added.

'No,' she said, smiling, 'I don't mind.'

She was winding the bandages into a tight ball around her forearm, concentrating hard on keeping the edges neat.

'It's quite simple really, and it's probably a cliché—'

'What's that?' I asked, wishing I had a dictionary.

'Oh, you know, something typical.'

I looked at her, puzzled.

'Like saying you and the other girls are all the same, or teachers all have buns and glasses, or doctors all have soft hands . . . that sort of thing.'

I still wasn't quite sure what she was on about, but I was getting the picture.

'I wanted to dedicate myself to something worthwhile, something meaningful,' she went on, 'and God seemed like the best idea to me. So here I am.' She smiled and shrugged, as if to say she could take it or leave it. It made me think: There's more to it than that.

'I always thought nuns were perfect, but they're not, are they?' I said.

'No one, except God, is perfect,' she replied.

'How come He's so mean, then?'

'Because we have to prove our worth.'

I couldn't help thinking I'd heard all this before, at Sunday School and chapel at Gunyah, and I wondered if that's what she meant by a cliché.

'You mean unless we prove ourselves we don't get to go to heaven?'

'If you walk with God now and ask His forgiveness, you are halfway there,' she said.

I didn't believe that one bit. It was like saying: You can do what you like, be cruel and sinful, then pray for forgiveness and He'll still let you in. And I thought: *You* might be halfway there, but the other old bats aren't. They haven't even got their foot in the door, not by a long chalk. Maybe that's why they became nuns in the first place, because they're so evil they knew it'd take a whole lifetime on earth to get there. I was surprised at myself, because in with all these thoughts I felt sorry for them.

It is such a relief to have the bandages off and feel the water on my whole body again. I wash my hair three times a day now; like plants, when you give them plenty of water, I hope it might grow back faster. It is over my ears already, but I still feel ugly, like a boy.

But it feels so good to be clean. To have my own undies and a bra. Mum sent some new Bond's Cottontails –

they're big and daggy, but I don't care, they feel like silk after the hairy ones at Gunyah. She sent two cakes of Palmolive, a bottle of Lustrecream shampoo, bathcubes and a bottle of Mum deodorant. Normally she wouldn't give things like that as presents, because she said it implied the person receiving the gift was dirty. But with me it didn't matter; she is my mother. There was a note inside the brown paper parcel, in a pink envelope. It said:

Dear Ellen,
    Looking forward so much to seeing you and having a fresh start. I'm so glad you took Sister Dawson's advice. I will see you soon, probably at the end of next week, to take you home.
    All my love, Mummy.

She didn't give *me* away. I'll talk her into it, she'll come round to the idea. I'll beg her, I'll cry and cry and cry till she says yes. I want my baby more than anything in the world. I don't care about anything else, I just want my baby.

A nun came in with Mary today. She looks awful. Her eyes are more sunken than ever, with deep, dark circles underneath, as though someone has punched her. She is so thin; even her bosoms have shrunk. Her hair sticks out as if she's had a terrible fright.

We are on our beds, reading comics, when she arrives. The nuns say they don't mind us reading comics if they are classic stories, like *Mutiny on the Bounty* or *The*

Hunchback of Notre-Dame. They say it might lead us to read good literature. I laugh to myself at that, because with Mrs McGrath I studied Shakespeare and Dylan Thomas, and she even smuggled in *Wuthering Heights* and some really beautiful Russian poetry.

I am surprised the nuns let us have women's magazines. Perhaps they don't know that, apart from recipes and knitting patterns, there are things that would make their habits wilt. I read them over and over. Especially the letters to Doctor Dorothy in *The Woman's Day*. There is one from a sixteen-year-old, about period pains. She says she's been told by friends that taking the contraceptive pill, whatever that is, can help relieve the pain, but her mother won't let her take it. Must be an awful mother.

Another letter is from a girl who has been to a special clinic to have a VD test and they told her she had genital warts. She says nothing gets rid of them, even surgical treatment doesn't work. Dorothy tells her to be careful about her personal hygiene. I can't stop thinking about it. It sounds repulsive.

And there is a letter from a woman who can't get pregnant. She goes into details asking about when is the best time to have intercourse, and to have a girl does she need to 'do it' a week before her period? Doctor Dorothy explains about ovulating and natural family planning and sperm. It makes me feel queasy. I don't show any of it to Kerry, it's too embarrassing. And we never mention our babies. It's as if nothing has happened, as if we are here on a holiday, reading magazines in a motel room.

'I like talking about sex,' Kerry says one day, out of the

blue. 'All my friends and me, we talk about it all the time. I've slept with lots of boys. They all used, abused and rejected me,' she says, laughing. Her voice sounds like piano keys, light and tinkly.

'Robbie's not like that,' I say. 'I'm going to see him as soon as I get out. He'll come with me to the hospital to get our baby.'

'Don't bet on it,' she says and rolls her eyes. 'They're all the same, blokes. All they want is one thing and one thing only. Once they get that they just dump you.'

Mary is on her bed curled in a tight ball. She stays like that all day without moving. I put *The Woman's Day* on the end of her bed.

'There's a magazine here, if you want it,' I say, but she doesn't move a muscle.

'She'll have to get over it,' Kerry whispers when I sit back on her bed.

'I feel sorry for her.'

'Life goes on.'

'I know. But something like that would take a long time to get over, I reckon. I hope she's all right.'

'She'll be okay. The nuns will sort her out. They don't like people who feel sorry for themselves.'

'You don't see them much except in the dining room. What do they do all day, pray?'

'They've got their hands full with that lot in the other block. Glad to get rid of us probably.'

'Do you think we should talk to Mary?'

'Nah. She'll get over it.'

*

At night I can't sleep.

I get up and down to the toilet at least twenty times. That feeling, like when you've lost a key or your purse, and you can't rest till you find it.

The rash on my arms has come up again; it burns like hot coals.

I cry a lot, wrenching, painful crying that rips at my ribs. My eyes are permanently red and swollen.

I try to think of other things. Reading helps. I like looking at the fashions. During the day Kerry does my face with her make-up. She can't do my nails, they are too chewed.

Every day I ask the nuns when I can see my baby, but they just snigger, or laugh and say, 'You can't look after a baby', or 'You're far too young to rear a child', or 'Hark at you, useless little slut, you're wicked and stupid.'

I am so ugly. I know I am. And so dumb. They are right. I can't look after a baby. Not even my own baby. I am being stupid and selfish to think I could. Sister Dawson said that without a proper mother and father she would die. I don't want her to die. I don't want her to be orphaned, either. I have to go back for my baby, I have to. She needs me, she needs her mother. Somehow I'll look after her. I will.

It's 2 am on the twelfth night. I sit up in bed and switch on the bedside lamp. I can't sleep, my mind is racing. I pad across to the book corner to find a magazine.

Back in bed again, I curl up on my side and flick through the pages; past the usual stuff about TV actors, past the cookery and knitting patterns and interviews with people who have done up old houses, looking for the Problem Page.

Towards the back there's a pull-out section: ENJOY YOUR BABY. There's a young mother with blond hair holding her baby. The baby is naked, the chubby folds of its arms make it look hand-made, in sections, like a doll. With my heart in a terrible knot and tears streaming down my face, I read the article:

> All new mothers feel it sometimes . . . a lack of confidence in their ability to cope. But motherhood should be enjoyable . . .

COMING HOME

A strange thing happens when a new mum leaves hospital: she feels fit and strong before departure, but by the afternoon she feels exhausted – perhaps it's the excitement and the thought that she's now responsible for the welfare of her child. If this happens to you, it's important to know that you need to take things quietly for a few days . . . 'Early to bed' is a must for the first few weeks. This is difficult to organise because babies work on a four-hour feeding schedule (around 10 am, 2 pm, 6 pm, 10 pm, 2 am, 6 am), and if you go to bed at 8 pm, you'll need to be up again at 10 pm – but even one hour's sleep is better than none . . .

Once you arrive home, you will suddenly find your doorbell never stops ringing – friends keep calling to see the new baby, and you find yourself making endless cups of coffee . . . One of the most boring chores we women have to face is the weekly shopping—

Shopping? I never thought of that. Where will I get the money if Mum doesn't help, if Robbie has decided to break up with me?

. . . And it would be fair to say that the prospect of shopping with a brand-new baby is terrifying . . . Remember, coming home is an adjustment period for all members of the family. The words 'slowly and quietly' should be written into every mother's brain. If she can observe this rule she must be on the right road to successful motherhood.

Successful motherhood? I haven't even seen my baby; not properly. I don't even know if she's healthy; she could be deformed, for all I know. There is more, lots more . . . I can't stop reading . . . under the heading HOW TO COPE. I bet it doesn't tell you how to cope if you've had your baby in another place and you don't even know where, and you don't even know if it's alive any more . . .

Giving birth itself does not make a mother. We have to learn how to care for our babies . . . To help them grow from self-centred infants into confident, happy adults . . .

How can a baby be self-centred? Am I self-centred? Am I being selfish, wanting my baby when I can't look after her? But I can learn, I can. From this article, from my mother, from experience . . .

> Caring for children can be tedious, time-consuming, repetitive and exacting. There are situations which would try the temper of the Archangel Gabriel himself, says the introduction to *Care for Your Child*, written by three doctors from Sydney's Alexandra Hospital for Children . . .
>
> The NSW Health Commission has published a booklet entitled *Our Babies* which is free to parents in NSW . . . Aware that many of today's mothers are highly educated, the authors – a panel of commission members – have prepared a very thorough and wide-ranging booklet. It is available from hospitals and Baby Health Centres . . .

I toss the magazine on my bed and sit up. I'm not well educated. I don't even have my Higher School Certificate and it's too late now, because I ran away. The Nurse's Entrance Certificate doesn't mean anything, because I hate nurses, that's the last thing I want to be. I've been stupid and selfish, and I've got no money, and Sister was right, I can't look after a baby. I've got no right to think I can.

I pull the covers over my head and feel my body go limp, then stiffen. All night it does this. By the time morning arrives I'm wound tight like a rubber band.

At breakfast Sister Agnes serves porridge in the small

dining room. I sit there, watching her. My eyes are red-raw.

She looks tired and distracted, and as she slops two scoops of porridge into my bowl she mumbles something under her breath.

Fuelled with a sudden fierce anger, I leap to my feet and shout, 'Why don't you say it out loud, go on! Tell us out loud we're useless sluts. That's what you're thinking, isn't it? Isn't it? All that bullshit about God and heaven. You hate us really, just like the others. Don't you?'

She puts the steaming saucepan on a table – Kerry and I are the only ones there, as Mary said she wasn't hungry – she crosses her arms and looks at me. I sit down and fold my arms.

I stare back, my jaw clenched. 'I'm not even a Catholic,' I say, haughtily.

'You think what you like, Ellen. But I'm telling you now: I know from experience that it is up to you, and no one else, not even God, to make something of your life. And blaming everyone else won't get you far, either.'

I push my porridge away and sit back in my chair with my arms crossed, glaring at her. She gives me an odd look: a quizzical frown, an irritated smile, that seems to mean: You're not that stupid.

I smile sarcastically. You know, the sort of look you give teachers when you know you're wrong but you don't want to admit it.

I sit there after Kerry leaves, sulking. Sister Agnes clears away my untouched plate and 'tsks' because I don't do it myself. I know she is thinking: You will have to snap out of it, Ellen, but she doesn't say it, thank God, and that makes me forgive her.

Back in the dorm I sit on my bed scratching my arm. Bloody nuns, bloody nurses, bloody officers, I hate them all.

The magazine with the baby special is on the end of my bed. I lent it to Kerry, hoping she might read it and want to talk about it. But she put it back without a word. I pick it up and open it to the pull-out section and carefully tear it out. I spend the rest of the day and half the night reading it over and over again, all the time thinking: I'll be an expert by the time I've learnt this off by heart. I'll surprise everyone, even Mum, with my knowledge.

At around midnight my eyes begin to sag. I write my name on the baby book and put it away in my locker.

Poor Mary has clammed up completely. Hasn't spoken a word in three days.

I'm getting around quite well now. A nurse took the stitches out yesterday. The scissors tugged at my skin like a fish-hook.

'Don't exaggerate', she said, when I flinched, 'it's not *that* bad.'

I've got my hair in a centre parting now, and I don't tease it on top like I used to – that look's gone out of fashion. When Robbie sees me he won't believe how much I've changed.

Kerry has taught me how to apply brown shadow in the deep part of my eyelids; she said blue's old-hat. Brown makes my eyes look sultry, she said. I'm trying not to bite my nails. I want to knock Robbie over when I see him. He'll be so amazed.

Sister Benedictine is standing by the door holding a parcel.

'Mary?'

Mary lifts her head from the pillow.

'What?'

'Get up and don't be so lazy.'

Mary gets off the bed and shuffles across the green lino to collect her package from the nun's outstretched arms.

'*Thank you?*' the nun says. She waits for Mary's answer, but there is none.

She glides away grim-faced, and Mary shuffles back to her bed to open her parcel.

Kerry and I are bursting with curiosity. Getting a parcel is really exciting. We can't control ourselves. Next thing we're sitting on Mary's bed.

'Come on, Mary,' Kerry says, 'open it, hurry up. It might have some goodies, Jaffas or Minties or Fantales – who's it from?'

'My friend, Carol.'

'Well, come on, come on, let's see what's in there, come on, Mary,' Kerry says eagerly. 'Never mind, Mary,' she adds, hugging her. 'Life has to go on, you know.'

'Yeah, you'll be all right, you'll feel better soon, don't worry,' I say. But the words sound hollow and I hate myself for saying them.

She slips the string over the corners. 'It feels soft,' she says. 'I don't think there's anything to eat.'

'Oh, come on, come on, there might be some make-up, or it might be a new blouse,' Kerry says.

'No,' she says, 'not Carol. She's too hard up.'

At last it is open. Inside are neatly folded baby clothes. Tiny, white, hand-knitted baby clothes.

'Shit,' Kerry says.

'*Oh*.' Mary stares at the bundle. Then she tosses it to one side and rushes into the bathroom.

'Leave her,' says Kerry, 'she'll come round.'

I pick up the garments and wrap them in the paper. I look at the writing. Mary Perry, it says; scrawly, childish printing. When it is wrapped again it looks exciting, full of promise.

I take it downstairs to the main office, a darkly furnished room off the wide, wood-panelled hall.

Sister Benedictine looks up as I burst through the half-open door. Her eyes look like the sea on a dull day, the colour of green mud.

I drop the parcel on her desk.

'I don't think Mary will be needing these,' I say, giving her a dirty look. 'You don't have any idea, do you?'

'I beg your pardon?' she says. She looks astonished, as if I've just stepped off Mars. 'How dare you—'

'How dare I? *How dare I?* You're so good at reading our mail, you knew what was in that parcel, *didn't you?* Why'd you give it to her? Why'd you let her see it? I hate you, all of you!' I shout.

Then I slam the door and run back upstairs.

Mary is still in the bathroom. She's been in there hours. I knock on the door.

'Leave me alone,' she says.

'Open the door.'

'It's open.'

'Oh. Okay. Fair enough.'

I lie on my bed. Poor Mary. I try to imagine how she must feel. I feel lucky. My baby is alive.

I close my eyes and drift. I think of the hospital. The fat nurse, the needles, the pain, people gawping as if I was a shop display.

I'm so stupid. Ugly, dumb, *dirty*. Sister Dawson said so. All the nuns say so.

'You are a dirty, wicked, evil girl,' Sister Dawson said the day she gave me that enema. 'You have *sinned*. You have let *filthy* things be done to you. Your body is spoilt and dirty. This will help to clean you out *physically*, but it's your *soul* that is tainted.'

I hate myself. I hate my life. I can't look after my baby. She looked so small and helpless in the cot, inside that dark laundry room. I'm glad there was another baby with her. Perry. The one called Perry. Perry? But that's Mary's last name, isn't it? I saw it on the parcel this morning. I remember now at Gunyah, Matron called her Mary Perry. It can't be, it's not right. They all said her baby was dead. But I saw it. It said Perry. It did.

The bathroom is at one end of the dormitory, tacked on like a sealed box. I knock on the door.

'Mary! *Mary!* Please can I come in? Mary, I have to tell you something, please, come out.' I turn the handle. I push the door open a fraction.

'Mary?'

It is dark inside because the light is off. There's a salty smell. I know what it is straight away; I've cut myself lots of times on broken bottles, swimming in the lake at home, and the butcher's at Coolamon smells of it, especially in the morning when the meat is fresh. Bodily fluids, stem the flow. *Jesus!*

I flick on the switch. Mary is lying in the bath. The water is red. Her head is slumped on her shoulder. Her clothes are ballooning like a parachute on the sea. Her face is white. Poor, pale Mary.

All night I lie awake going over and over the day. I can't stop thinking about the look in her eyes when she slammed the door, the choking, painful croak of her voice, the animal sounds echoing in the bathroom followed by a long stretch of silence.

After I dragged her out of the bath, all the time screaming for Kerry to get the nuns, I wrapped a damp towel around her wrist, but it was soaked through in minutes because the blood flowed so fast. I sat with my legs stretched either side of her, like open scissors, and lifted her head on to my lap. I felt helpless and stupid because I couldn't stop the flow, and I hated the nuns with all my heart for making Mary hate herself so much that she would do this.

I knew, I just knew, it had nothing to do with thinking her baby was dead; not deep down, although I knew it would be a terrible thing to go through. It wasn't that with Mary. She just hated herself so much she'd given up.

The nuns came – four big, burly ones – and put her on a stretcher and they carried her to Sick Bay. It seemed like hours before the ambulance came purring up the front drive, and I couldn't help thinking, as I stood at the window watching them slide her in, that they were taking their time.

The nuns chatted for a few minutes to the driver, then off they went, carrying Mary through the city to God knows where, as though it was a pretty ordinary, everyday thing.

'Will Mary be all right?' I ask Sister Benedictine at breakfast.

'Oh yes,' she says, with a bug-eyed look, 'don't you be fooled, Ellen Russell. This is not the first time Mary has tried to hurt herself. Her records make very interesting reading. She'll be back, don't you worry about Mary.'

The next day Mary arrives back with white bandages around her wrists. Sister Benedictine delivers her to the dormitory.

'You should be ashamed of yourself, Mary Perry,' she says, then thumps off down the stairs.

'Mary!' I cry, jumping off my bed.

She slumps on her bed, head bowed.

I sit next to her and stroke her shoulder.

'You silly old thing,' I say, 'I thought you'd died. You gave me an awful fright. It's not worth it. And anyway I was coming to tell you.'

'What?'

'In the hospital. I found my baby in a laundry room, in

a cot, with another baby. They were ours, Mary. They had wrist bands with their names printed on. I saw them, Mary. Honest, I did.'

She looks at me. Her face is crumpled. 'Why the fuck are you telling me this?' she says. 'I don't wanna hear this shit.'

'Honest,' I say. I put my hands over hers and squeeze them.

'Are you sure?' she says, peering into my eyes.

'I was in a state, I know I was, because all the medicine made me dizzy. But I remember seeing them, both of them. I didn't dream it, I know I didn't. Honest. You can go back for your baby, to the hospital. Kerry told me. We've got thirty days. I'm going. So's Kerry. You can, too.'

'No,' she says, shaking her head. 'No, I can't.' She stares at her lap. There are brown stripes on the bandages where the blood has stained them.

'But, why not?'

'I'm no good. I'm hopeless. Anyway, I don't believe you. I told you, my baby's dead. *Stillborn*. That means fuckin' *dead*.'

Eight

I'm invisible! Invisible!
MIKHAIL BULGAKOV,
The Master and Margarita

Will I be a good mother?

I've asked myself this over and over again. I've read the pull-out on babies over and over again. The thing that sticks in my mind more than anything is the bit that says: *Giving birth itself does not make a mother*. What does, then?

Is my mother a good mother? She gives me lots of presents and clothes. But she's always criticising, as though she doesn't like me, not really. It's almost as if she feels she *has* to love me. Once, years ago, when grown-ups were always saying kids should be seen and not heard, I overheard her telling Cousin Pam that I was a bribe, to entice my father back from his piece of stuff on the side. But it didn't work, and now she's stuck with me. I'll love my baby even if she's ugly. And I'll never criticise her.

I love my mother – it's easy to love her, because she's so perfect. Except that when I'm around her I can't relax, I'm aware of all the ugly things about myself. She's a good mother, I suppose, but I didn't like the way she dated different men before she married Jack. And I hated it when she went away.

She went off to America once and put me in a boarding school for a few years. I was eight. I wet my pants when we walked up the long driveway to meet the headmistress. My granny was too sick to look after me, and Mum said it was all my fault because I was such a handful. Granny had something called angina. It gave her terrible chest pains.

I am lying on my bed staring at the white ceiling. I am a castaway on a waterproof bed; my baby is asleep in a fruit box.

'What do you think it'll be like, being a mother?' I say, turning to face Kerry. She is sitting on her bed with her legs crossed, holding a mirror. She applies brown eye shadow, a dark sweep of blusher and bright-red lipstick.

'I dunno. Hard, I s'pose. But you won't even think about it once you've got your baby. When you see its face, when you hold it, you won't even think about any of that stuff. You'll just do it.'

'You reckon?'

'Yeah. You won't have time to think about it. My friend Barbara, she's only eighteen. She's got a kid. He's two years old now. She's been all right with him. She can't go out much, that's the only trouble. She lives with her mum and dad. They've been great about it.' She curls her lips to examine her teeth in the mirror. I'm dying to ask how come her teeth are so bad, but I don't in case it hurts her feelings.

'What do you think will happen to Mary?'

'She'll be all right. She'll probably end up inside again, though. She seems the type. Institutionalised.'

'What's that?'

'When you're in and out of homes. Like me. I'm institutionalised. But this is the last time. I'm not getting put away again.' She shoots me a look that says: I mean it.

'I can't believe they let Mary go today, so soon after she did that to herself. It was only two days ago. She looked so white, all that blood she lost. She didn't have anywhere to go. What will she do?'

'Probably go up the Cross. A lot of the girls end up there. She gave me the phone number of a friend who lives up there, so I s'pose that's where she'll go. I dunno. I did it once, y'know. But I didn't like it. The guy was a fat businessman. Japanese. He wanted to do weird things, y'know?' She pulls a face, remembering something disgusting – I hate to think what.

'Where are you going to go when you get out?' I ask her.

'Get a live-in job, housekeeping or babysitting.'

'What about your baby?'

'I've decided not to keep her,' she says. She opens her mouth as if she is yawning, and stretches her eyes wide to apply mascara to her long lashes.

She is a damaged porcelain doll with a heart-shaped face and yellow silk hair.

'But Kerry, I thought you were going back for your baby? You said. I thought we could go together.'

'Why don't you go with Mary? You reckon you saw her—'

'I did! I saw them both, hers and mine.'

'Here, take Mary's number,' she says, scribbling on a slip of paper. 'Go and find her. You haven't got long. It's nine days now since you came in. You'll have to hurry when you get out, or the thirty days will be up.'

Later, after lunch, the dormitory is empty. I sit on my bed wondering if the nuns are giving Kerry another good talking to in the office.

And I wonder where Mary is now, how she will eat, where she might sleep. I can't believe she's gone, with no money.

I think of my baby. I imagine the nurses caring for her. She won't know me when I go to the hospital; I won't know her. I wouldn't know her if I fell over her.

It's weird, being let out. The noise of the traffic hurts my head. Everything seems fast and hectic, as though speeded up. I can't focus properly, it's like being on a fairground ride: when you jump off everything shimmies and sways for a while, until you get your bearings.

I imagined I'd be so excited when they let me out, but when Sister Augustine opened the big front door and I saw my mother standing next to her car in the bright sunshine, I felt frightened – everything seemed magnified and bright, and I wanted to run back inside where everything was familiar.

In her blue Holden we head out of the city at the top of George Street and join the stream of cars pouring over the Harbour Bridge. Mum is elegant at the wheel in a red and navy-blue dress with a pleated skirt. Her nails and lips match the red in the dress. Her dark-navy shoes with red trim and matching handbag complement the whole outfit. Her perfume, an expensive Estée Lauder one, fills the car with a tropical smell, like sun-warmed mangoes.

I lean forward to turn on the radio. It's playing the theme from *The Saint*. I turn the dial to 2UW. A song I haven't heard before is on. *Gotta get back to the spirit in the sky*, go the lyrics. The beat is catchy, the guitars grating and loud. I tap my feet and nod my head in time. I reach for the dial to turn it up.

'Turn that racket off!' my mother says. Her voice is impatient, like a school teacher's.

'Sor-*ry*,' I say, switching it off.

'Thank you.' She clicks her tongue in that teacherly way that makes me want to tear at my skin. 'I don't want you listening to that rubbish any more, Ellen. You've got to put all that behind you. I want to look to the future now. You have no idea what I've been through. I can't believe you have done this to me.'

She looks more beautiful than ever, like a film star. *Done this to her.* Her dark arched eyebrows, perfect skin, deep-brown eyes, everything about her is perfect and polished and tasteful.

'Thanks for the clothes,' I say, awkwardly. As though she's a stranger sitting next to me. 'It was great to have my own things for a change.'

'You're welcome,' she says, smiling. 'I've bought you some more things. You can try them on later, when I'm out, if you like. Your skin has cleared up, hasn't it? All you need to do now is get your figure back and let your hair grow. We can get it shaped at a salon, if you like. We'll have dinner together at the weekend. Won't you enjoy a steak after all the stodge at school?'

'Where are you going?'

'I have a date.' She smiles.

'With Jack?'

'He's long gone.' She flexes her jaw and tosses her head a fraction, nervously. 'He told me it was either him or you. I said: You know where the door is, Jack. My daughter comes first.'

'I hated him,' I say. 'He was always going off to the club with his mates. And I hated going on his boat every Sunday. All we did was sit there fishing, not talking. He hated me, Mum.' I stare out the window, hoping, *praying*, she won't ask me any questions about why I hated him so much. She'd kill me if she knew, and Granny always said, 'What she doesn't know won't hurt her,' so I've kept it to myself all this time.

He was horrible, this other bloke she moved in with for a while. A floor polisher; I called him Mr Baloney. He came to do our floors on the verandah and, next thing I knew, we were sharing a crummy flat with him down near the beach. He used to get up early for work and drag me out of bed with his hand over my mouth. Then in the lounge he'd put his big, hot hand down my panties and touch me. He whispered loud in my ear while he did it, 'Don't tell your mother, or there'll be trouble.' Then one day I caught him in the kitchen twisting Mum's arm up her back; she was screaming in pain. We got away, somehow, and fled in the car. He followed us in his car, then when he saw we were pulling up outside the police station he drove off at top speed and we never saw him again. But I used to worry that Jack would do the same.

'Jack didn't know how to handle a teenager,' Mum says, and she tosses her head slightly, as though that explains everything.

'Who are you going out with tonight?' I ask hastily, trying to change the subject.

'Just a friend.'

'Can I phone some of my friends?'

A serious look crosses her face. 'I don't want you phoning any of those people you were mixing with before all this happened.'

'You mean Robbie.'

'I don't even want to hear his name.'

'But Mum, he should be told about the baby. He might marry me when he finds out he's the father.'

She lets out a snort that makes my blood boil. 'How do you know he's the father?' she says.

'Thanks a lot!' I snap. I cross my arms and look out of the window. Tears well in thick pools along the bottom rim of my eyes and balance there, like the time I left the tap running in the concrete laundry tub at home and Granny arrived just at that moment and shouted: Quick! Before it overflows! I blink them away and stare at the blurred colours whipping past.

'That creep hasn't been near the house since you were put away,' Mum says with venom in her voice. She takes a deep breath, then says calmly, 'I think you will have to forget him, Ellen darling.' She tilts her jaw. The tone of her voice seems to indicate that she's convinced I've learnt my lesson and that I'm listening to her at last: I *will* wear that pleated tartan skirt she bought from the Scottish shop in the Imperial Arcade; I *will* be a nice girl.

'He doesn't know where I live,' I say, flatly.

'He could have asked at the police station.'

'Miss Riley probably told him to keep away from me. She hates me.'

'Well, if he really wanted to find out how you were, he would have.'

'But Mum, I want to see him.'

'Well, you can't. You are under-age. You can't marry him, even if he does ask you. I don't want to hear any more about it. I've had enough of your nonsense, Ellen. You will have to knuckle down and get a job and make a new life.'

'I want to get my baby from the hospital. I know where the hospital is. In King Street. This girl at the hostel said I've got thirty days to go and get her. After that they'll give her away. I don't want to give her away. I want her with me. She belongs with me. No one else.'

'Honestly, Ellen, you are being ridiculous. You can't look after a baby.' She frowns at me and shakes her head. 'You're only a young girl. You have your whole life ahead of you. And I certainly can't afford to bring up another child. Life is hard enough without another mouth to feed.'

'I'll go out to work. You could look after her.'

'You can't earn enough to feed three mouths.' She pauses. 'You didn't see the baby, did you?' She sounds as though she hopes I'll say no. As though I had no right to see her, as though I might have contaminated her.

'I found her in a laundry room, with buckets and mops. With another baby.'

I watch my mother's face closely to see her reaction. I suppose I'm expecting her to be shocked at this news, at the image of my baby in a cold laundry. I hope it might stir some sort of loyalty towards me, against the nurses. But she just stares at the road, unmoved.

'The nurses dragged me back to my bed and stuck a needle in my bum. I put up a good fight, but I was in agony, from the stitches.'

'Really, Ellen. Do you have to mention such details?'

'After that I didn't see her.'

'Well, it was probably for your own good,' she replies in that know-all tone that makes me want to scream.

'I don't think it's doing me much good not letting me see my own baby.'

'Ellen, listen to me. You are only fourteen. You are too young to bring up a baby. I have to go out to work to support the two of us. You will have to get a job. You will have to accept that you made a terrible mistake, and put it behind you. The baby will go to a good home, with two parents who will give it things you can't.'

'I can give her love. What more does she need? She won't starve. I read a pull-out from *The Woman's Day* magazine about babies. We can look after her. If I got a job you could stay at home. Or I could work at night somewhere, waitressing. Please Mum. I want my baby.'

I bury my face in my hands and begin to sob quietly, *oh, these tears, why won't they stop?* My heart feels as if a stone is stuck there.

'There is no use crying. You have to forget what has happened and get on with life. I don't want to hear another word about it. Please, Ellen. Life is hard enough.'

I look at her in despair. 'Please, Mum. I want my baby. I don't feel right. It feels like I've lost an arm or something. As though she's dead.'

'Don't be so silly,' she says, 'it's not dead.'

Suddenly the taste of salt and the scent of the sea, fresh and clean, hits me. We have reached The Spit. I dry my tears on my skirt and stare out at the blue water, which sparkles in the sun like a silver plate. Contented fishermen in their dinghies and smart cruisers dot the river. The waterfront houses look modern and bright after the gloomy Victorian buildings at Gunyah. The sun is hot on my arm. I push my face further out the window to let the warm breeze finger my hair.

'I can't wait to get in the water,' I say. 'I'll take her with me, like Granny did with me.' I think of my baby, swaddled, *trapped*, in those blankets. Tears roll down my face. I look at Mum. She glances at me several times, nervously. The car hits the kerb and she turns the wheel to steady it again.

'Phew,' she says. Tiny beads of perspiration appear on her forehead. She clutches the steering wheel tight, in the ten-to-two position. She leans forward to concentrate. 'Ellen dear, you will simply have to put it all behind you now.'

'I'm going back for my baby, Mum. She's mine. I'm going back for her.'

My bedroom is just the same, with its frilly white curtains and three-mirrored dressing table. The doilies are freshly washed, and the blue Wedgwood trinket dishes that Granny gave me are arranged neatly along an embroidered runner on my dressing table. My china doll and three teddies are grouped on my pillow. My mother has taken down the posters on the inside of my wardrobe doors: one of David McCallum from *The Man from Uncle*, two of Hayley Mills and Sally Field and the one I loved most, of a golden labrador. Apart from that, nothing has changed.

I put a record on my record player, *Make It With You* by Bread, and lie down on my bed. It is soft and familiar under my body. I turn over, snuggle into the cool cotton pillowslip, and push my hand underneath. It is still there: the lavender sachet Granny made me. I press it against my face and take deep breaths. A few minutes later I am fast asleep.

When I wake, night has fallen and my mother is standing by my bed holding a glass of milk, a plate of Arnott's biscuits and a banana. I rub my eyes and sit up. She is dressed in a long, dark-red evening dress, halter-neck-style, which glitters under the light. She looks like Elizabeth Taylor. Sometimes, when she hasn't coloured her hair for a while, she reminds me of the Queen.

'I'll be home late, Ellen. Why don't you try on the things I bought you? If they don't fit we can take them back to DJ's on Saturday morning.'

'Can I phone my friends?'

'Yes, if you like. But I don't want anyone here at the house unless I'm here. And don't phone that boy. You're to forget about him, do you hear? Miss Riley and the social worker Mrs Turnbull have both been in touch with me already this week to find out if you have come home. They are going to pay us a visit soon, so I don't want you seeing that boy or there'll be more trouble. Do you understand, Ellen? I don't want any more of your nonsense.'

'Yes,' I say, pouting. When she tries to kiss me, I shrink away and say, '*Don't*.'

She sighs. 'Why are you doing this to me?'

'Because you won't let me have my baby,' I snap. I cross my arms and look up at her. 'If you love me you'll help me get her back.'

'It's because I love you that I'm trying to help you.'

'Don't I get a say in things?'

'I told you in the car, you are far too young. Now *stop* going on about it. You are behaving like a spoiled brat, Ellen. I try to do my best for you and this is all the thanks I get.'

She leans down to try and kiss me, but I turn my face away sharply.

'I'll see you in the morning before I go to work,' she says, straightening. 'I want you to get up early and go down to the newsagents and buy the *Herald*. You should be able to find a job.'

'Where? Where am I going to work?'

'I thought you were going to be a nurse?'

'No thanks.'

'But you passed your examination—'

'I don't want to be a nurse. I hate nurses.'

She sighs. 'Honestly, Ellen, I don't know what I'm going

to do with you. You have to do something. What about factory work? Or a chemist's shop?'

'I don't want to work in a factory. Or a chemist. I don't know what I want to do. I thought about being a vet.'

'You have to go to university for that. It's no job for a girl, anyway.'

'I'll find out about it. But not until I get my baby.'

'Ellen!' she wails. 'Please, you have got to forget about it. You are torturing yourself. And me. It's too late—'

'No, it's not. It's not too late at all. I've still got a few weeks.'

'Well, I don't know what you're going to do. I've got to work.'

'I'll get the train and the bus. I'll find it.'

'I'm not giving you any money to go gallivanting all over the city.'

'I'll hitchhike.'

'You will not! You'll be raped. There are some dreadful types out there with their long hair and surfboards and loud music. I won't have you hitchhiking, young lady, or I'll call Miss Riley.'

Being threatened with Riley makes me snap, finally. I leap off the bed and push Mum out of the room.

'Get out!' I scream. A horrified look comes over her face, as if I've gone mad. But I'm not mad, I'm angry. And sick of being told what to do. No one – not my mother, not Miss Riley or any of those fucking social workers – is going to stop me from getting my baby.

I slam the door shut and turn the key. 'Leave me alone!' I yell.

'Ellen, oh Ellen, why are you doing this? You'll be the death of me.' Her voice is cracked and thin.

'Go away,' I yell. I flop on to my bed and sob into the pillow.

A few minutes later I hear the car engine start up. I peek through the curtain and see her reversing out of the car-port.

Before turning the wheel to swing out on to the road she stops, glances up at the house, blows her nose, then wipes her eyes with a hanky. I can tell she knows I'm looking. Then she slips the car into first gear and drives off slowly. When I can no longer hear the engine, I unlock the door and charge into the lounge.

It takes a while to find the number, because I don't know where to look: under Hotels, Motels, Boarding houses, Private lodging or Accommodation? Eventually I find it, under Boarding Houses: Searles Court, Private Rooms, East Esplanade, Manly, it says, with a list of prices and a phone number.

'Who's this?' The landlady's voice sounds suspicious. She saw them leading me down the stairs in handcuffs that day, like a criminal.

I put on a voice: 'I was wondering if you might be able to help me?' I say.

'That depends.'

'Pardon?' I say, playing dumb.

'I don't want your sort coming round here.'

'I'm looking for a Mr Robert Clarke,' I say, calmly. 'Does he still live there? This is his sister speaking.'

'No, he doesn't live here. He left months ago. After that girl he was with got arrested. Seemed like a nice girl to me, till they told me she was under-age. I don't know where he is. You could try the beach, he goes surfing over at Queenscliff. Nice young boy. Except for that hair.'

'Thank you,' I say, and slam the phone down.

I go back into my room to find the piece of paper Kerry gave me with Mary's phone number. It is still in my bath-bag, hidden.

In the lounge I sit on the floor with my legs crossed and dial the number. It rings for ages, and I am about to hang up when a sleepy voice answers.

'Is that Mary?'

'Mary's out. Won't be back till late tonight. Who's that?'

'I'm a friend of hers. Can you tell her I called? Tell her I'm out. It's really important. Tell her I'll call again tomorrow. What's your address?'

'Gotta pen?' the girl says in a dopey voice. She sounds as if she's been drinking.

'Yep,' I say. 'Shoot.'

'When are ya coming?'

'I don't know,' I say, while scribbling down the details. 'Tomorrow, maybe. Tell Mary it's Ellen, Ellen Russell, from Gunyah. Tell her I want to help her get her baby back; she thinks it died, but I saw it. She's *got* to believe me. *Please* tell her, it's urgent. We've only got two weeks. Please tell her.'

'Rightio,' the girl says. She sounds a long way off, as if she is drifting off to sleep, then snapping awake again. 'I'll tell her . . . don't worry. See you.'

I hang up and sit there for a while, wondering what to do next. Then I decide to ring my friend Louise.

Her mother, Fiona, answers and my heart sinks. She has never liked me, I can tell. Thinks I'm common. Louise and I went to primary school together. Someone once said we were like chalk and cheese, because I had long dark-brown hair and she had short ginger hair, her family were snobby and well-off, mine were poor and down-to-earth. But we never let any of that get in our way.

'Hello?' Her mother sounds like the Queen.

'Hello, Mrs Robson. It's Ellen speaking. Ellen Russell. Please may I speak to Louise?'

Silence.

'Hello? Are you there, Mrs—'

'Louise is not available,' she replies coldly. I can picture her spine straightening as she speaks, the tilt of her head, with its neat blond bob, the gathering of her lips into a stiff pucker. 'And she won't be available at any other time, either. Not to you, that is.'

'What? I mean, pardon?' I add quickly, remembering my mother's advice about never saying 'What.'

'Louise has made other friends now, and I believe Jenny-Jane Clarke has, too. I suggest you do the same. We don't want your sort in our home and nor do the Clarkes.'

'But . . . Louise and me are best friends,' I burst out.

'I suggest you find another friend to replace her. Goodbye.'

Click.

I put down the receiver. I have a strong urge to crawl into bed and sleep for ever.

In the kitchen I sit on one of the bar stools; it lets out a loud fizz.

Outside a noise on the roof makes me jump; probably a possum. I lock the back door and turn on all the lights, till the house is buzzing.

Back in the living room I switch on the TV and sit cross-legged on the floor, staring blankly. But I can't keep still, it's like having insects under my skin.

No one cares. No one.

Nothing on Nine, or ABC. On Channel 7 there's a new family show, about a woman who sings in a rock 'n'roll band with her kids. The mother is blond and bubbly and having fun with them. I think: Why can't my mother be like her, at *home*?

I don't know where it comes from, it just happens. Something about the way the mother smiles at the little kid with freckles, her voice when they hug. I don't know. The insects are prickling my skin: like the day I got put away, when the walls seemed to crush me, that sensation of being pushed under by a wave and held there. My forehead is oily with sweat, the rash on my arms is swelling and my mouth tastes of Dettol and BO.

I can't breathe.

I run through the kitchen, unlock the door and tear up the yard, cursing the ugly stars. There are no sounds in the garden except the knocking of my fists on my skull. Bone on bone.

When the pain is too much to bear, I stop.

The air is still, the heavens quiet. Nothing but my warm breath touches the emptiness around me, and even that irritates me. I want to snatch it and bury it.

I am crouching on the ground on my knees, like a

Sunday worshipper. I lean forward to push myself up and realise I'm kneeling in a mound of ashes and rubbish.

Even in the darkness I recognise my things: my green maxi-coat, my paisley toilet bag, my hairbrush, my underwear. Charred and shredded by fire.

I hitch a ride outside our house. I don't care if the neighbours see. Usually I walk for a while before sticking out my thumb. But not today.

It is the next day. Mum went off early to work as usual and I promised to buy the paper and look for a job.

My jaw and my head are bruised and I have a terrible headache that makes me squint in the sunshine. Through the trees on the other side of the road, shreds of blue lake flare like irregular flags in the wind.

I must look all right, because a guy in a suit stops. I hop in. He is driving a snazzy sports car, silver, with two seats. He's up himself, he keeps flicking his long, lanky blond hair with one hand. He eyes my legs. I am wearing one of the new dresses Mum bought. A knee-length yellow-and-white, sleeveless shift. I hate it, but it's new and all my old stuff . . . My legs are bare and pale and I didn't bother to shave them. I tug at the hem to try and cover my knees.

The inside of the car smells of feet and dogs. He lights a cigarette, a Marlboro, and switches on the radio. A man announces the next song. Someone called Jimi Hendrix. I can't sit still. My mind soars with the guitars. I lean out of the window, tapping my fingers to the beat.

'Shame he died,' the guy says, nodding at the radio. 'Where you off to anyway?'

'The city.' On my lap is one of Mum's handbags, a big brown leather one that even she says is old-fashioned now. Inside is a toothbrush, hairbrush, change of underpants, some Kotex, because I'm still bleeding, my make-up bag and the five dollars that I took from my mother's purse when she was in the bathroom this morning.

'How old are you?' he asks. He glances at my knees.

'Fourteen,' I say, and leer at him.

He drops me at Wynyard without saying another word the whole way to the city, about fifteen miles.

I don't know what to do next. The hospital is near Paddington, Mary said, in King Street. I wouldn't know it if I saw it.

The traffic roars past. I flinch at the noise; everything is so loud and fast. The fumes make my throat close up. People hurry along the footpaths looking rushed and worried.

Halfway down Castlereagh Street I ask a girl in a mauve shift the way to Paddington. She points and tells me to turn left up Liverpool Street to Hyde Park. I set off. The air is cool along the shaded footpath, the skyscrapers block out the sun.

What if I can't find the hospital? What if those nurses are there and I have to argue with them about my baby? All of a sudden I feel desperate to give her a name. Any name. So it seems more real. So she is real.

Trudy? No, too common. Jody? Too tomboyish. Alicia? I like that name, it's pretty and light, like her upturned nose. I'll call her Alicia. What will she be doing right now? Sleeping? Having a bottle? Crying?

I hurry up the street, panting. At the top of the hill

shoppers are ambling up the broad steps to the elaborate entrance into Mark Foy's. A woman is going up the steps backwards, heaving a large blue pram. I stop and stare. My heart is speeding.

I don't know what makes me do it, but suddenly I am racing across the road, dodging cars, and I am face-to-face with the woman. She stops and blinks at me.

'Can I help?' I say. My hands tremble as I lift the front of the pram. Together we lift it to the top, and I think vaguely of Cleopatra and rickshaws.

'Phew,' the mother says, smiling, 'thank you so very much. That really was kind of you.'

Her voice sounds far off, as if she is under water. I peer in at her baby. It is looking at a string of yellow plastic ducks pulled tight across the pram. It has big blue eyes and a thatch of pale hair that sticks out like ragged feathers. It gurgles and coos. I want to pick it up and hold it close, bury my face in its neck and breathe in its smell.

'Is it a boy?' I ask.

'No, a girl, as a matter of fact.'

My heart lurches. I reach into the pram and touch her head. It is hot and silky. I can smell curdled milk and skin like ripe peaches.

'Are you all right?' comes the woman's voice from somewhere far off.

'Pardon?' I say.

'Excuse me, young lady, *are you all right?*'

I straighten and look at her. She is frowning. She manoeuvres herself behind the pram and grips the handle, then scurries away without another word. Just before she catches a gap in the revolving door into the shop, she glances over her shoulder at me. Her face looks astonished.

At the bus stop I feel sick. A man in a grey suit keeps looking at me. A woman with a howling kid stares. Do I look odd? Is my hair sticking out? Is my dress dirty? The kid's whingeing gets on my nerves.

I decide not to go to the hospital. It's too scary, going on my own. What if they call the police? I don't want to go back to Gunyah. What if they lock me up there and then, and I'm taken somewhere else, like Myalla?

'Excuse me,' I say to the grey-suited man, 'how do I get to King's Cross?'

He raises an eyebrow, as if to say: Thought so. Then he says, 'Go that way through the park and you can either walk up William Street or catch a bus. It's a half-hour walk, five or ten minutes by bus.' He gives me a funny look, sort of fatherly, as if to say: You shouldn't be wandering around by yourself, at your age.

'Thanks,' I say and set off.

Hyde Park is scattered with business people sitting in groups on the grass munching sandwiches; some have pulled off their shoes and socks, they wriggle their pink toes at the sky. The midday sun is so hot my arms are turning a deep brown. There's a Bird Man standing ankle-deep in pigeons and seagulls by the Pool of Remembrance, and a mother with a kid in a push-chair, wide-eyed and dribbling ice-cream, kicking its legs at the sea of pecking birds. Thank God it's not a baby, I think, thank God for that, and I hurry on towards the east side of the park.

On the bus I look at my reflection in the window and

frighten myself. It isn't me staring back. It is someone with swollen, red-raw eyes and a miserable mouth. She has a deep crease between her eyebrows. It's not the girl who was always laughing. It's not the girl who loved life. It's someone different altogether. Someone sad and fretful who looks much, much older.

At the top of William Street I get off the bus, feeling slow and weighed down. Ahead of me, on the brow of the hill, a huge neon billboard advertising Coca-Cola flashes a gaudy red design at the oncoming traffic; it seems to mark the entrance into a different world. The red-light district Mum calls it, and I think that must be why, because of the red Cola ad.

From Mum's bag I take my street guide and the piece of paper with Mary's address. According to the map, Curtis Road is at the far end of King's Cross, but I'm dismayed to see that the easiest route will take me right through the main street.

I went to the Cross with my mother and one of her friends, years ago. I can't remember his name, or even what he looked like, but he treated us to dinner at a posh restaurant. When the waiter put the bill on the table, folded in half, I picked it up to read it. I remember Mum being furious. She said it was the height of bad manners, looking at the bill when you're not paying. I wanted to crawl under the white tablecloth and melt.

Afterwards we went for a walk, 'just out of interest,' my mother's friend said. I was shocked at some of the people on the streets. Hard-faced women in shop doorways flaunting their bosom; manly women with stubbly chins and chicken-legs; guys who reminded me of gangsters I'd seen in old movies; young girls hanging around street corners, smoking.

The main street is still packed with similar weirdos, even though it's daylight. Somehow it seems scarier in the harsh sunlight. The pavements are filthy, the make-up on the women caked on and too bright; in the harsh glare their eyes look unearthly. A brawny bloke in a black suit is standing outside a doorway just ahead of me. He is trying to entice a group of giggling young men inside. You can tell they're from the country by their daggy clothes. They give him a wide berth, almost stumbling in the gutter and bumping in to one another in their haste to get away. I hurry by, pretending to look at the shops across the street, but he calls out, 'Hey, love, looking for work, are ya?'

I almost run. I hate this place. Mum said it was seedy, whatever that means. I think it's just plain scary. In every doorway stands a red-lipped woman; some are so young. I try not to stare at the older ones, who frighten me. I think one might ask me for something; they look as if they might try and steal my purse. I walk past quickly pretending not to look.

At the end of the street there is a small square with a pretty fountain. I cross the road to it. There are some park benches, but on one a scruffy old man holding an empty bottle to his chest is stretched out on his back, asleep; on another two girls wearing thick black eye make-up and pink hot-pants sit whispering.

I sit on the concrete wall of the fountain to read my map, in case someone thinks I am one of them. The sound of the water drowns the traffic. A fine, cool mist of water settles on my burnt arms. Three pigeons land at my feet and peck at the path. It hurts to sit on the cold stone because I am still sore from the stitches.

I am glad to leave the busy part of the Cross. The street I head down is tree-lined and narrow. Handsome, old blocks of red-brick flats, and elegant sandstone houses with broad verandahs and manicured gardens. Cabbage palms sway in the light breeze, and now and then I catch a glimpse into rooms crammed with exotic furnishings.

Mary's flat is in a 1930s' white-painted building that reminds me of a cruise ship. It looks run-down: the blue paint on the windows is peeling, the scorched lawn is littered with rubbish. Inside the lobby, which is dingy and smells of urine, I press a button with the number thirty-two on it. A few seconds later a buzzer breaks the silence and a crackly voice, the girl I spoke to on the phone, I think, says, 'Who is it?'

'It's Ellen. Ellen Russell. I rang yesterday. I'm a friend of Mary's. Is she home?'

'When you hear a click over near the door, push it hard and come up. Third floor, turn left at the top of the stairs.'

Their room is a cupboard. There is one single bed, a wardrobe and a sink. It smells of tobacco, like a pub; in the centre of the bed a large ashtray with TOOHEYS printed around the rim is stuffed with lipstick-stained cigarette butts and grey ash.

One end of the bed is piled with clothes and toiletries, make-up, dirty underwear and wet towels. At the other end, with her back against the wall, knees up to her chest, and her head resting on folded arms, sits Mary. She is wearing a long tie-dyed Indian dress with strings of tiny coloured beads draped around her neck.

After letting me in, the other girl – Carol, I guess – who is wearing bell-bottoms and a T-shirt with LOVE printed across it, slumps on the floor by the sink and presses her back on the wall, bare feet against the bed. She seems wedged there.

Cigarette ash and butts also line the bowl of a sink. Next to the soap by the hot tap is a plastic hypodermic syringe and a dessertspoon, blackened, as if left in the hot ash of a fire.

'Mary?'

Slowly, she raises her face to look at me. Her eyelids are droopy, her face white. Her head swivels and nods as if it isn't connected properly to her neck. I can see she is trying to figure out who I am, but there is no hint of recognition.

'Mary, it's me, Ellen. Ellen Russell. From Gunyah. And the hostel. Remember? I've come to see you.'

The other girl is asleep, I think, head buried in her folded arms on her knees.

'Whadya want?' Mary says, blinking at me in slow motion.

On a small space of candlewick pink, I sit chewing my nails furiously. Everything in the room seems dirty because the window, draped in a grey length of torn rayon, blocks out the clear Sydney daylight.

'What's wrong, Mary? Are you sick?'

She blows air out of her nostrils at my question, and her

head rotates backwards, as if I've asked the most stupid question in world history.

'What's the needle for? Are you sick?'

'Heroin,' she says, grinning. 'Don't you know anything?' Her speech is slow and slurred.

I look at her thin figure, slumped on the bed like a broken-winged bird. The marks on her arms. So that's what they are. She's on drugs. Robyn in Gunyah told me about heroin, said she'd tried it once, but the needle hurt and all it did was put her to sleep and turn her off sex.

'Whadya want?' Mary drawls.

'Mary, you've got to listen, you've got to believe me. I saw your baby, *and* mine. I'm sure it was yours. Won't you come with me? There's still time. If we go together we wouldn't be so scared of the nurses.'

I don't like this room – there's a nasty smell, like burning tar.

Mary grins, as if I'm a complete idiot.

'Please, Mary.'

Something bites my ankle, and I look down just in time to see a tiny black flea. A red lump erupts on my skin and itches. I scratch it, then wet my fingers with saliva and rub it on the bite. I want to get out of here as soon as I can. When I look across at Mary again, her head is slumped, like her friend's. Silence.

For a long time I sit stiffly on the corner of the bed, sweating and gnawing at my nails. My throat feels parched. What should I do? Wait for them to wake up? I don't know what to do. Then I think: I'll leave a note.

On the bed, amongst the wreckage, I spot an address

book. Inside the front cover Mary's name is printed, with an address in Marrickville. I copy it down in my own address book under M for Mary. Then I write my name and address in hers under E for Ellen. I find a piece of paper; it has a few things scribbled on it, names and phone numbers, a shopping list: tampons, tissues, Wetchex, lipstick, bread.

There's just enough space for me to write:

Dear Mary,
I came to see you but you were too tired to talk. I am going to get my baby from the hospital in King Street. Ring me – my number's under E in your book. Take care, I hope you and your friend will be all right.
From Ellen Russell.

If I leave the note on the bed, they won't see it. The walls are covered in torn posters. I rummage through the stuff on the bed. I can't find any sticky tape, but there's a safety pin. I pin the note and the five dollars in my purse to a poster of a man holding a guitar. He looks like Jesus, with a hairless chest. At the bottom it says: Jim Morrison.

Mary's friend has sagged sideways against the wall beneath the window. She stirs and tries to lift her head, but it nods like a thirsty flower.

Should I call a doctor? I don't want to interfere or get them into trouble. I don't know. I haven't got a clue what to do. All I know is: I want to get out before they wake up and try to give me some.

Nine

Courage is the thing. All goes if courage goes.
J.M. Barrie

It takes me over an hour to walk from King's Cross to Wynyard. As I hurry alongside tired city types, their suits crumpled, their faces strained after a long day, my own sense of purpose seems echoed in theirs – I want to get home fast, too. I begin to imagine I'm one of them, that I've just put in a day filing and typing, that I'm dressed in high heels and matching handbag and I'm off home to a square meal; I'm like them, I'm normal and not caught up in this mess of trying to get my baby back.

If I'm not home when Mum gets in from work she'll be furious. Breathless and hot, at last I reach the narrow stretch of road that broadens into several lanes on to the bridge. I stand in the gutter with my thumb stuck out at the traffic. After a few minutes a white lorry pulls over and I climb up into the cab.

The driver, a big burly bloke with massive hairy arms, is

on his way to Coffs Harbour to pick up a load of pineapples. He is friendly and harmless, I can tell, because he talks about his wife and kids the whole time.

He makes a long detour, miles out of his way, and I'm sitting there thinking: Kerry was wrong, men aren't all bad. He pulls up at the top of Coolamon's main street.

'Thanks a million,' I say, reaching for the door handle. Just then he reaches over and places a stocky hand on my right breast. I lift my right elbow and whack him square on the nose, then I bolt out the door.

I run down the street, and when I glance back at him he is leaning forward on the steering wheel, nursing his bleeding nose with a rag.

At a newsagent's I buy a *Sydney Morning Herald* with a few cents I have left in my purse, then sit on a bench at a bus stop reading the Jobs Vacant columns. The sun has set, but inside the tin bus shelter it's hot and airless. I wipe the sweat from my forehead with the back of my hand. I draw a circle round some of the ads: one for a Milk Bar Assistant; another at a Veterinary Hospital in Mosman, helping to clean the cattery and kennels; and one in an old folks' home at Mona Vale, for a nursing assistant. They all have one thing in common: NO QUALIFICATIONS NECESSARY. My hands are black from sweat and newspaper ink.

I walk the rest of the way home, about two miles along the edge of the lake. Now and then I catch a glimpse of the silvery black water shimmering through the trees. It's dark now. In the distance, way out in the middle of the lake, torch lights scour the dark – fishermen gathering prawns. I glance at my watch: ten o'clock.

When I get near our house, I stop dead. Parked outside on the grass verge is a police car.

Now what? I stand there for a few minutes, my heart banging. A car turns into Parkhurst Road and its headlights hit me full on. I duck behind a clump of bushes.

Through the branches I can see the police car. If I go in, they will probably arrest me again for being uncontrollable, for not having a job, for being out late. I'm not going back to Gunyah. I can't believe my mother has called them – again! She must hate me, she must. When they get in their car and turn around towards town, the headlights will shine straight into the bushes and they'll see me, I know they will. They'll catch me and push me into the police car and lock the doors, and I won't be able to get out. They'll send me back to Gunyah, I know they will.

I run towards town, not stopping until I get to Pittwater Road, which will take me into Manly. A few cars whoosh past; I keep glancing over my shoulder to make sure the police are not coming. I stick out my thumb and hitch.

After a few minutes a car stops. I peer in at the driver, a bloke wearing shorts and a T-shirt; he has a beer-belly and is wearing thongs. He could be a fisherman; because I can smell fish. He grins at me.

'Where you off to at this hour, eh?' he says.

'Manly.'

He shakes his head. 'Sorry, love, can't help ya. I'm only going up the road to Long Reef.'

'Thanks anyway,' I say, smiling. He drives off.

A few more cars whizz past. I run for a while, till my

ankles hurt; my sandals are too high, and my feet keep twisting sideways. I stumble along the gravel at the edge of the bitumen, glancing nervously over my shoulder in case the police are coming.

The unmistakable lights of a big truck approach. I stick out my thumb, then I start waving, as if I am hurt and need help. The driver sees me and pulls over, the wheels spinning on the gravel, scattering stones across the bitumen.

'What's up?' he asks. He is leaning out of the passenger window. He's a young guy, in his twenties, with sandy hair and a stubbly chin.

'I need to get into Manly. The police are after me for being out late, and I'm too scared to go home or they'll put me away,' I blurt.

I'm amazed, and so relieved, when he says, 'Hop in.' I can't believe my luck.

'Are you going into Manly?' I ask, settling down into the deep bucket seat inside the cab.

'Am now,' he says, smiling.

'I don't want to take you out of your way or anything.'

'Don't worry about it. I was on my way out west roo-huntin'. Makes no difference if I make a detour. Want a smoke?' He hands me a packet of Craven-A. I hate smoking, but I take one anyway, for something to do.

'Thanks,' I say. He reaches across and lights it for me. My hands are shaking.

The cab smells of fur; he is sitting on a fur seat cover.

'What's happened to you, eh?' he says. 'Fuckin' cops, they're always sticking their noses in other people's business. If they weren't cops, they'd be robbers. They're all cunts.'

'I know.'

'What happened?'

I tell him everything, he is easy to talk to and a good listener.

'I reckon you'll have a hard time gettin' your kid back,' he says, 'but good luck. Don't let the authorities push you around any more. This is supposed to be a free country.'

He takes me all the way into Manly.

'Thanks a million,' I say. 'I'll never forget this. Here, I haven't got any money, but have this.' From my neck I unhook a turquoise necklace that my mother gave me from one of her trips to America. I press it into his hand.

'Good luck,' I say.

'Same to you.'

The beach is deserted and dark.

A light breeze lifts the hairs on my arms. It's so good to smell and hear the sea again.

I take some deep breaths and realise I am hungry. It is 2 am. Above me the sky is a deep purple helmet flecked with stars.

I settle on the sand against the shelter of the warm sandstone wall that overlooks Manly beach. Mum's shoulder bag is lumpy and hard under my head, but there's a hint of her smell on it that is sort of comforting. The dull ripple of the waves on the sand is soothing. I feel safe here. Safer than I've felt in ages.

In the morning I'll walk along the beach, climb the

stairs against the cliff and hotfoot through the streets to Queenscliff. If the surf's up, Robbie might be there. It won't matter if I look a mess; when I tell him what's happened, he'll help. He'll be so glad to see me. He'll come running out of the water, surfboard under his arm, body glistening with seawater, and his eyes will light up when he sees me on the shore. I can't wait to see him. I've missed him so much. He'll help me get my baby back. Our baby.

Next day I awake to a frightening sun – it is so big as it emerges over the horizon that I can almost see the flames flicking the sky. I am mesmerised by the changing tapestry above: purple, red, pink. In Gunyah we couldn't see the sun rise or set, the walls were too high. A hint of pink was the most you could hope for.

At the water's edge I curl my toes into the cool, wet sand. A wave slides up the smooth, hard slope and tickles my ankles. Further along a few eager surfers arrive, carrying their boards and towels. A cheeky oystercatcher is playing a game of chase with the waves. Above me the sky has dissolved to a brazen blue.

I feel grubby after my night on the sand; my eyes are full of grit, and sand has found its way into every crack. I can feel it in my bottom. Salt baths, ha! The sea will fix me, better than anything. The sun, now quite high in the sky, has shrunk to its normal size and turned corn-yellow; already it is burning my face.

I run back to my bag and strip down to my underwear. I don't care if anyone sees me; I have to get in that water, feel the coolness against my skin, let it heal the cuts and wash away the blood.

Half an hour later I lean against the warm wall till the sun dries me. Then I pull on my dress, slip a clean pad in my panties, stuff my sandals into my bag and set off towards the steps at the northern end of the beach.

The beach is already quite busy with more surfers and a few beer-bellied men with huge fishing poles, serious-faced at the water's edge.

A group of blond-headed boys on boards weave in and out of the transparent waves. The sand is hot under my feet, and it squeaks as the ball of each foot twists into it, but my feet are fireproof.

The surf is up at Queenscliff and the place is packed with surfers. I stand at the top of the cliff looking down. It won't be easy to spot Robbie, even if he is here.

First, I look for his blue panel-van in the car park flanking the beach, but it's not there. I pass a group of boys on their knees next to an orange Combie van. They are busy waxing their boards. As I walk by, two look up and whistle. I try to look calm, but my face turns red and I feel as if I've fossilised. I walk on quickly, almost tripping over my feet, which are suddenly two cumbersome lumps.

I wait on the beach all day, studying the surfers in case one of them is him. I'll know him the minute I see him – I know his style, the way he leans forward, bent at the waist, arms stretched to his side, like a bird.

By mid-afternoon there's still no sign of him. I'm starving and about to give up. I've already spent the few coins I had left on fish and chips. What next? Should I go home and say I'm sorry to Mum? What if the police are there, waiting? No. I'm not risking it.

What about Lizzie? Maybe I should march straight into the boarding house, straight past the landlady, *old bag*, up the stairs, and bang on Lizzie's door? She'll help me, she's always got money, she works at a dry cleaner's in Balgowlah. Why didn't I think of that earlier? I'll go and find her, if she's not at work, hopefully she'll be at home.

It's 4.30. People are packing up their umbrellas and towels, and some are examining their sunburn; kids have already come home from school and are arriving for a dip or a surf before tea; the banks are closed and workers in the city are already gearing up for knock-off time. The car park is half empty. I am just about to nip between two pine trees to cross the road when I spot Robbie's van. I freeze. I dash back across the dust-blown car park to the wall to look for him in the water. The surfers all look the same sitting astride their boards, brown backs to the shore, waiting for a wave. The water is calm, the sky a deep grey. Soon the sun will set. It has dropped behind the cliff, and the beach is shadowy and quiet.

Soon a wave swells, and one by one they paddle towards the beach. The wave is small and slow, and the guys aren't tempted any more; a few paddle ashore and sprint up the sand.

A long-haired blonde girl hugging her knees on a towel is staring at the guys in the water. That was me, not so long ago, waiting for Robbie. All day I'd wait, in between swimming and sunbathing. Sometimes I'd take a book, or a magazine. But I was waiting for Robbie, really.

It's no use, he's not here, it must be someone else's van. Or maybe he's at the Milk Bar across the road, or the pub. I stand on the wall and look towards his panel-van; it is still there.

When I sit down again to scan the beach, I see him. He is jogging up the sand with his board under one arm, hard legs muscly and tanned, long blond hair dripping like wet straw on to his shoulders. He is smiling.

I lift a hand to wave, he's seen me!

I stand up on the wall, my heart racing. Then he drops his board on to the sand next to the blonde girl, bends down to her face and stops. He is staring straight at me.

Lizzie and Robbie. Robbie and Lizzie. There are too many 'ie's and 'z's and 'b's, but it doesn't matter, they sound okay. My heart has turned blue. Not green, like you'd expect in this sort of situation.

They have a small flat above a bottle shop off The Corso. There's a lone palm tree outside with bitumen right up to the roots, and cigarette butts and Coke cans. The floor in their tiny white flat has that sea-grass matting that my mother says attracts fleas. She says all the dirt falls through and you can't suck it up with the Hoover.

Robbie says he's sorry, but he thought he'd never see me again.

Lizzie says, 'Yeah, we thought you'd disappeared off the face of the earth.'

'That's okay,' I say. 'It's not your fault. Your hair's grown,' I add.

When I tell Robbie about being pregnant, he says, quick as a whip, 'It's not mine, I used Wetchex.'

I say, 'Well, it didn't bloody work, because I – *we* –

have a baby. She's at a hospital in King Street, in the city. I want to go and get her. Will you come with me?' And the whole time we're talking he's moving around the room looking at record covers, lighting a cigarette, peering at the contents of his wallet, checking his matted hair in the cane-rimmed mirror, and I'm perched on the very edge of the couch, heart pumping, chewing my fingers, shoulders hunched.

'Why should I? It's not mine,' he says, looking over one shoulder at me while flicking through *Surfing Now*. He chucks it on the floor, then walks across to the window, which is smeared and cracked in one corner. He pulls the faded floral curtains. He switches on the light. He sits down on the ripped velvet armchair, but only for two, maybe three seconds, then almost sprints into the kitchenette.

Leaning against the wall in the lounge is his surfboard. The floor is strewn with LPs. A brand-new stereo system is stacked on a length of board supported at each end by bricks. The walls are decorated with surfing pictures, torn from magazines. In one corner there's a clothes-horse with Lizzie's undies, skinny bikini pants, black and red, really sexy. They've thrown their his and hers beach towels on the couch. I can hear Robbie fill a kettle, then rifle through the fridge; now he's chopping something.

There's a bedroom, *their* bedroom. I can see through the half-open door. Above the bed there's a big surfing poster. The bed's a mess, the covers pulled half off on to the floor, the bottom sheet exposed, as though they slept with nothing but their bodies keeping them warm.

Lizzie is sitting on the floor next to a drooping rubber plant, with her chin resting on her knees. She is looking at me as if to say: It's nothing to do with me.

'What are you gonna do?' she asks.

'It's Robbie's baby. He'll have to help me.'

'I'm with Robbie now,' she says, staring at me coldly. She gets up and goes into the kitchen. I sit there, wondering what to do next.

Eventually I get up and walk across to them. I stand in the doorway watching while they make salad sandwiches. Robbie is still in his yellow board shorts and bare feet. There are white patches on his deep-brown back where the salt has dried. In the middle of his back, right in that central spot where your own hand can't quite reach, there's a cluster of red pimples that look as if they've been squeezed. I can't take my eyes off them. And then it hits me. They are sharing much more than a scungy flat and a water-bed. They are doing what my mother would call Being Intimate.

'I thought you'd do the right thing, Robbie,' I say thinly. 'It's your baby. She's *our* baby. If you don't help me they'll give her away.'

He shrugs and ignores me.

'Is that all you can do, shrug?' I say.

'What do you want me to do, jump for joy,' he drawls over one shoulder. 'Just because my olds are rich, doesn't mean I am.'

He looks at Lizzie for back-up. She is busy shredding a lettuce. She pushes a tendril of blonde hair away from an eye and tosses her head, giving him a quick glance that says: You tell her, Robbie. Together they stand with their backs to me constructing two salad doorsteps. I am half expecting them to offer me a cup of tea, because that's how my mother brought me up. Suddenly, from a narrow crack in the wall behind the sink, a black cockroach scuttles out and nose-dives into the mountain of dirty crockery.

In their wretched kitchen I can suddenly see exactly what's going on. No matter how long I wait, Robbie has finished with me. He probably finished with me the day he saw me crumpled and egg-stained at the police station – months, aeons, *oh*, light-bloody-years ago. I should have guessed he wasn't going to wait around for me. It wasn't like we were engaged or anything. He probably got lonely. Can't say I blame him for picking on Lizzie: she's gorgeous with her long blonde hair, slim brown body – and those perfect round bosoms. All the guys drool over them at the cleaner's, so she reckons.

No, there's no point getting angry or begging him to help me, it wouldn't do any good. He's set up house with Lizzie. They make a great couple, really, in spite of their sing-songy names. I can see that. I'm not a dummy. I can tell they wish I'd go. And I know that – whatever has happened to me, no matter how scary, how wrong, how unfair – they don't care. Matter of fact, nobody does. No one wants to help me get Alicia back. Because it's my problem. Because she's my baby. Because it's my fault.

I turn and walk out the door, down the concrete steps and into the car park.

It is full of shoppers loading up their cars with groceries. They don't have a clue what's happened to me; as

I walk along the rows of cars I could be invisible. I am invisible.

There's a woman packing boxes of food into the boot of her white Valiant. Inside the car, strapped in matching small seats, are two kids with snotty noses, screaming their lungs out. The woman looks flustered and strained. She's got a huge trolley-load of stuff, it'll take her ages to unload it. I stop to help her, because that's how I was brought up. She barely looks at me. When it is all in her car, she mumbles 'Thanks', as if she expected to be helped and wasn't surprised one bit.

I walk away without saying a word, guiding the empty trolley towards the back of Woolies. I begin to imagine it's a pram I'm pushing. I begin to imagine Alicia is in it, gurgling and smiling up at me, that I am smiling back. Then I imagine I am taking her home. By the time I get to the trolley point tears are gliding down my cheeks and my palms are burning on the handle.

Granny used to say to me: There's no such word as can't, it's just an excuse for laziness.

When I get Alicia back I'll find a way to look after her. I can be a good mother, I can. I can be strong and good, and I'll work hard and I'll do it, somehow.

But first I'll get Mum on my side.

If I say I'm sorry and if I beg her, she'll give in and help me. She *has* to. She just has to.

All the windows have been nailed up. I can't open any of them. Even my bedroom window, which is never locked, because where we live there are no worries about burglars. And my key doesn't work because the lock's been changed.

When I got home last night the house was in darkness. My mother's car was in the car-port, so I crept up the front steps to the verandah and dozed on an old cane chair.

Early this morning, before the sun came up, I could hear her padding about inside, having a shower, making tea and toast. I could tell by the sounds of her cup being rinsed at the kitchen sink, the gurgling noises coming to a halt down the drain, that she'd go into the bathroom to clean her teeth next, apply her lipstick, check herself in the bedroom mirror, then leave for work. At the point when she went to do her teeth I hid in the grove of sugar bananas out the front.

It's no use – every window has been nailed tight. I tiptoe round the side of the house, past the jasmine that grows like mad in the shade, careful not to make a sound in case the neighbours hear. In the shed in the back yard I find a rusty screwdriver and a hammer.

The wood splits and bruises when I try to jemmy open my window. I realise it's not going to work. *Shit!* The nails must be huge. I sprint softly to the shed again and find an oily rag amongst the stiffened paintbrushes and bottles of turps. I'm wary in there because of spiders and snakes and lizards. Once, when I was little, I went in to get something for Granny and a frill-necked lizard hissed at me as I turned on the light. It was clinging to the wall right by the switch. Its neck flared out like a fan and when it spat I could see its firm grey tongue. Granny came out with her axe and chopped its head off.

Back at my window, I stand in the depths of Granny's blue hydrangeas and press the rag against the glass, then firmly tap with the hammer. The glass fractures into long shards – I push them with the rag and they clatter noisily on to my eiderdown.

I climb in and sit on my chair, my heart pounding. I feel shocked and numb that my mother could do this to me.

There's no money anywhere in the house. I check every handbag, suitcase, pocket, drawer and cupboard. Nothing.

In the top drawer of Mum's dressing table there's a folder with papers and letters, bills and receipts. Maybe there's a few dollars in there, or a cheque book.

I'm intrigued by the stuff in the folder. There are some old sepia photos of Mum holding me as a baby, surrounded by kids I've never seen before, cousins probably. Standing next to her in one is Cousin Pam, the hard one who works as a nurse. She has a square jaw that sticks out haughtily, and a false smile that hides a multitude of meanness. Her two blond sons are by her side in grey shorts and sandals, giggling, their shoulders hunched as if they'd really like to loosen up a bit, but they're too afraid in case their mother gives them a bloody good clip round the ear.

There are some letters in the pile – some from me, written in Gunyah. And others I wrote when she put me in boarding school, in big, childish printing, with drawings of the trees I liked to climb. I was always in trouble for climbing trees, and the headmistress made me stand for hours under the hall clock where visitors and staff walked past.

I check every envelope but there's no money. Inside one there's a typewritten letter that catches my attention. It is addressed to Mum, and I'm amazed to see it is from Sister Dawson. There's another one with it, from someone called Mrs Gannon, on official-looking headed notepaper. The name Gannon sounds familiar, but I can't pinpoint it. Both letters are about me and my baby. Sister Dawson's is dated 29 August 1970.

Dear Mrs Russell,

I am pleased to inform you that I have found a suitable placement for your daughter Ellen's baby. They are a lovely young couple from the country. He is a sheep farmer, and his wife helps out on their property. They are unable to have children of their own and are thrilled at the prospect of adopting. I am quite confident they will be excellent parents. They have a modest but steady income from their property, and I feel sure you would be delighted to see the baby go to such a secure environment. After discussing the matter at length with myself, Ellen expressed a desire to give up the baby, as she conceded the child would have a more secure future with a married couple. I outlined the stigma of illegitimacy to Ellen, and as she is a reasonably intelligent girl she did not have any difficulty understanding the possible repercussions of attempting to keep the child.

> *I trust you will be happy for me to proceed with the adoption and that you are satisfied the matter has been dealt with according to your wishes.*
> *I remain, yours faithfully,*
> Sister Iris Dawson

Shaking, I put the letter on the table and begin to read the one from Mrs Gannon. It is pretty similar to Sister's, but the date is more recent, only a few weeks ago, around the time when I first went to the hostel after having Alicia, I think. It says something about me signing the release papers: '*Ellen has signed the release papers; now it is a matter of a few weeks before the baby can be handed over to its prospective parents.*'

I put the letters back in the folder, my mind racing – I can't believe these people are writing to my mother about me and my baby. I can't believe my mother has ganged up against me with those witches. I hate her for this, I *hate her*. Release papers? I remember Sister got me to sign something the night she sent me to the hospital – she said it was to confirm I was happy to have the baby at a certain hospital, and if I didn't sign she wouldn't be able to take me in the ambulance, and I'd end up having my baby at Gunyah without proper maternity facilities.

In the kitchen I make a peanut-butter sandwich. I am starving. There's a bowl of fresh fruit. I make a big fruit salad and by the time I'm finished the bench is littered with scraps of peel and the room smells tropical and exotic. I can feel the fruit doing me good. If I'm going to get Alicia back I will need the energy. I might have to walk fifteen miles into the city if I can't hitch a lift.

I am just eating the last few chunks of pineapple, all the time thinking about my mother and those letters, all the time hating her for doing this, when I hear voices.

In the dining room, where the letters and bills are strewn on the table, I peek between the curtains, trembling.

Walking up the driveway is my mother and her cousin Pam. What's she doing here? With them is Miss Riley.

I can see by their faces that they know I'm inside – the neighbours must have phoned them – and I begin to panic. Then suddenly I know *exactly* what to do.

I charge into the kitchen, unlock the back door and run up the garden. Right up the back there's a short flight of concrete steps built between two rocks. I leap up them three at a time, scramble over the wire fence at the top into the thick bush that stretches for miles behind the house. The route is imprinted on my mind: every stone, rock, tree, bush, because I ran out the door like this lots of times when Mum nagged or criticised me, or when Jack and I were home on our own and I got nervous, then I'd run away and hide all day.

It was easy, then, because I scarpered a few times a week, so the path was pretty clear from me tearing through it like a wild boar. It's grown back with a vengeance since then: the lantana and blackberry rip at my arms and legs, but I just keep fighting my way through, because I'm not going to let them get me, I'm not going to let them send me away again. My feet are bare and feel tender because of being in shoes at Gunyah, but I ignore the pain as I scramble over the rocks and down steep gullies, panting, staggering now and again, but not looking back, not once looking back.

At last I reach Snail Rock, about half a mile from the house. I lean with my back on the warm rock, panting.

They'll never find me here, and when I'm sure they've gone – I'll be able to see if their cars are there from the top of the cliff – then I'll go back into the house, have a shower, change my clothes and head into the city to get Alicia.

The entrance into Snail Rock is via a small opening at ground level, like a low tunnel. Even when I was a kid I had trouble squeezing through it on my tummy.

I start digging at the soft, dry dirt, and it takes a while, but eventually there's a shallow ditch; before crawling through I break off a leafy branch and leave it by the entrance, so that I can reach out later and cover the hole.

On my tummy, I start to wriggle through. My heart is pounding. The raw rock grazes my shoulders and the top of my head, and for a few awful seconds I think I am stuck. I lie flat and try to relax. My mouth is pressed into the dirt, which smells of bull ants. I begin to panic, but manage to stretch my arms and grip with my fingertips on to the shelf of rock in front of me. I wrench myself forward into the cave, leaving bits of skin and hair clinging to the rock. Inside it is pitch-black and cold. The air is heavy with the smell of possum shit. There's a thin sliver of dust-flecked light shining through a crack in the cave ceiling. I used to sit here for hours with a torch and a book, *Bush*

Christmas usually, because it was comforting to think other kids had been all right in the bush without grown-ups.

They won't find me here. I reach my arm through the opening, wrap my fingers around the broken branch and pull it across the hole. Then I scramble up to the ledge at the back of the cave and sit there hugging my knees.

No one likes me. Not even my mother. They all hate me. Especially Sister Dawson. I never said I wanted to give my baby away – she made it up, she did. I never said: Give my baby away. *Never*. I'm so stupid and ugly.

No one can see me here, and I can do what I like to myself. There might be a snake that will bite me. It can bite me all over and I won't care, because I'm not worth anything, I'm full of shit.

It's amazing what the human body can stand. Beneath the beam of light I carve ALICIA on my leg with a sharp piece of stone. It stings like hell, and the blood dribbles down and drips like a tap on to the crumbly earth.

When I've finished I sit there shivering stiffly, listening.

In a corner of the cave there's a soft scuffing sound. Two huge, round yellow eyes are staring at me from a black corner. A possum! It is probably more scared of me, but I'm still worried, because if possums panic they scratch with their sharp claws. It's one thing to hurt yourself, quite another when it's done to you by something unknown in the dark.

I find some stones and start hurling them towards the poor creature, but I don't shout in case there's someone outside, hunting for me. And I am careful not to hit the possum. I don't want to hurt it, I just want it to leave me alone.

After a while it blinks and is gone. I can hear rustling as it picks its way through the branch across the entrance. At last, I am completely alone.

The house is silent and empty when I get back.

There's a sheet of plastic stuck with sticky tape across the shattered window. I peel it off and climb in. The slivers of glass on my bed have gone and the eiderdown has been smoothed and straightened; in the kitchen, the fruit scraps are in the pedal bin, the papers on the dining table cleared away. Everything is back to normal. So like my mother: can't stand any mess.

Quickly, I undress and pad into the bathroom. The hot shower stings the scratches and the tattoo, but when the dried crusty blood has rinsed away I'm quite pleased with the result. I even managed, in the dark of the cave, to do one of those fancy As that I like to practice, with squiggly curls.

After drying myself I quickly slip back to my room to dress. I want to get out fast, in case they come back. In my top drawer I find clean underwear, but I'm surprised at how empty the drawer is. And when I open my wardrobe, there are hardly any clothes hanging up. I guess Mum decided to burn the lot.

The only thing that fits me is a pair of jeans and a short-sleeved broderie anglaise blouse, and even that pinches at my arms. There's an old pair of sand-shoes at the bottom of the wardrobe, and a hand-knitted bobbly cardigan that

Granny made. It was always too big, but now it fits perfectly.

From my jewellery box I take the heart necklace Granny gave me – perhaps it will bring me good luck. Then I brush my damp hair and apply some pale-pink lipstick. I want to look decent at the hospital or they'll turn me away. But in the mirror I see reflected a scruffy, spotty mess of a girl.

I sit on my bed, crying into my hands. It's no use. They'll take one look at me and laugh. I can't look after Alicia. I'm not a mother. I'm just a kid, really.

I know! My mother's clothes. I'll wear something of hers. I'll make myself look like Mum. She's got suits and frocks and jackets, there's bound to be something that will fit me. Her wardrobe is chock-a-bloody-block with clothes. I pull out an armload and dump them on her bed. They all smell of her – Estée Lauder and Palmolive soap. I try on everything: swirling dresses with cross-over bodices and low necklines; tight-skirted suits with little box jackets; navy-blue slacks with a pale pink twinset. I decide on a white pleated skirt, below the knee, and a navy-blue top with a white trim along a soft collar. Her shoes are a size smaller than mine, but I squeeze my feet into them – the navy pair with punched holes around a white trim. Then I comb my hair and pin it back at the sides with bobby pins. In an old powder-stained make-up purse in her top drawer there's a powder compact. I dust my face with this, then pat with the sponge to try and cover my pimples. It looks quite smooth when I finish, so long as you don't look too close, because the powder has built up over the spots into dry, cracked nobbles, like an erupting desert landscape. I apply more lipstick and some mascara. Only a bit, because I'm not used to applying it and it keeps smudging under my eyes.

When I look in the full-length mirror it doesn't look like me. And it doesn't look like my mother. But one thing's for certain, I look . . . *straight*. That's what Robbie would say. He hated people who looked straight. But that's exactly what the people at the hospital will want – someone who is straight. Someone respectable. That's what Sister Dawson said to me: The baby deserves to be brought up by respectable parents. I'm respectable. I am. And I'll show them I can be a good mother. I'll dress like this all the time. I don't care about fashion, or music, or boys, or any of those stupid things. I just want to get Alicia and hold her close to me, love her and touch her and smell her. I want her so much. Please God, help me get her back.

By the time I am ready to leave it is mid-morning. The littlies at the local primary school will just be lining up to get their halfpint of sun-warmed milk from the crates outside the classroom door; in the distance I can hear the soft drone of the first speedboats dragging bent skiers across the glassy lake; my mother will be walking to the deli for some sandwiches, fuming probably; freshly-permed pensioners will be emerging from the hairdresser's to eat lunch at one of the RSL clubs, before spending the afternoon pulling the slot machines. I can't help wondering what everyone's doing. Even Jack – where will he be right now? At work, I guess. Or maybe he's taken the day off and he's got his feet up on his boat, fishing. My friend Louise – she'll be at school, studying hard, because her parents are rich and sent her to one of those posh secondary schools.

Me? What am I doing? I'm looking for my baby. That's a funny way to spend your day. I can't stop thinking about her. She must feel so confused; she must be crying for her mother, for *me*. Would they be bathing her now? Or giving her a bottle? Or hugging her? I can't bear the thought of those nurses touching her.

I shut the front door and tread carefully in my mother's shoes down the steps. I totter on Jack's concrete handiwork like a criminal leaving the scene of the crime.

At the bottom of the driveway is my blue suitcase. I stop dead and stare at it. Tucked under the handle there is an envelope. It has my name printed on the front. Inside, a note says:

Ellen,
    As you are not prepared to live by my rules I am no longer prepared to help you. You will have to fend for yourself from now on.
    Mum

PS Here is $100 to help you get started. Find a place to stay and get a job, then I might consider having you back one day. Mum.

I tuck the note into my bag and struggle down the drive with my suitcase. There are no tears, just a deep sense of being unloved. It is very heavy, my bag, and I don't know how far I will get. I put it down on the grass verge. I think about dumping some of the contents. My fingers are already red and pinched.

When I look up again, I notice a yellow Holden on the other side of the road, parked in the shade of some paperbark trees, their trunks ghostly, as though draped in shredded muslin. Sitting in the front of the car on the driver's side, staring straight at me with a stern face, is a dark-haired woman.

I recognise her straight away, even from a distance. It is my mother's cousin, Pam.

Ten

I'd forgotten how much Pam can talk, but at least she is giving me a lift.

All the way into Manly she never shuts up. On and on about how unfair I am to my mother, about how selfish I am, about how much my mother suffered when I was put inside. Her voice is confident and clear; she seems so in control, so right, so bloody right about everything, that I don't argue. I don't say a word.

At Manly wharf she draws up in front of the taxi rank to drop me off. My hand is on the handle and I'm just about to get out when she turns to me and says, 'Your mother's far too lenient with you. I told my boys if they ever play up they'll be sent packing. Your mother should've done this a long time ago.'

I open the door and get out. She sits at the wheel while I open the boot and lift out my bag. I walk off without a word. Not one.

*

I've got no choice. I decide to go back to Mary's. She's the only person I can think of who might be able to help me find a place to stay. Even though she's given up on finding her baby, she might let me sleep on her floor for a few nights, or tell me where to look for a room.

As the ferry pulls out of the quay I settle on the middle deck, outside. The ferris wheel on the jetty is slowly spinning, young kids are splashing in the public swimming baths enclosing the inlet. I can hear the pinball machines at the fun fair being jabbed by teenagers, and as we draw away another ferry bumps against the creaking timber wharf to deposit passengers from the city. I lean over the front of the boat to stare at the soft green waves. A salty, fishy smell fills my nostrils. A fairy penguin is crisscrossing at the bow, like a black-and-white arrow. It's hard to feel sad on this glittering harbour, with the sun pelting down and the fresh air in your lungs. I know the people sitting behind me are staring, and I can feel their eyes on Mum's clothes, but somehow I don't care. I know I'm alone, truly alone, and it doesn't seem to matter what anyone thinks. If it was Alicia watching me, now that's a different thing. If she was here, looking at my skirt and my hair and my make-up, that'd be different. I'd want her to see a good mother, a good person, a kind and sensible person. Not a mixed-up kid who has just been thrown out on her ear.

At Circular Quay I take a taxi to the Cross and ten minutes later I'm standing on the parched lawn in front of Mary's, listening to the dull roar of the city traffic, wondering what to say. Hi, Mary, I'm back. She won't even remember me being there. I wish I had somewhere else to go; I've never liked Mary. She is so sure her baby is dead. Maybe I did dream it all. Maybe it was another name I saw, like Berry. So much of what happened is a dark blur, so much of it is blank. But why would I dream it? I remember Alicia's nose. I touched her head, felt her soft hair, heard her breathing, *smelt* her. I saw the name *Perry*. I saw the name *Russell*. Didn't I?

There's no reply when I press the buzzer, so I sit on the front step, wondering what to do, hoping Mary might arrive home any minute. It's a long time before anyone comes, and when they do it's only the cleaning woman. She opens the door behind me and pushes a bucket through with one foot. Soapy brown water slops on the tiles. She has an armload of brooms and mops.

'Who you lookin' for, love?' she says, eyeing me suspiciously under wrinkled eyelids.

'Mary Perry and her friend Carol. Flat thirty-two.'

'Oh, *them*,' she snorts, 'you don't wanna know their sort, do ya? Nice girl like you.' She looks at my mother's shoes. 'You their sister or something?'

'No, I'm a friend, sort of. I don't know them that well, but I'm looking for somewhere to stay.'

'You don't want to stay here, my girl. Too many druggies and prostitutes. That Mary, she's been put away again. Cops caught her with heroin.'

I look at her with my mouth open.

'And you know what that means, don't you?' she continues, frowning. She reminds me of Granny a bit, with her large bosom and floral dress.

'Trouble,' I say.

'Too bloody right! She's in for a long stretch in the slammer, that girl. Heroin is the worst. The other girl . . . ?'

'Carol.'

'Yeah, her. She took an overdose. The ambulance took her away, but she carked it before they got to the hospital. You stay away from people like them. That young Mary, she's lucky. At least she's safe in an institution.' She lifts her broom and begins to sweep the floor. ' 'Ere, why don't you look in the window at the newsagent's up the hill, next to the Bottle-o? They have ads for rooms. You might find something decent if you're lucky.'

'Thanks,' I manage weakly.

I struggle up the hill with my suitcase. The pit of my stomach feels queasy. Did Carol die after I was there? Should I have called a doctor? Is it my fault, for being so stupid, for not seeing the danger? Tears begin to flow down my face, but I wipe them away angrily, because I don't want to cry any more. I want to be strong and fight the whole world till I get Alicia back. The old woman's words keep echoing in my skull, over and over again: *That other girl carked it, that other girl carked it.*

At the top of the hill there's a phone box. I find the newsagent's and take down five numbers. I buy a newspaper so that I've got some coins for the phone.

Inside the sun-baked telephone booth on the curve of the hill the first three numbers don't answer and the coins keep spitting back.

A man answers the fourth number and the coin is gulped. He sounds older, says his name is Frank, he's a pharmacist in the Cross. He has a flat at Rushcutter's Bay, there's a small garden and a balcony. I'd have my own room.

'I haven't got a job yet. I've just left home. But I'm looking.'

'Come over for an interview,' he says. 'Two o'clock.'

I write down the address and he gives me instructions for getting a bus.

Frank comes straight out with things. Things I don't know anything about. But I sit there listening, trying to pretend that I do.

'I do a lot of illegal stuff for addicts in the Cross,' he says. 'The police know. I give them backhanders to keep the heat off. Those young kids need my help. I give them what they want when I can, so they don't get too sick. The other thing I do is abortions. In a small room at the back of the chemist shop. I'm telling you all this now because I want someone I can be honest with. No point you living here otherwise, because you'll see and hear things you won't understand, and that might get you talking to your friends. I don't want anyone snooping around. The arrangement I have with the police is satisfactory at the moment. There are reasons I do what I do. For a start, I know what it's like to have an addiction. I'm addicted to drink. And I can imagine what it must be like to be pregnant when you don't want to be. When you can't afford to be. When you don't know who the father is. When there's a risk of disease. So, that's what I do. As well as dishing out the usual cough medicines and tinea cream.' He laughs. I see that his teeth are false – the little silver clips are visible in the roof of his mouth.

He is sitting opposite me on an enormous apricot pouff, his long, slim fingers clasped between his knees. He looks like the golfing or bowling type.

'Well?' he says. 'Do you think you can handle an old dodderer like me?'

'I don't know. I suppose so. How much is the rent?' I mutter, nervously.

'How does twenty dollars a week sound, plus some housework? I need someone to put in a load of washing now and then and keep the place reasonably clean and tidy in case I entertain.'

'Sounds okay to me,' I say, though I'm not sure. I hope he's not a dirty old man or anything. He looks all right, with his sleek grey hair, blue slacks and open-necked shirt. He looks like I imagine my father might look these days, old and harmless. But you never can tell with men. That's what Kerry said, anyway. You can't trust any of them.

'Tell you what,' he says, 'I'll make us a cuppa while you think about it. I don't want any down-payment, by the way, just pay me every Saturday.' He gets up and walks into the kitchen.

'I haven't got a job, yet,' I call after him, 'but I've got enough for a while. And . . . well, there's something else.' My heart is in my mouth, because I don't know if what I'm about to say will put him off, and I need a bed – I need a home – badly.

The room is light and airy, with a wide window overlooking the balcony and garden. I could easily live here, it's more comfortable than Mum's. The floor is carpeted in pale-grey shag, the couches are plush, with apricot flowers and silk scatter cushions. On the glass coffee table there are travel books and magazines – *Australian Vogue*, *Homes and Gardens*, the *National Geographic*, and on the floor a stack of magazines called *The Lancet*. The one on the top has a close-up photo of some white tablets spilling from a brown bottle. Along one wall there's a beautiful white bookcase, full of serious-looking books. Wooden artefacts, African or Asian, peer down from the top shelf. Leading off the lounge are several doors; one is slightly ajar, and I can see a double bed, crumpled and unmade.

Frank is filling a kettle. I can see the back of his silver head, his tanned, blond-haired arms moving across the bench to turn on the switch, then arrange cups, saucers, milk on a tray. It reminds me of Robbie. In the kitchen with Lizzie.

'What's the something else?' he asks, briefly turning his head over one shoulder towards me.

'I have a baby,' I blurt. 'Well, not yet. But I will, when I get her. She's still at the hospital. In King Street. I have to get her before thirty days.'

Suddenly the kitchen is silent. It's as if the last breath of air has been drawn out of the living room into the kitchen through Frank's false teeth, and he is holding it there, in his diaphragm.

Now he is at the door staring at me, grim-faced.

'Are you one of those breeders?' he says.

He can tell by the look on my face I haven't got a clue what he means.

'Let me just get our tea,' he says.

A few minutes later he appears carrying a tray with a teapot, two cups and saucers and a plate of Monte-Carlos. My mouth waters at the sight of them.

'Help yourself,' he says, noticing my hungry eye, and I do. I eat three, one after the other, without stopping.

'Did you put yourself in a hostel voluntarily?' he says, watching my face closely.

'They put me away. In a place called Gunyah, out west. It's a training—'

'Yes, yes, I know,' he says, impatiently. 'What did you do, rob a bank?'

'No! Course not,' I giggle at this, the thought of me, robbing a bank.

'No, of course you didn't. Let me guess – shoplifting?'

I shake my head. 'Two more guesses.'

'You smoked some pot and got caught.'

'No, not me. Can't stand the smell of it.'

'I know,' he says, beaming, 'you committed the unutterable sin of having searingly hot sex with your boyfriend. You were under-age at the time, about fourteen I'd say, and your boyfriend is about, ooh, twenty. But he got off scot-free. He walked away a free man, because he told the cops you lied about your age. *And* I bet he's a surfie.'

My mouth is wide open. 'How'd you know?' I mutter, dumbfounded.

'Just a wild guess,' he says, winking.

'I have to try and get Alicia back. I can't just leave her there. She's mine.'

The tears are coming again, I can feel them.

'Here,' Frank says, 'catch.'

He throws me a clean hanky from his pocket. It is one of those huge check ones. It smells of tobacco and whiskey. I blow my nose hard, but the tears start flowing like tap water.

For a long while we just sit there, silently, while I sniffle and blow my nose. When the hanky is soaked and my eyes are dry but raw, Frank says, 'Why don't you go and unpack? You've got a lot of talking to do. And I'm just the person to listen.'

I tell Frank everything.

Somehow, he draws every little detail out of me. He doesn't seem surprised, or shocked or anything. In fact, he seems to know what's coming next. As though he's heard it all a thousand times before. As though this sort of thing happens all the time.

'You're not alone in this,' he says, when I finally feel ready to drop.

We've had plate after plate of food. Frank kept disappearing into the kitchen to make more: Sao biscuits and cheese, tomatoes and celery, a Greek dip called hoummus that he said was coming into fashion and a sweet pastry called baklava that was dripping with honey.

'What do you mean?'

'I'll tell you exactly what I mean. It's very simple. Those other girls, at the hostel, I'd be very surprised if any of them kept their babies. The nuns and the nurses, and those battle-axe social workers are very clever at persuading unmarried mothers to give up their babies for adoption. If a young girl can't support herself, they figure, how can she bring up a child? There's a lot of sense in that, really. But they don't go about it the right way, as far as I am concerned. You should not have been given so many injections – the drugs they use are powerful, mind-altering barbiturates. It's a wonder to me you can remember anything at all.'

It is late now, about seven o'clock, and I feel full and comfortable. More comfortable than I have in ages. Months. For ever. I am listening to Frank, but a lot of what he says doesn't make sense, and he keeps using words I've never come across, like barb . . . whatever it is.

'Didn't you have to work today?' I say, suddenly conscious of the time I've taken up talking about my problems.

'No,' he laughs, 'not on a Sunday.'

I didn't have a clue. My mind begins to run, trying to figure out how many days I have left to get Alicia. Between us, Frank and I work it out. Sixteen days. I only have sixteen days.

'I'll take you,' Frank says, sitting next to me. He places a hand on mine. I tense. He pulls away.

'Don't worry, Ellen, I won't hurt you. I've got two daughters of my own, you know. They live in England. One's a university lecturer, at Cambridge. The other is a primary-school teacher in Manchester. I miss them both terribly.'

'But, where's your wife?'

'She died eight years ago. Cancer.'

I look at him. There's a genuine sadness in his eyes.

'Sorry,' I say, softly.

'Oh, that's all right. You weren't to know.'
'Frank?'
'Yes?'
'How come you know so much about things?'
'I used to be a doctor. A gynaecologist, actually. I worked for a time at Cannonwood hospital, but not in obstetrics. I was on the clinical side, hysterectomies, cancer of the uterus and cervix, that sort of thing.'

I look at him blankly.

'Why'd you leave?'

'Because of Maggie, really. She had cancer of the uterus, you see.' His voice is low. He is wringing his hands and leaning forward over his legs, staring at the floor. He looks up at me and I'm sure there are tears in his milky-grey eyes.

'I should've diagnosed it sooner, you see. If I had, she might still be here today.'

It's the next day.

My bed was comfortable, Frank put clean sheets on it, and I slept okay, with the feeling I'd had a nagging pain cut from my body.

My room is blue and slightly dark because of the block of flats next door, but there's a pretty clump of pink hydrangeas outside my window, and a cabbage palm and two small gum trees. I wake to the sound of lorikeets feeding noisily from a bird-feeder on Frank's balcony.

In the sun we eat bacon and eggs and cereal. Frank pours the tea, and in my dressing gown and slippers I feel like I'm rich or something, sitting like a film star with my director. I stretch my legs and place my feet on one of the empty chairs. My pink dressing gown slides apart over my legs, revealing Alicia's carved name. I know Frank has seen it, but he doesn't say anything.

'We can go tonight, if you're ready.'

My heart starts to thump.

'You'll have to be brave. I won't come in, in case someone I know sees me. I'll wait in the car. Dress smartly, like you were yesterday. And think carefully about what you want to say. You can tell them you have a place to live, that a friend is going to help you, and that you are going to get a job.'

'But . . . what will I do with Alicia when I'm at work?'

'Pay someone to mind her.'

'But that will cost a fortune.'

He narrows his eyes. 'Do you want your baby or not?'

'Yes, of course I do.'

'Well, you had better give it all some very serious thought today. A baby is a huge responsibility. I'll do what I can to help, but she's your baby. I don't mind her living here, I'm out all day anyway. But you'll have to find a way to support her and yourself at the same time. It won't be easy.'

The whole time we're talking, Frank is concentrating on spreading butter and jam on his toast, pouring tea for us, taking bites and sips. He's not looking at me as if I'm weird or different from anyone else, and it strikes me how unusual it is, to be talking to a grown-up who doesn't judge me.

'You know, Frank, you're wrong about one thing.'

'What's that?' he says, shoving a piece of jam-laden toast into his mouth. He has those slightly full, wrinkle-free lips that look as if they've been polished. On anyone else they'd repulse me, but on Frank they seem okay, they suit him, because he's so easy-going, so broad-minded.

'The sex wasn't like you said. It was pretty awful really.'

'The first time's never up to much.'

'Or the second, or third . . .'

'Good God, what was wrong with him, too rough?'

'Too pushy. And he put it in my . . .'

'Mouth?'

'Yes.' I look at my lap, embarrassed. I'm amazed at myself, telling all this to someone I hardly know, but there's something about Frank; he makes it seem natural to talk openly.

'You didn't like it?'

'It gave me a bloody shock when he – you know – I don't know what he did. I nearly choked. I had to run to the bathroom and I threw up in the toilet. Then I washed my mouth out with soap and drank nearly a bucket of water.'

'I suppose he was terribly wounded at that.'

'He was really angry. But I didn't know. I thought he'd done a wee in my mouth.'

'Heavens, you've lived a very sheltered life.'

'My granny brought me up. And I was in boarding school for a while. And where we lived, we didn't really know our neighbours. I spent most of my time in the bush or swimming in the lake. There was a family up the hill, the Footes. The kids were covered in boils and when the mother popped them with a hot needle you could hear them screaming miles away.'

'How ghastly.'

I nod solemnly.

We both sit there, staring at the table, me remembering, Frank imagining. But with the bad memories there's a new feeling creeping up on me, one I haven't felt for ages, not since before Granny died, anyway; an optimistic feeling, like I'm on the brink of something better, but it's mixed with a sort of nervousness, because I still don't really know this elderly man with whom I'm sitting having breakfast. He could be a murderer for all I know. Or a rapist. Or both. I look across at him. He looks so harmless.

'I was going to tell you, Frank . . . The thing is, you seem so different from all the adults I've known. I was beginning to think I'd never find anyone to listen or be on my side.'

He smiles and huffs a little puff of air from his nostrils, as if to say: We're not all bad, you know.

'I think teenagers are treated very badly these days,' he says. 'Terribly misunderstood. Your parents are on the tail-end of the Victorian era. Too much for their constricted little brains to take in, all this. What with the emancipation of women, the homosexual issue, Vietnam, the whole hippy thing – they don't know what's hit them. But it's too bad when kids like you are caught up in the cultural revolution. You're no wiser than your parents, and it's because they don't tell you things . . . you become victims.'

'Victims?'

Suddenly I have this picture in my head of my mother's brain being squeezed by a gloved hand, and Officer Wyndham hitting me. Beads of sweat swell on my forehead and my palms begin to feel sticky. A small plug of vomit rises at the back of my throat. I swallow it and my stomach rumbles in retaliation. I take a few deep breaths and I'm just about okay. My body is hot under the chenille, but I leave it tied up tight because of Frank.

Now I have a whole long list of words I don't know – emancipation, cultural revolution, gyna . . . I can hardly keep up. But one thing about Frank, he doesn't make me feel small for not knowing. He just takes it in his stride, as if I'm not to know, because of my age. A lot of the words I can't remember any more, but I still remember abortion, because he said he does it at work. I want to find out what it is because of what he said about the police. I want to make sure he's a safe person to be sharing a place with.

'Sure,' he says. He takes a big sip of tea. He is so casual about it all, as though we're discussing the price of bread. 'You're a victim all right. The social workers should have helped you through the last nine months, given you some guidance and support. Instead, they just stuck you in that place and left you to get on with it. I dread to think how you were treated,' he goes on, adjusting the sleeve of his shirt. He is smart this morning in grey slacks and a business shirt and tie.

'I'll clean up,' I offer. 'Then I'll tidy the rest of the flat and get ready to meet my baby.'

All day I think about what Frank said, about being a

victim. I'd never thought of it that way, till now. I just kept thinking I was bad, that the police and the magistrate and the officers at Gunyah and the nurses and social workers, that they were right, and I was wrong. That I was stupid. But Frank has helped me see it all in a new light. In a light that makes me seem an all-right sort of person again. I'll say that to them, if they are nasty: My friend, *a doctor*, says I'm a victim and *you* should be helping me more.

I'm beginning to feel so much better than I have in ages, and while I'm dusting and polishing and choosing something to wear to the hospital, I put on one of Frank's LPs, an old Frank Sinatra record; it was either that or Frank Ifield.

I spend ages getting ready, styling my hair different ways – with Frankie warbling in the background about dancing in the dark – it's quite long now; I pluck my eyebrows, steam my face over a bowl of boiling water at the coffee table, even shape my raggedy hair a bit with some kitchen scissors.

When the nurses see me they'll realise I'm making an effort. Even though I've got no job, I've got a place to stay, and that's a start. I can use some of the money Mum gave me to buy some nappies and clothes. They'll be surprised and impressed when they see me, dressed up and wide awake.

At twelve o'clock everything's done and I'm ready. I'm wearing the same white pleated skirt belonging to my mother. It needed sponging where I spilt some milkshake on the ferry, and it dried a bit brown, but it'll do. And instead of her blue top I've chosen a new blouse she put in my suitcase, a yellow puff-sleeved one with a big collar, and my own leather sandals.

Frank won't be home till five-thirty, so I sit on the balcony in the shade of an umbrella, reading magazines. An ad about nappies makes me suddenly remember the pull-out. Now's the time to be reading about baby care, because in a few hours I will have Alicia with me. I'll need to know what to do, how to make up a bottle and change a nappy. I should go shopping! I find the pull-out in my toilet-bag, I always hide private things in there; it is crumpled and water-stained from my flannel. I make a list.

There's an ad in the pull-out for Three Baby Cuddles to send away for. One is a Buggycuddle that fits on to strollers or chairs; one is a Cosycuddle to keep baby snug and warm in the winter; and the third is a Carrycuddle. This is the one I think will suit me best, because I won't be able to afford a pram or a buggy, not yet. It costs $10.95. I write it on my list. There's another ad for nappies, $12.99 for a dozen terries, available at leading pharmacies or babywear shops – that's it, I'll find a baby shop. In one of the lounge cupboards near the phone I find a Pink Pages and look up B for Babywear. There are lots of shops listed, and there's one at Rose Bay. I'll take the bus.

The shop assistant looks at me as if to say: You're one of those unmarried mothers with no money and no idea how to bring up a baby; what do you think you're doing, coming into my shop?

The shop is decorated with mushrooms and gnomes

painted on the walls in pastel shades, and from the ceiling hang prams and buggies and fluffy animals. I've never ever been in a babywear shop, it's another world of complicated-looking gadgets, accessories and toys that I never knew existed. I remember the tin of pebbles Granny made me that I dragged around the garden with a piece of string, and I think kids are pretty lucky to have all this stuff. Oh, I forgot the bike that Mum gave me when I turned thirteen, along with the book about periods and unsightly body hair.

'I need some things for my baby,' I say, shyly.

'How old is baby?' she inquires smoothly, looking at a point beyond my right shoulder. She is concentrating so hard on the spot that I glance behind me, thinking there's someone there, but there's nothing – only shelves stacked with baby clothes and teddies.

'She's only a few weeks old.'

It feels weird, saying that. As though I'm making it up. As though none of it has really happened, and I'm in a dream.

I think of Mary, locked up in Gunyah again. And Carol, dead in the ground somewhere, with her feet pressed against the end of a box instead of the bed in that room. I feel guilty and sad and angry that no one helped them. If only I'd known. If only I wasn't so dumb, I could've helped them.

Maybe I shouldn't be here at all, kidding myself I can do it, be a mother. Maybe Alicia would be better off with a proper family. I don't know. But I can't help it, she's mine. I have to see her and love her.

'What exactly do you need?' the woman in black and red

says, finally looking right at me from under a set of dark lashes. She has one of those hairdos I've always wanted – a square bob with a straight fringe. My fringe will never stay like that; it springs up with a mind of its own.

'A Carrycuddle.'

'Pardon?' she says, as though I'm speaking a foreign language.

'To carry her in. On my back.'

'Oh, I see.' She walks across to a wall of shelves and pulls down a backpack with an aluminium frame and a blue canvas liner with holes in the bottom, for the baby's legs to go through, I guess.

'This model is $29.99.'

I let out a gasp. 'But the one I saw in *The Woman's Day* magazine was only $10.95. Have you got anything cheaper?'

'I'm afraid not. We only stock the better-quality items. You might be better suited in Coles or Woolworths, perhaps.'

'Oh. Is there one near here?'

'The nearest one is in Bondi Junction. You can take a bus.'

'Thanks.'

I open the door to leave, but I'm so nervous I walk straight into the edge of the door and bump my nose. She sees what's happened and looks at me as if I'm a complete ninny. I'm suddenly conscious of my arms. I don't know where to put them, and I know I'm walking clumsily as I skulk past the broad window, red-faced.

*

In Coles I find just about everything I need.

As I push the trolley along the aisles I tick off each item on my list: a dozen terry nappies, a packet of safety pins, two bottles with a packet of four teats, Johnsons baby powder, a sterilising unit and baby lotion. I find a section that sells baby clothes and choose four terry-towelling baby-grows and four singlets. They smell fresh and clean as a spring morning, like the ads say.

I remember the advice in the pull-out: *'slowly and quietly should be written into every mother's brain'*. But it's hard to remain calm, because my skin feels as if it has been peeled back, exposing the nerve-endings to the air.

There's a backpack for $15.99, pink-and-white checks. A suspicious assistant with a Doris Day hairdo tells me which powdered milk to get and explains the quantities to use when making it, and how to use the sterilising unit. The whole time she's talking she is glancing at my hands.

There are other mothers, all much older than me, filling their trolleys with all sorts of paraphernalia. They give me sneaky looks as they stroll past, and I can tell they know I'm not married; I can tell they know I've been dirty and wicked, like Sister said. I look away from them and think: It doesn't matter, not a bit, I can do it. If I'm old enough to get pregnant, I'm old enough to be a mother.

I walk tall to the check-out. Because I'm beginning to feel excited and more confident. And when I queue up behind the other mums I think: That'll be me soon, tomorrow probably. I'll be a real mother.

The bill comes to $48.98. When I hand over the money there's a hard lump in my throat. My money's not going to last long at this rate. I will have to find a job. It might have to be a job where I can have Alicia with me – maybe one in a babywear shop? Or a milk bar? Or a kindergarten? I don't know. Something will turn up. It just has to.

Back at Frank's I lay everything out on my bed. Then I suddenly realise there's one important thing I forgot. A bassinet.

I sit on my bed, crushed. I saw some in the shop in Rose Bay – big, fancy cane cots, with price tags to match, and then I must have forgotten about them because I was worried about everything.

In Frank's laundry, which smells of Sunlight soap and makes me gag, there's a plastic clothes basket – that'll do! I run into the laundry and empty the pegs on to the concrete floor. Then I find two soft towels in the linen cupboard and fold one in half to line the bottom of the basket. The other one will make a good blanket – the nights are warm, she won't get cold. I place it on the floor next to my bed with the small teddy I bought in Coles tucked up inside it.

Everything is ready.

There's an hour and a half to go until Frank gets home from work.

I sit on the couch with my feet up watching *My Three Sons*, and while I'm staring at the screen my mind wanders back to the things Frank said, about a revolution and abortion and being a doctor.

I switch off the TV set and start searching his bookshelves for a dictionary. It is chock-a-block with big heavy books with complicated titles like *The Complications of Medical, Surgical Gynaecology, Psychosocial and Perinatal*; *Therapeutic Trends and the Treatment of Venereal Diseases Before 1900*; and *Prostitution in Europe* . . . I don't understand a lot of it.

Wedged between *The Oxford Medical Companion* and a book with the longest title I've ever seen – *The Other Victorian: A Study of Sexuality and Pornography in Mid-Nineteenth-Century England* – is a Medical Dictionary. I pull it out and place it on the coffee table. If I'm going to live with Frank I might as well try and understand what he's on about.

On the front cover it says: *A Vocabulary of the Terms used in Medicine and the Allied Sciences, with their Pronunciation, Etymology and Signification*. It's an old book, it smells musty, and along the edge of the pages are little black index shapes with each alphabet letter embossed in gold. The word I want to look up is on page five, but it's not spelt how I thought, it's 'ion' on the end, not 'shun'.

First there's the word *a-bort*, 1. *To bring to an end before full development.* This seems pretty obvious, and it makes me think of all the homework I never finished, and leaving school so suddenly when I was just about to study for the School Certificate – two things I brought to an end before full development. But what's it got to do with medicine and illness?

There's another word, *a-bor'ti-cide*, 1. *The killing of a foetus in utero*— now I will have to look up *foetus* and *utero*, and my spine has turned to ice at the word killing and my hands begin to tremble: what's Frank up to? Am I boarding with a killer?

I glance at my watch: 4.30. Only three-quarters of an hour till he gets back.

I quickly look down the page: *a-bor'tion, 1. The expulsion of a foetus which is not viable; miscarriage. By some authorities the term abortion is used when the ovum is expelled during the first three months of gestation, and the term miscarriage from the end of the third month to the time of viability. In law, the term denotes any premature expulsion before full term.*

Are they talking about when you get expelled from school? I nearly got expelled from boarding school once, after I pinched some biscuits from the kitchen, but I was only suspended, which meant being in disgrace at home for a few weeks.

Abortion may be classified as spontaneous or accidental, where it is not due to artificial means, but results from (1) paternal aetiological factors, like syphilis – there's that disease from Sister's poster! – *alcoholism* – Frank said he was addicted to alcohol – *sexual excesses* – Christ, what does abortion mean? – *extreme old age or youth, etc.; (2) maternal causes, like violent exercise, traumatisms, surgical operations, coition* – God, now I'm really flummoxed – *hot baths* – hot baths? – *tight lacing* – huh? *acute infectious diseases, mental emotions, uterine displacements, vomiting, diarrhoea, tumours, etc.; (3) ovular causes, which induce the death of the foetu*s.

I skip a few lines, because it's all foreign to me, *neoplasm* and *polyhydramnios, diseases of the decidua* –

sounds like a tree. Then my eyes come to rest on the words: *Justifiable, where it is induced to save the life of the mother, and Criminal, the unlawful delivery of the ovum, foetus, or child from the uterus at any time of pregnancy.*

I sit there, paralysed.

I'm not stupid. I don't need to look up any of those other words. That's what Mary was up to, with the razor blade. The girl in the quadrangle that day, she said to Mary: Did you try and get rid of it, Mary? And Mary said: Yeah, but Matron took the razor blade off me. That's why they put her in lock-up for so long, because she tried to kill it herself on the way to the dormitory on our first night. They locked her up for her own protection.

Abortion – the unlawful killing of an unborn baby. Christ, why doesn't the dictionary just come right out with it, instead of beating round and round and round?

And Frank, that's what he does.

He'll be back soon. I hate him. I don't want to live here with a man who does that.

For the next half-hour I read the baby pull-out over and over again, with my heart stuck somewhere at the back of my throat, like a blunt knife.

*

'What did you mean when you asked: Am I one of those breeders?' I say as lightly as I can.

Frank has just come in from work; he looks troubled and tired. I can tell he knows I've been snooping, his eyes are darting this way and that, my voice sounds strangled, and I can't look him in the eye.

There's a splattering of dried blood on his shirt that I can't take my eyes off. I wonder what I should say next, and think 'Did you have a nice day?' might not go down too well, because I know what he's been up to, killing babies – how does he do it? What does he use, a knife? A long needle? Or poison, poured into the mother's opening? I can't bear the thought of it, it's too horrible. But he said he'd help me get Alicia, and he's been so nice to me and no one else cares, so I have to stay. At least until I get her.

'Been doing some reading, have you?' He is looking straight at me. I gulp loudly. Then he says, 'If there's anything you don't understand, just ask. I've got nothing to hide.'

'Oh no, that's okay, I just wanted to look something up about babies.'

'Did you find it?'

'Yeah, I did. I found it. Thanks.'

'That's what they call the unmarried mothers,' he says, pouring himself a large glass of whiskey. 'Breeders.'

He opens the fridge to find some ice and bangs the metal container hard on the bench. The ice clatters, then slides across the bench. Frank's hands scramble after it. He drops two big cubes into the glass. Clink! Plop!

I look at him, frowning.

He shakes his head, and his face changes, as if he can't believe I don't understand.

'It's not a very nice term, I grant you that. But it's honest, if nothing else. It means you are a breeding machine, to put it bluntly.'

Frank wanders casually into the lounge. I follow, like a puppy, eager to hear more. But he is tired, I can tell, so I sit impatiently opposite him, pretending to read a magazine, trying not to talk, with the colour of blood in my eyes and the smell of it, salty and hot, in my nostrils.

After a while he sighs and says, 'I'd better get ready, I suppose. I'll have a quick shower, first, if you don't mind.'

'Sure,' I mutter, conscious of his sullen mood.

While he's in the shower I imagine the babies he's killed today, landing in a bucket, then being flushed away down a stinking back-room toilet or buried in a hole in the corner of a bare back yard, where stray cats meow pitifully in search of their murdered litter – my mother's gift shop had a small yard like that, with bald grass and dirt like concrete – but wouldn't the other shopkeepers notice when they stand in the sun for a cigarette? Maybe he puts them out with the rubbish. Or gives them back to the poor mother, wrapped in a towel?

I shudder and try to block it out. But I can't help thinking he is under the shower washing away the evidence. And I wonder about the word 'breeder', trying to figure out why he looked so worried when he asked me if *I'm* one.

Later, in the car, I ask again, because he seems in a slightly better mood now, and I'm dying to know exactly what he meant. His window is down, and as we drive through the Cross with the sound of music and laughing, car horns and shouting, the liveliness on the streets helps to evaporate the tension. The night air is warm and smells of hamburgers and urine.

'If a girl wants to keep her baby they wouldn't call her a breeder, would they?'

'I suppose not,' he says.

'And if you decide to keep your baby they tell you what to do, don't they? How to feed it and everything?'

'Probably. As I explained, I worked in gynaecology. I have a few colleagues in obstetrics. I hear through them. But they don't give away too much.'

'What exactly do they mean by breeders, then?' I ask, determined to understand.

'Some of the nurses call the unmarried mothers breeders because they give up their babies for adoption.'

'Like in a factory? A breeding factory?' It makes me think of that Three Stooges episode where they put an abandoned baby on a conveyor belt and hands appeared from above to wash, dry and powder it. 'I could never do that,' I say firmly. 'This mean Sister at Gunyah tried to talk me into giving Alicia away, but I said no. I think it's unfair on the baby, giving it to strangers like that.'

'Life was never meant to be fair, you know,' Frank says.

'You sound like my mother. I always say: *What*, then? What *is* it meant to be? But she can never answer that one.'

'I can,' he says.

'What?'

'A bitch of a challenge, that's what,' Frank replies, and he shifts into low gear down a steep hill towards the hospital.

I can't believe I had my baby in such a confusing place.

It is more like a town than a hospital. A few nurses are

walking up the driveway, chatting noisily. At the front there's a large circle of grass with a sign that says ACCIDENTS and EMERGENCIES.

Frank parks the car up the street and points me in the right direction. All the way here I've been stiff with fear, thinking: This is crazy, I'm sitting next to a bloke I don't even know, who kills babies, and he's taking me to the hospital to find my own baby. Where's the sense in that?

'Ask for the Maternity Wing,' Frank says. 'It's a long walk inside the grounds. Good luck.' He squeezes my hand before I get out.

When I bend down to say goodbye at the window he is lighting a cigarette and switching on the radio, as though he's done it before, waited like this for someone to go and get their baby.

Eleven

Lightly was her slender nose
Tip-tilted like the petal of a flower.
　　ALFRED, LORD TENNYSON

I don't know where I'm going, and some of the buildings just have letters on them – J block, K block, L block; one has a sign that says: Radiology; another says: Physiotherapy Unit, Day Patients Only.

I am rigid with fear and my throat seems to have closed up. I'm sure if I try to speak my voice will sound feeble and cracked. So I just keep walking, past groups of nurses and visitors, hoping that I might see the maternity ward without having to ask someone. I wonder who'll be on duty. I wonder if anyone will recognise me, now that my hair's grown and I'm all dressed up with make-up on?

I'll say, 'Hey! Remember me?' No, that sounds silly, like an annoying kid who won't go away.

How about, 'How do you do? My name is Ellen Russell. I was a patient here a few weeks ago. I had a baby girl. I've come back to get her.' No, that sounds too formal and stiff.

I'll smile and be friendly, of course, like I always am to people. Mum always told me to be polite and friendly, but to be myself, too. But if I'm going to be myself, it might be an angry self they'll see, and that's no good – they might get angry back and tell me to go away.

What about, 'Hello. I'm Ellen Russell. I've just come to collect my baby.' No, that sounds ridiculous, as if I'm collecting dry-cleaning, or shoes from the menders.

What do you say to someone, when you've come to get your baby, a little human being, so helpless and small, how do you put it? I don't know. And what if they don't believe me? *Oh God*, I should've brought my birth certificate with me. I stop walking, frozen with doubts. They won't remember me, I know they won't. I look so different. And what if the nurses on duty are different: how am I going to prove I am who I am? Maybe I should come back tomorrow with my birth certificate. I don't even know where it is – in my mother's top drawer? I'll have to go back for it and break my window again. God, why didn't I think of it before?

Then I think: they'll know I'm not kidding, because I'll tell them about Gunyah and Sister Dawson. I'll tell them I remember the bleached blonde nurse who was always sticking needles into me, and I remember seeing Alicia, with my name on her wrist. No one would know all this, unless it happened to them, so how could I make it up?

I walk on, straining in the dim light to read the signs. Then suddenly I see it: Maternity Unit. And a sign underneath that says: Reception.

It is a tall building, quite ugly, of modern construction –

white-painted concrete. The windows are metal-framed and rusty at the edges. Underneath are water-stained blue panels – as if the whole building is crying.

Some windows are in darkness, others brightly lit; some have drawn curtains, and through the cracks I can see nurses moving about inside. It is four storeys high, and on the roof steam pours from a narrow chimney, silver against the dark sky.

At the front there's a square of immaculate lawn surrounded by a wide driveway. I stop for a few moments, staring at a set of double doors with a neon 'Emergencies Only' sign glowing red and yellow in the dark. An ambulance has reversed up in front of the entrance, the engine is off and the back doors left wide open. I try to imagine being ejected from the ambulance on a trolley, lifeless, the night Alicia was born. It's as though it never happened, that part, as though I was magicked here at the click of Sister's bony fingers, and I think: Is that what is meant by your mind playing tricks?

But it happened all right. I'll never forget the pain. I'll never forget the terror of waking up blind in the dark of the ward with a flat, empty belly. Then waking again to the sound of Mary's unseen crying, and again to the smell of my vomit and the blood, and I'll *never, ever* forget the scent of Alicia's skin in that laundry.

Just then the double doors swing open and two men in white uniforms stride out. They shut the doors of the ambulance and climb in the front. I stand there watching with a lump in my throat, and they drive off to bring in another victim.

For a while I daren't move. For a while I can't. Then somehow, after a few deep breaths of air, I find my feet and walk towards the entrance, '*quietly and slowly, quietly and slowly . . .*' and I think: The pull-out didn't mean *now*, it meant when you get home. With your baby. My pace increases. My fists are clenched, shoulders thrust back. My head is up. I'm thinking: Alicia's in there, Alicia's in there, she's mine. She's *my baby*. I want my baby. Next thing I know I'm running. I hurl my shoulder against the door. It bursts open into the reception lounge. The brightness inside makes me stop dead.

The room seems noisy with the sound of my breath and the thump of my pulse through my veins. The stink of medicine and Dettol enters my nostrils and strikes my memory. The pain and the weakness are inside me all over again.

Behind the reception desk a nurse is sitting with her head bowed, writing. She glances up at me, checks her watch and waits as I approach. Her head is tilted and she is frowning, as though she is trying to figure out who I am. I walk towards her, shakily, dreamily. When I'm within a few feet of her I'm just about to speak, when she says in a cold voice that sends a shudder down my spine: 'Can I help?'

I don't recognise her. She is wearing one of those hats that cover all of her hair, like a nun's veil. She has small, inquisitive dull eyes, like a mouse, and a small puckered mouth.

'*Can I help?*' she repeats, irritably.

'Yes,' I reply, firmly. I look straight at her and try to

smile, but my mouth is self-hardening like clay, it won't co-operate and the corners are quivering uncontrollably.

'I . . . I've come to get my baby.'

At last it's out, and the sound of my own voice seems strangely comforting.

'I had her a few weeks ago. I was sent to a hostel near Bondi Junction after leaving here, then my mother came to get me. I haven't been able to come any sooner, because I was looking for a place to live. Now I've got somewhere, and my friend who's a doctor, he's brought me here to get my baby. My name is Ellen. Ellen Russell.'

'Which ward?' she says, icily. 'And when?'

'I don't know. It was upstairs, overlooking the front, I think. I don't know the exact date, but it was two weeks ago.' As these words leave my mouth it hits me for the first time that I don't have a birth certificate for Alicia; I don't have any proof of her existence, or mine, we're both like ghosts.

'There are quite a number of wards, you know,' she says. 'I can locate your baby more quickly if you can tell me the name of the ward and the baby's date of birth.'

'I don't know. Sorry.'

'Take a seat,' she says.

The seats are gummy, like the ones at the police station. I perch on the edge, waiting.

The nurse gets up and goes to a corner where I can hear her opening a file.

'What was the name?' she calls out.

'Ellen. Ellen Russell. Number Three, Stacey Street, Coolamon.'

After a few minutes she shuts the file, the metal runners make a loud screeching noise like the steel wheels of a train pulling up. She stands behind the counter and stares at me.

'There's no file under that name in our records,' she says. 'Are you sure you had your baby here?'

I stare at her, dumbstruck.

'Yes, I'm sure,' I blurt. 'The girls at the hostel said it was the King Street hospital.'

'I wouldn't believe what they tell you,' she says, with a look that seems to mean: I know all about those girls.

'Where were you before you had the baby?'

'At Gunyah Training School for Girls,' I say, biting my lip.

'I see,' she breathes, giving me a knowing look.

'She must be here,' I say. 'Can't we go and look?'

'I can't allow that, I'm afraid. I need some proof of identity before we go any further.'

My heart hits the floor. I should've known this would happen. Now I'll have to go back to Mum's for my birth certificate. If only I'd thought of it. But why haven't they got my notes? Maybe they are somewhere else, in another file?

'Could my notes be somewhere else, on the ward, maybe? Or in someone's office?'

'All the admission files are kept here. There are other files on the wards, with medical details. But if you had your baby here we'd have your admission notes in this file.'

There is something odd about her face that I've noticed

while we're talking. She is finding it harder and harder to look me in the eye.

I stand up and walk across to her at the counter. I want to get a good look at her, so that next time I come back I'll remember her. Because I feel as if I'm losing my mind and I might forget where I've been and who I've talked to. There's a name tag pinned to her chest; it says Sister Lynette Reece.

'You will have to bring your birth certificate and evidence of income before we can release your baby,' she says in a voice that reminds me so much of the officers at Gunyah. A voice that means: I'm the boss round here, and you're *nothing*.

'*If* it is here, that is,' she adds. 'As there is no evidence in the form of records in our files, I'm afraid there's not a lot I can do to help you. Perhaps you'd be better off going back to Gunyah with your mother or your friend, and finding out *exactly* where you gave birth. There are many hospitals with maternity wards in Sydney and the outer suburbs. Perhaps you had your baby nearer to Gunyah. It seems highly unlikely they would bring you all this way when there are hospitals much nearer the institution.'

I am staring at her open-mouthed and paralysed. I can't believe I've got it so wrong. *Mary* said. *Kerry* said. *Sister* said. 'You will be taken to a hospital in the city,' she said.

'Sister Dawson, at Gunyah, she said I was going to a city hospital,' I finally say through trembling lips. 'And the girls at the hostel, they all said it was King Street. My friend Mary, she was at Gunyah with me, she had her baby at the same time; we were in the same ward right next to one another.'

'Well perhaps Mary got mixed up. These things happen you know. Especially when you've just given birth. And it is likely that you and your friend were under strict control, coming from an institution like Gunyah.'

The urge to scream surges inside me, but I resist, I push it back. Tears fill my eyes, but I blink and rub with my fists to banish them. There's no point in crying. I know that. And Frank said I would have to be strong. I *can* be strong. I *will* stay calm now, and then I'll come back tomorrow.

'I'll bring my birth certificate tomorrow. Is that all right? Can I have my baby then?'

'I *said*, we have no record of you *or* of your baby in our files.'

Her voice has a catch in it. And that's when I know. That's when I realise she's the same nurse whose lips quivered the night I had Alicia. It's a strange sensation, as if I've got something she hasn't. Yet it should be the other way around, because she's got my baby – well, the hospital has – and she knows. It's as though I've been given a key to my brain, as though a light has come on in my head. I know exactly what's going on. I know it's all a game, a serious game. And I'm ready to play.

For a moment or two I stand outside the door fighting the urge to run back in, past the desk and up the stairs to find Alicia. Because I know that if I do they'll call the police, and then I'll be put away again and Alicia will disappear into thin air. So I resist, I fight it with all my strength. I can't be sure if Sister Reece recognised me, because I must have looked a mess the night I gave birth, but she'd remember my name, wouldn't she? If she did know me, she was good at hiding it. But then I was pretty clever at hiding it, too. I didn't let on I knew her at all.

It was one of those weird moments when you and the other person know, really, but neither of you is going to let on. Just like when you get caught for something at school – the teacher knows, and you know. And you know the teacher knows. And the teacher knows you know. It's so stupid; it's a power game. And you both want to win, so you keep it up. Well, this is one game I'm going to win. It's a game called Find Your Baby.

The double doors where the ambulance men came out earlier is locked. But around the corner of the building, down a dark alley strewn with boxes and giant metal bins on wheels, there's a small landing at the top of some steps and a door that says FIRE EXIT. From behind a bin I can see two nurses leaning against the iron railing. When they gesticulate with their hands their cigarettes glow like fireflies.

I crouch down amongst a stack of cardboard boxes, where the smell of vegetable scraps is overpowering. The nurses are chatting and laughing, but I can't make out the words. After a few minutes they stub out their cigarettes with their shoes and go inside. Please, *please* don't lock the door. I wait. Then I tiptoe up the steps and push the door.

I can't believe it's open! It leads into a long, narrow passageway lined with sealed cardboard boxes. Dettol and Handle With Care is printed on them. I can smell it again, pungent and strong, and although it's a smell I hate, somehow it spurs me on because Alicia seems connected with it.

There's a set of stairs in front of me, the fire escape, and I climb it to the first floor. At the top I turn left down another passage and stop in front of a door with a metal handle across it. The words PULL UP are printed behind the bar. Gently I pull it up, and the door snaps open. I freeze in case the noise alerts anyone. I can't hear anything, so I slowly push the door, hoping it won't creak. There's a long, wide corridor with a polished blue linoleum floor. I remember that cold floor, the sticky suck of my bare feet on the lino when I went hunting for Alicia. I'm not hunting for her now. I just want to make sure I've got the right place, that the nurse at Reception is the same one, that this is the hospital where I gave birth. And I know how.

I know this is the wrong floor, because the lino is blue. I'm looking for brown lino. And I remember thinking I must have been on the second or third floor when I had her, because the footsteps outside sounded a long way away, and they echoed as if in a deep gulley. And when the magpies sang it sounded as if they were right there outside the window in the branches of a tree.

But that's not all. I want to find the laundry room where I found Alicia. I'll never forget the smell in that room, a mixture of wet mops and Dettol, urine and Lux flakes. I'll never, ever forget the shape of the room, or the shelves, or the laundry tubs, or the sticky clawing air.

Whenever I'm about to open the fire door I hear footsteps and voices, and I freeze. I decide to sit it out on the stairs until the night shift takes over.

Nine o'clock. The nurses will be giving out pills and settling the mothers down to sleep. I shudder at the thought of some other poor girl like me being jabbed with needles and pushed, helpless, on a stretcher, away from her baby.

Soon the lights will be turned off and all will be quiet. I listen at the door. It is silent on the other side. I remove my sandals, tie the strings together and sling them around my neck. I push down the handle. Clunk! It opens and I step out into the corridor on to brown lino. This is it.

My breathing is regular but fast as I tiptoe past the blue-lit nursery, glancing anxiously, longingly at the sleeping white bundles. I know it's hopeless trying to recognise her. I would have to check every single wrist band, because I wouldn't know my own baby. They all look the same, like wrinkly old men, purple-faced and ignorant. Anyway, the door is locked. Sealed up like incubating silkworms.

When I reach the laundry door I hesitate. What if Alicia is still in there with Mary's baby? My heart has tightened into a knot. I push the door. The cool air creeps over my skin. No life here. Nothing but buckets and mops and towels. Just to be sure I stand right inside the room, to capture the memory of that moment when I first saw my baby. I know it was real, I know I didn't dream it. But oddly I don't feel as upset as I thought I would. I feel like a detective might feel – sort of practical, as if I'm working my way through a complicated case. I wonder if it's because the room is cold. So far I've been lucky, there are no nurses around. Probably scoffing biscuits and tea in the staffroom.

Now that I know it's true, that I didn't dream or imagine any of it, I can get my birth certificate and bring it back. I'll come up here to the ward and speak to the Sister. I might even try and see the bleached blonde nurse, wait till she's on duty, or I'll ask when she'll be here and come back then.

Downstairs, I burst through the main door again. I'm surprised to see a group of nurses standing behind the reception desk chatting earnestly to Sister Reece, who looks anxious. She looks up at me, startled. They all stop talking and turn abruptly to stare. I gulp, take a deep breath and walk steadily towards them.

'I just wanted to let you know, Sister,' I say, staring straight at her, 'that I've just been to the ward on the third floor where I gave birth to my baby. I found the laundry room where I saw my baby and where I saw Mary Perry's baby. Mary was told her baby died, but I saw the name tag. It said Perry. That's her surname. I don't know what's going on around here, but I want my baby and I'm coming back for her tomorrow, with my birth certificate.'

No one says a word. I look at the other nurses. One of the thin nurses is here – the one who wheeled me off like a sacrifice that night, and she is open-mouthed. And next to her is the bleached blonde one, aghast but composed, which is an odd combination, but true – I can tell she is in shock, but resisting the temptation to make it too obvious.

'Don't you recognise me?' I say to her.

She simply stares, then glances at Sister for help. Sister Reece frowns and shakes her head a little, as if to say: Don't answer.

'Well, I recognise you,' I say sharply to the fat one. I am surprised at myself. I didn't think I'd be this brave. I thought I'd be too afraid of them. But something is different now; they've lost their power because I am free, I'm not their victim any more. 'And you,' I add, glaring at the thin one. '*You* tied me down to a stretcher.'

She turns bright red and looks as if she wants to bolt down the corridor, but she fights the urge. I notice her hands clenching and unclenching, while one shoulder moves up and down nervously.

'I'll be back tomorrow with my birth certificate to get my baby. You'd better find my notes and have her ready. I've got a place to live. I'm boarding in a flat with a doctor. He knows all about what goes on here, so you'd better watch out.'

With that I turn and walk out the door, shaking stiffly like a rattle. In my heart I feel a deep stillness, because I know that they know I know.

A few minutes later, as I walk down the footpath towards Frank's car, I feel amazed at myself. I breathe in the warm night air – big, deep lungfuls.

Someone is shouting and running behind me.

'Excuse me, excuse me! Wait!'

When I stop and turn around, I'm surprised to see Sister Reece rushing towards me waving a folder.

'We just found your notes,' she cries, breathlessly. 'They

were on the ward. Russell, you said, didn't you, your surname is Russell?'

We stand there in the dim light. I am breathing heavily, because I am suddenly overcome with a sense of longing for Alicia. A surge of excitement floods through my veins. I almost begin to cry with relief. But then I see that her eyes are hard and black.

'You'd better come back in,' she says, coolly.

Inside, the other nurses have all gone, and the reception area is empty and quiet. She leads me into a small, neat office, with a desk, filing cabinets and a telephone.

'Sit down, ' she says, gesturing at a chair in front of the desk. She seats herself behind the desk and clasps her hands together on top of the folder. She stares at me for a few seconds, then opens it. I shift in my chair, but I stare back. She pushes a piece of paper towards me across the desk and stabs at a signature at the bottom with a finger.

'Is that your signature?' she asks.

I lean forward to look. The writing is untidy, shaky. But it clearly says Ellen Russell. And my name is printed at the top of the page.

'I . . . I don't know. It's my name. I *suppose* it's my signature. But it looks more untidy than mine usually is. What is it?'

'These are the release papers.'

Before I can get a closer look at the rest of the typewritten words above my name, she slides it back inside the folder.

'You mean, the ones Sister Dawson got me to sign, to say I agreed to have my baby here?'

'No. These are release . . . or rather, *consent* forms. Giving your permission for the baby to be adopted. You signed them yourself when the social worker visited you. This is only a copy, Mrs Gannon has the original. And here, on your medical notes, which were written up daily while you were in here, at the bottom, it says: Socially Cleared. See?' She slides three sheets of paper towards me and points to some hand-printed words at the bottom of a list of dates and columns with numbers and scrawly writing.

I slide my eyes quickly over the page, trying to read it all. It says Nursing Notes at the top, and Remarks: Bleeding, fits, sleep, general condition, etc. Underneath that someone has written, *1.15 am Normal delivery of living girl > tearing to perineum following induced delivery. Third Stage complete. Sedation. 200mgs Pentobarb. 2. 45 am Stilboestrol 20mgs.* The rest of the page is a jumble of spidery scribble that I'd have to study for a while to work out. I didn't have a clue what it meant, except the bit about the medicine and the normal delivery. Normal delivery. There it was, in black and white. I had a baby. It was a strange feeling, looking at the notes, to think I'd been given that much attention when they all hated me so much. You don't expect to be left rotting in a hospital bed, but that's how it felt at the time, except when they wanted to stick needles into me. Now this. It doesn't match with the way I was treated at all. All those nurses, all the notes they wrote, I couldn't believe it.

'"Socially Cleared" means that you agreed to adoption and that your signature was taken,' she says.

I stare at the words near her finger. My heart goes cold. Socially Cleared. I think: What a strange way of putting it. As though I had a disease, but now I am better. Or I was naughty, but then I was good. Good enough to go home. Good enough to give my baby away.

'But . . . I don't remember signing the other papers.'

'It's your signature, so you must have. Is this your home address: Stacey Street, Coolamon?' she points at my address on the front of the folder.

'Yes, but—'

'There are no *buts* about it. Your baby is not here. It has been placed with a proper family. Now why don't you toddle off home and be a good girl and stop causing trouble, eh?' She narrows her eyes. 'Before I call the police. You wouldn't want that now, would you?'

Twelve

I cried for two solid days after getting back from King Street.

Frank just left me to it. He was good that first night – the poor thing was still sitting in the car when I got back. He had smoked a whole packet of Stuyvesant – and he knew by the look on my face that it was too late.

'They told me at the hostel I had thirty days to get her back,' I said when I got into the car.

'Who?' he asked.

'The girls,' I said.

And he said nothing.

I felt as though I could sleep for ever.

Some mornings I couldn't get up; my body felt like a dead weight on the mattress, and the room was dull and uninviting.

If I did get up, to go to the toilet or make some toast

after Frank had gone, the sunshine on the balcony would entice me out. I'd sit on the hot concrete hugging my knees, just staring at the ants busily retrieving crumbs.

Sometimes a lorikeet would land on the railing and hop up and down the length of it, cocking its head at me, as if to say: Any bread today? But not even that cheeky gesture snapped me out of the blackness. I knew that, along with Alicia, something of me had gone for ever.

Frank tried cheering me up with exotic dinners, and he introduced me to some of his friends, but they were mostly his age and boring. And they all looked at me as though I was some sort of pathetic creature, like a stray dog. They'd all try to jolly me along, saying things like, 'I had an aunt who adopted her first baby out, and *she* got over it eventually, when she had three more children.' Or 'Never mind, it could be worse, she might have died – at least this way you know she's safe and growing up with love and attention.' Or 'Cheer up, worse things happen at sea.'

And I wanted to scream at them and punch their chests with my fist when they said these things, because they didn't have a clue how I felt. They didn't know what it felt like to have your baby taken away for ever. They didn't know what it was like to have what is rightfully yours wrenched from your body, then whisked away. They didn't know that all I remembered of my own flesh and blood was the shape of her nose and the smell of her skin. I walked around Frank's place in a tense dream, as though I'd been winded.

One Sunday afternoon there was a crowd of people

over for a barbecue. I said hello to everyone and listened to their bloody advice, then slunk away to lie on my bed and read magazines. I could hear their voices in the garden, and the jazz band that Frank had hired to entertain everyone. The music sounded staid and self-righteous to me, although I was probably being unfair, because Frank's friends were generally pretty broad-minded. After a while, when I'd read all my magazines twice over, I got up to go out for a drink. I sat on the verandah sipping it, with my legs dangling over the edge.

There was a woman whom I'd met once before called Vera, tall and dark-haired, sort of masculine-looking in a way, but the blokes all seemed to love her, probably because she was fascinating to talk to.

She'd travelled all over the world and spoke as though she was reading from a travel brochure or a history textbook. I pretended not to listen, but with my ears straining to hear her voice above the music, I managed to catch a lot of her banter.

She was talking about inner strength and faith, and stuff like that. She kept quoting people I'd never heard of. I loved things like that, that's why I liked the book of Proverbs. I wasn't interested in religion, not really, because I thought people who preached, like the nuns, were hypocrites. Sister Dawson, too, raving on about how I'd sinned and was wicked – how did she know what was in my heart? How did anyone? I have love in my heart, I know that. I know it won't get me a job, but it's important. I will always love Alicia, wherever she is, and I still think my love would have helped us survive.

It was the philosophy of the Proverbs that I liked. I used to read them and think: If people lived by some of these ideas, the world would be an all-right place.

'You know, Frank, I admire people with guts,' Vera was saying in a loud voice. 'The battlers of this world. Never give up, that's my motto.' She turned and winked at me. There was a gleam in her dark eyes, which held in them something else besides those few sentences, as though she was sending me a message. It took me by surprise, really, because I felt like such a fool. I felt dirty and useless, and I thought my life was going to drag like an old dog's, that my days would be lived out in deep sighs and the sinking of my body on endless surfaces – the couch, the floor, the bed, the beach, a sun-warmed rock. When I thought of the future, which wasn't often, I couldn't see myself being enthusiastic about anything.

Vera went on talking about a medieval philosopher whose name I didn't catch. She said he was thrown into prison for treason and wrote that the only way one man could exercise power over another was over his body and over what is inferior to it – his possessions. But you can't impose anything on a free mind.

The music was irritating in the background, one of those annoying jazz tunes that have no shape, with a warbling saxophone that makes the song sound disjointed and jarring.

Suddenly I felt alert. I straightened and stared across the lawn at Vera. She was leaning against a palm tree. She was wearing navy slacks and a blue-and-white striped shirt. Around her neck was a bright pink scarf: It's hiding a scraggy neck, I thought, unkindly. My heart was hammering hard, because she was a lot older than me and I hardly knew her, and I was scared of women older than me, but what she said made my blood rage.

'I've got a free mind,' I said loudly, staring straight at her. 'But that didn't stop them taking my baby. They imposed that on me.'

Everyone lowered their voices, and a few people glanced over at me. My face was burning and I wanted to get up and run into my room. But Vera said, 'Excuse me, will you?' to her friends and sauntered across to me. She was holding a drink in one hand and a cigarette in the other. She had a full mouth, with a hint of pink lipstick, and waxy white skin that her blusher clung to like chalk – two thick stripes of powdery pink along each cheekbone. She smiled up at me, not in a condescending way, more in understanding.

'You know,' she said, 'Frank's told me all about what happened. You must feel bloody awful.'

I lowered my head and kicked my feet in and out a few times against the concrete. My heels felt rough on the stone, and I rubbed them hard to smooth them.

'Are you going to get a job?' she asked.

I shrugged.

'You have to carry on, you know, Ellen; you can't give up. You've got your whole life ahead of you.'

'If anyone else says that to me I'll scream,' I said.

'There's no point feeling sorry for yourself.'

'What do you want me to do, celebrate?'

I flinched when I said that, because I expected her to

hit me or shout, but she just took a sip of her drink and stirred it with the swizzle stick a few times. Then she said, 'They might have taken your baby, but you can't let that infect your heart. Imagine your baby is watching you and you can't see her. She'd want to see a strong, gutsy mother, a mother who never gives up, a mother who wants to make the most of herself. Not someone who is a loser. You might feel bad now, Ellen, but give it time, love. Make up your mind to get through it, not over it.'

With that she went back to finish talking to her friends and I sat there, like an awkward kid at a grown-up party, thinking: How does she know, how does *she* know how I feel?

Later on I was flat on my back on my bed, staring at the ceiling, when Vera came in.

'I didn't mean to interfere out there,' she said, sitting on the end of the bed, 'but I don't like to see anyone unhappy. Life's too short.'

God, I thought, how many more clichés will this woman come out with?

'You know, life throws all sorts of ghastly life things at people. It's how you handle life that counts. If you let things get to you, then life's got the upper hand. If you let this destroy you, they've won. They might have taken your baby, but they can't take you.'

'Yes, they can,' I said, quick as anything. 'They took me, all right. They took me and put me in a gaol for kids.'

'So that's the end of your life, is it?'

I shrugged.

'That's right,' I said, then, giving her a hard stare.

'Can I tell you something?' she said.

'What?'

She stood up and put her drink on my dressing table, then sat down again, leaning forward over her knees with her hands clasped.

'I was married to a policeman once,' she said. 'We couldn't have children, so we adopted two newborn babies. We were very happy with them, and I brought them up as if they were my own. Then my husband had an affair. The children were in their early teens by then. I adored them, of course, but he turned them against me. I was heartbroken. The girl went off to England and my son is in Perth, so I'm told. I've heard through friends that they both got in touch with their real mother recently, through the adoption agency. Maybe that will happen to you.'

As I listened to her voice I began to seethe inside. I couldn't bear the thought of her looking after someone else's babies, and that was all I could think of at that moment. In my mind I saw her breastfeeding Alicia, and it repulsed me.

'Leave me alone,' I muttered. 'Just leave me alone. Tears slid down my cheeks.

She shrugged and said, 'Suit yourself,' then she got up. She was over by the door when she turned around and said, 'Frank says your mother sent you to Gunyah and that she threw you out. You know, you should go and see her, try and make up with her. She's probably heartbroken. She probably thought she was doing what was best for you. We can't help the way we are, us oldies. We come from a different time, more old-fashioned. Your mother probably didn't mean to hurt you.'

'Go away,' I said, and turned my face to the wall.

I didn't talk to Frank for days after that, because I blamed him for telling Vera about everything in the first place, for talking about me behind my back, as though I wasn't old enough to be included.

'Not everyone's bad, like the officers and the nuns you came across,' he said to me more than once. 'You've got to learn to trust people again.'

Apart from Vera's stupid advice, I learnt a lot at Frank's place. In his books I read about diseases and medicine. It turned out he had lots of younger friends as well, they were a mixed bunch – there was a woman called Stevie who was waiting to have a sex-change operation. I didn't even know there was such a thing. She had a voice like a man's, a five-o'clock shadow and muscly calves. Apart from that she looked just like a woman: shoulder-length blonde hair, beautiful blue eyes, full lips and big breasts. At first I wasn't sure if she wanted to be changed from a woman into a man or the other way round. I must have looked puzzled, because she took my hand in hers and said, 'Here, feel.' She placed my hand down the front of her blouse. I stiffened. 'Stiff, just like you,' she laughed. I withdrew my hand as though it had been dipped in fire. 'Silicone implants,' she said. 'Twelve months ago they were just another pair of all-Australian male tits. Now they'd make any red-blooded bloke get a hard-on.'

There was a girl called Delilah, a stripper who worked as a prostitute after-hours. 'That's my stage name, dahling, my real name's Sybil,' she said by way of introduction one Saturday. I'd never seen such an exotic-looking person – she swanned into Frank's laden with wine and flowers, wearing a long, floating Indian dress and enough beads and bangles to decorate a Christmas tree. '*Sybil* wouldn't attract too many customers, would it? They'd be expecting a nurse or a school teacher. Not my scene. All that domination stuff gives me the heebie-jeebies. *Delilah* means delicate, you know.'

Then there was Libby, and her jovial boyfriend Scrub, with their matching Afros and vibrating Harley Davidson. They seemed to spend their whole lives touring between Melbourne and Sydney, or Sydney and Brisbane, just to feel the rumble of the engine between their legs and 'meet other bikers en route, if ya know what I mean, *route* with a double-o,' Libby said, winking.

And sometimes Frank would bring home a young girl, usually tear-stained and frightened, and I knew when they shut the kitchen door for hours that they were whispering about abortion.

It took me a while to work out a lot of things, especially the stuff Stevie talked about. But gradually, over the next few weeks, it all came together. I began to understand the things I saw on the streets in the Cross, and I began to feel less and less frightened by it all.

One night I was having a long talk in the kitchen with Frank and a dark-haired seventeen-year-old girl called Cathy. She wanted an abortion, but didn't have the money. I could tell by her scruffy jeans and worn leather sandals that she was telling the truth. She was so thin her skin hung off her bones like webbing.

'Don't you worry about that,' Frank said, kindly. 'I'd rather do it for nothing than have you end up like Ellen here.'

I looked at Frank in shock. 'What do you mean by that?' I said. We were sitting on the bar stools, sipping pineapple juice. Frank was swigging a large glass of whiskey and ice.

'Don't get me wrong,' he said, 'I don't mean to diminish what you've been through. I don't mean it that way at all.'

'*What*, then?'

'I mean the *not knowing*. At least if a girl is offered the option of abortion then it is over and done with – *buried*, so to speak.'

You mean flushed down the dunny, I thought, feeling repulsed.

'In your case, you know your baby is alive, somewhere. In a way that must be worse than losing a child through death. There are so many illegitimate babies in our society that are not cared for properly; it's not fair to bring a child into the world unless it is born in to stable circumstances. You girls don't know what's involved. The responsibility lasts for years.'

'Thanks a lot, Frank. I thought you were on my side.'

'I am on your side,' Frank said. 'But I do think that in the long run you would've been better off getting rid of it.'

Better off? I sighed. How could I be better off, unless it had never happened? If I was still at home, with Granny, *then* I'd be better off. But she's gone, and now Alicia's gone – both of them, gone for ever, and even my mother's my enemy. Whichever way I looked at it, Alicia was gone from my life. She was never even in it, not unless you count the nine months when she was inside my body.

There was a bowl of fresh fruit on the bench, delivered by Delilah the day before. Peaches and pears and grapes. I noticed Cathy's hungry-eyed look and the way she kept licking her lips. The fruity smells filled the room. I reached for a peach, took a knife from the drainer and began to slice it in half. I could feel the blade scrape against the stone inside the soft flesh. When I prised it apart the stone remained firmly seated in one half, surrounded by stringy bits of red pulp. I gently slid the knife under the stone. It was stubborn, but after a last determined twist of the knife it shot out of its soft nest, scuttled across the bench, clattered on to the floor and disappeared under the fridge. I bent down to try and find it, but Frank said, 'Don't worry, you can get it later.'

'That's okay,' I said, 'I'd rather get it now before it goes rotten and the cockroaches come.' I pushed a flattened hand under the fridge and felt for the stone. My fingers found it, wet and firm, but already bits of dirt had clung to it.

I put the peach stone on the counter, then rinsed my hands at the sink and sat down again. I divided the peach into quarters and offered them on a clean plate to Cathy and Frank. While we sat talking and eating, I couldn't help picking off the bits of fluff and dust from the peach stone, returning it to its original perfection.

Cathy sniffed. 'I've got no help,' she said. 'I couldn't handle a kid. I don't even know who the father is. And my parents don't know. If I told them they'd kill me.'

Frank took a gulp of whiskey. I could see his pearly pink lips through the glass, like a camel baring its teeth.

The kitchen suddenly felt hot and suffocating. It was so hot that the backs of my legs were stuck to the plastic cushion. When I lifted myself off it felt as though the top layer of skin had peeled away – I almost expected to see it there, like tracing paper.

I opened the window behind the sink. The air outside wasn't much cooler. I turned on the tap and splashed water on my wrists. What am I doing, I thought, sitting in this kitchen listening to two people plan a murder?

I dried my hands on a tea-towel, all the time thinking: Frank has dried his hands on this. Frank has turned this tap on. Frank has pressed his lips against this glass, that cup, and the prongs of all those forks on the drainer have passed between his lips.

I said good night and went to bed. Just before I switched off my light I opened the little pink-bound copy of the New Testament, given to me by a man from the Church Missionary Association, who visited us at Gunyah every Monday. I took it into class with me the day he gave it to me, and under the desk on my lap I wrote in the back 'Judge not, that you be not judged.' Matthew 7:1.

As I drifted into a tense sleep I could hear Cathy sobbing softly in the lounge and Frank's reassuring, deep voice saying, 'Don't worry, love, it'll be over before you know it.'

When I woke the next morning I opened my eyes to an unexpected wedge of sunlight streaming from the balcony right across the living room, through a crack in my open door. Frank must have opened it in the night to check up on me.

He was already gone. The kitchen smelt of stale fruit. I ate a bowl of cereal and went back to bed. I tried to sleep. I touched myself down below, to see if the stitches had healed properly, but the skin still felt rough and lumpy, and tender. I tried to relax, but my head was full of blood and screams, and Frank in his business suit plucking a naked baby from Cathy's belly.

Some days, when I felt a bit better, I went to the local newsagent, bought a paper and read the ads while I drank a milkshake at a milk bar. And sometimes, if the jobs were local, I'd walk to the places that advertised for a shop assistant or hairdresser's apprentice or a door-to-door canvasser – anything that didn't need qualifications. Frank said I should go by bus to save time, but I was more worried about saving money.

'Someone else will get the job while you're still walking,' he said.

But I didn't care. Sometimes, when I arrived, I didn't even go in. I just stood on the footpath, staring in the window of Curl Up 'n' Dye at the purple-headed ladies having their hair rolled and teased, or up a smelly stairwell leading to an encyclopaedia sales company. I knew if I went in they'd take one look at me, guess my age and wonder what had happened to me. I knew my chewed nails were a dead give-away. And on really hot days when

I wore something short or sleeveless, they'd be fixing their eyes on my home-made tattoo, thinking bad thoughts and labelling me a slut. Or I'd soon prove I'm a dummy and they'd sack me, because the truth is I can't do maths, so even in a shop I'd have to embarrass myself by adding up the bills on paper.

Sometimes I didn't even get as far as leaving the milk bar. Instead, I would sip my chocolate milkshake in its big silver container, pretending to read the news, because the Italian proprietors kept giving me suspicious looks while they served customers and flipped hamburgers.

One day, a humid Monday that held the sticky, still promise of a southerly buster, I was pressed against the wall in an empty booth with a copy of the *Sun Herald*. I began to turn the pages. On page two there was a story about a pro-abortion march on the streets of Sydney. CHANGE THE LAWS read the banners being held up in the photo. FREEDOM OF CHOICE. I sat there, reading about women and their 'back-street' abortions. One said she didn't want future generations to suffer the indignity of illegal abortions. I thought, legal or illegal, it would still be undignified.

I had this idea in my head that I wanted to do some good in the world, to make up for being so wicked. So later, when the owners of the milk bar started giving me dirty looks for sitting there so long, I went into a St Vinnie's charity shop to offer my services. There was a permanent notice in the window saying: Volunteers Always Needed. The mauve-headed lady who interviewed me said they wanted someone to sort through the bags of second-hand clothes. She took me into a back room where the smell of thick clothing full of body odour, cigarettes and mothballs made me feel nauseous and claustrophobic. It was like you'd imagine it might be at a funeral parlour – the cast-offs of dead people. I lasted half a day and staggered into the purple afternoon gasping for air. When the first crack of thunder snapped over the Cross and sent rain as heavy as Niagra Falls on to the dusty streets, I walked home to Frank's with my feet in the swollen gutters and my face upturned to the sky.

When I got home the flat was empty, thank goodness. I'd begun to hate Frank, he seemed so weak. He thought he was doing people such a big favour, killing their babies, but somehow I just couldn't agree with what he did when he came in with the evidence on his clothes, the money in his pocket and the sadness in his eyes.

I went to my room, climbed into bed in my wet clothes and lay there under the covers, shivering.

Thirteen

In some ways I wish Alicia was dead.

Frank was right. At least that way I'd be able to get over it – you know, cry and cry and cry till there were no tears left. Instead, I'm on tenterhooks all the time, wondering if this baby or that might be her when I'm out shopping (not that I do that much, because my money's running out fast), when I go to the park. Sometimes in my dreams I imagine her with her new family, but mostly she's with me, safe, on my island. When I wake up I always remember what Sister Dawson said: *She's in the country somewhere*, and I close my eyes again, wishing I could just sleep for ever.

She could be anywhere. Sometimes I imagine her in Queensland, where the ferns and mountain mist curl mysteriously in the valleys. Then I see her in some barren desert bowl, in the shade of a pathetic sun-stripped gum tree, watching the dappled shade play tricks with her eyes.

Or she could be quite near, just beyond the Blue Mountains, in Orange or Bathurst maybe. I could find her quite easily if she was in a town like those. I could walk down the main street and find her parked in a pram outside Woolies and wheel her away.

It's four weeks now since they told me. I'm still living at Frank's, but I can't find a job, because I haven't tried very hard. I was offered one working for Glamour Homes, selling that pretend brick cladding for timber houses, but I only lasted three days because people kept slamming their doors in my face and I couldn't hack that.

They paid me for the three days, $23.95. That was two days ago. I had to give some of it to Frank for my rent.

My money's all gone now. I'm going home to Mum. I've got just enough for the bus to Coolamon. I don't want to hitchhike any more. I haven't got the energy. I feel dead inside.

'Come home, dear,' she said, when I phoned to tell her what happened at the hospital. 'Come home and you can start again.'

She sounded sorry for me. There was real warmth in her voice; it surprised me and made me think about what Vera had said, that Mum was probably heartbroken. She didn't sound heartbroken to me, but her voice was comforting and tempting, that's for sure. So tempting I agreed to go home. Just like that.

I took all the baby stuff to St Vinnie's in the Cross. The lady tried to sound grateful, but she said she didn't think they'd find anyone who'd want it, because nearly all their customers were druggies or derros.

'Most mothers like to buy things brand new,' she said.

'But it is brand new,' I said. 'None of it's ever been used.'

She shook her head as if to say: Sorry, but your things are soiled and no one would want second-hand baby things. I knew she remembered me from the day I helped out. That beneath the excuse she was just trying to get back at me for walking out on her. So I stuffed them back in the plastic bags and on my way home to Frank's I chucked them in a bin down an alley.

When I said goodbye to Frank the next day he shook my hand. It felt limp and clammy in mine. He stood on the balcony with hunched shoulders and I felt guilty for not trying harder to find a job.

'Just give me a ring if you're in trouble,' he said. 'I mean it,' he added, looking me square in the eye.

'You'll soon find someone else to replace me in the spare room,' I said.

'I'm not worried about that,' he replied. 'It's you I'm worried about. If you need someone to talk to, or if you need a bed, there's always the couch.'

My mother was at work when I got home. The windows were still nailed shut, but my bedroom window had shiny new glass. With a sharp stick I carved Alicia's name in the soft putty.

I sat on the front verandah waiting for Mum. I tried to imagine what she might say. What I would say.

The two ribbons of white cement Jack laid to drive his ute up to the front door were freckled with hell-bent bull ants. When Granny was alive there was a path over which her lavender spilled. It was the first thing Jack did when he moved in: dug up all the plants and hired a mixer. I *hated* him for it. It was as if he'd concreted over her soul.

Mum came home and drove her car into the car-port at the bottom of the garden. Even when she was loaded with shopping she didn't have the heart to drive up to the door. She walked up the driveway, trying to smile. We hugged one another, stiffly, and went inside.

I've been home two months now. I still haven't got a job. Christmas was boring and hot, and Mum gave me new clothes I don't like. A new social worker, Mrs McCreedy, has been to see me three times; she doesn't seem too bothered about me not working, so long as I help round the house and don't stay out late. That suits me fine. I'm good at cleaning now; in fact, I can't stop sometimes. Mum's amazed at how spotless the house is when she comes in, and says the training at Gunyah did me a lot of good.

She hasn't mentioned Alicia, and nor have I. It's as if she doesn't exist. It's as if she was never born.

Most days I stay in bed till eleven or twelve, drifting in and out of sleep. I love the feel of the cotton against my skin, it's so comforting. And I hold Granny's lavender against my cheek, always. Mum doesn't nag me at all about getting a job. She acts sorry for me, and she seems lonely.

We sit together in the evening, eating a simple meal like grilled chops and salad, and talk about the gift shop, or the weather, or some of her customers. The conversations are stilted and awkward, as though there is barbed wire all round us. Sometimes she puts her hand on mine and I let it rest there for a few seconds before pulling away.

She can't figure out why I wear long sleeves every day. It says *I Love Alicia* inside a heart on one arm. On the other arm I carved her initials, AR. Four tattoos now, altogether. Robyn would be impressed.

Sometimes at night I sit in the bath and squeeze my nipples to see if there's any milk left; if I squeeze hard enough clear stuff trickles out. I wipe it on to a finger and put it on my tongue. It tastes sweet and wholesome, a bit like that sweetened condensed milk in tins that Granny made toffees with. Once, I put my china doll's hard pink mouth against my bare nipple and pretended to feed her. And I found an old scarf and pinned it on her like a nappy.

I telephoned my father today. Found his number in the phone book. There it was, bold as anything, under Greaves. A. Greaves. A for Anthony, Mum told me, at long last. She said he likes to be called Tony.

When I dialled the number I thought I might faint with shock if he picked it up at the other end. I was expecting a deep, manly voice. When a woman answered my heart missed a beat and I stuttered and jumbled my words.

'He's down the club,' she said. 'Who's that?'

'His daughter. Ellen.'

'What do you want?' she snapped. 'How dare you ring up making trouble. I heard you're a troublemaker. Word gets around, you know.'

'I just want to speak to my father. That's all.'

'What for?'

'Be . . . because he's my father.'

'Are you after money?'

'No. I just want to talk to my father. I'd like to get to know him,' I said.

'Well, what you don't know you won't miss,' she snarled, and hung up.

Next day I was feeling pretty low, but I forced myself to get out of the house and go for a walk. I was heading towards the shops along the unmade edge, where snakes sometimes venture out of the blue morning glory and blackberries, to slither across the bubbling tarmac. Sometimes the tar is so hot they get stuck there in the melting road and the cars iron them flat. Behind me I heard a car pull up. I turned around and was surprised to see Louise at the wheel of a battered beige Mini. I kept walking, but she opened the door, slammed it and started running after me.

'Wait, Ellie!' she cried.

I stopped dead and looked at my feet. My toes were covered in a film of grey dust, just as they were the day I arrived at Gunyah and weed on myself in front of the governor.

'I've left home,' she panted. 'I'm living in Manly! Left school and everything. I've got a job in a milk bar on the Corso. I've been sick.'

I glanced at her when she said this, but she looked okay to me, so I kept walking and she kept pace with me.

'I had gonorrhoea, I had to go into the city to this awful clinic to get it treated. I'm sorry about my mother, Ellie. *Please* can we be friends again?'

I kept walking and still she trotted alongside like a puppy. I could feel her looking at me closely, but I refused to look back. I didn't believe her – *Gonorrhoea*! Only *bad* girls get that.

I didn't want to be friends with her any more, I didn't want to risk being hurt again. But no one else wanted to be my friend, and I thought: Maybe we could go out together. I was getting bored at home and I felt like having a laugh, even if it was false.

'Okay,' I said, finally. 'But not today. I'll see you down at the milk bar in Manly on Friday. Is it the one at the beach end?'

'Great! It's the one near the pictures. I finish at five-thirty. See you there.'

She turned to walk back to her car and I kept straight on. When she was a good distance away, I turned and called out, 'By the way, did you know I had a baby?'

The following Friday I waited outside the milk bar on a bench. The Corso was closing down for the night, and shoppers and workers were rushing to catch the ferry across to the city. The sea was heaving like a man's chest and dumping itself heavily on to the beach. I was glad the surf wasn't up, otherwise I'd have been craning my neck to try and spot Robbie. All the same, I was nervous in case he or Lizzie walked past. Their flat was way up the other end, but the chances of bumping into them were still high.

When Louise finished work we headed back to her new place.

'Hurry up, will you?' I snapped. She was fumbling with her shoulder bag, stuffing in her white overall.

'What's the rush?' she said, scurrying to catch up.

'I might bump into Robbie.'

'Who's he?'

'No one,' I said. 'Just hurry, will you.'

Finally we reached the esplanade overlooking the water. We slowed our pace, and Louise began to tell me about her brush with the clap, how she had this awful rash down below, how it smelt and she knew it was serious.

'I never even knew what it was till a few weeks ago,' I said. 'I looked it up in a medical dictionary.'

'After the results came back, my doctor told me I'd have to go round and tell all the boys I'd slept with,' she said solemnly. *'Imagine!* I didn't know where to start. I got my friend Alana to help. We went to all the discos I'd been to in the last six months, looking for the guys I remembered screwing. It was pretty embarrassing. And that's a fuckin' understatement.'

I looked at her as we walked. Her ginger hair was shiny in the sun. Her freckled nose was camouflaged with foundation. From a distance she looked stunning, but now, close up, I thought she looked haggard, especially around the mouth.

'What about you?' she asked. 'What happened?'

'I was put away in Gunyah for nine months, and after that I had a baby and they took it. Simple. Now forget it. I'm trying to. I *have* to.'

'Okay,' she said softly, and we walked the rest of the way in silence.

She was living in a shabby bungalow with a wide verandah at the front overlooking a broad, sweeping lawn. Inside there was worn matting on the floors, and Indonesian batik cloths pinned to the walls, and enormous potted palms and glass-bead door curtains. The lounge beckoned with masses of bulging floor cushions, three threadbare velvet sofas and two sagging armchairs that looked as though they might swallow you alive. The other thing I noticed was the smell. The same smell that hung in the valley at Ourimba – I thought at the time it was gum leaves burning, or someone's foreign cooking.

Louise was sharing with three blokes. Two were surfies, Shane and Peter, and the other was an American called Jim, who was studying at university in Sydney.

I could tell Louise fancied Jim, because she thrust her breasts out and giggled a lot in front of him. We stood in the kitchen with Shane and Peter, talking and smoking Marlboros. I didn't say much; I'd almost forgotten how to have a proper conversation after being in Gunyah for so long.

'Sydney's so beautiful, and so are it's women,' Jim said, smiling at me. 'You're so lucky living here, with the harbour and all. I couldn't think of a nicer place to study.'

He was a short guy, dark-haired, with an annoying little moustache that had no substance – the hairs were fine and sparse – but he had intelligent, dark eyes.

'What are you studying?' I asked.

'Anthropology,' he replied. He could tell I'd never heard of it. 'The study of the origins and beliefs of man.'

'We've all descended from apes,' Shane said, snorting,

'what more do you want to know, mate? Or do you think you might discover some sort of secret super-species, never before known to man, and you're really at Uni to find *that* out, not to learn about the rest of us monkeys, eh?'

Jim ignored him. He described how he'd been watching some laboratory mice go round and round in a maze, trying to find the exit where bits of cheese lay waiting.

'They are very intelligent creatures, you know. At first they were really confused, but after a few tries they found it. Next time I took the cheese away, but they still found the exit; without any hesitation they went *exactly* the right way.'

Jim came with us to a disco in Manly that night and we danced till one in the morning. In a dark corner he sat close and talked to me as though I was an interesting person. He wanted to know all about me. He seemed really impressed when I said I knew the bush where I lived like the back of my hand.

'Where I come from, Kentucky, it's pretty boring – flat, dusty plains, wide streets in dull towns. You're lucky growing up here. It's so beautiful.'

'That's not everything,' I said.

'Well, at least you can be miserable in style,' he laughed.

'I don't want to be miserable,' I said.

'Tell me about it,' he said, kindly. 'Tell Uncle Jim all of it.'

I didn't want to spoil the night by going on about my problems. I wanted to forget them for one evening at least, but Jim was so easy to talk to and he seemed to really care; he wasn't judgemental either. When I finished the whole story he said, 'So, how does it feel in your head? How has it affected your psyche, and your self-worth?'

I didn't know what psyche meant, so I ignored that part of the question and said, 'I hate myself.'

'But you didn't do anything wrong,' he said.

'Well, it must've been wrong, because I was punished for it. And so was Alicia. That's the worst part. She's been punished for my mistake. It's not fair to hurt her.'

'You need something to take the pain away,' Jim said. He placed a hand over mine. It felt strong and warm. I pulled away, gently, so as not to hurt his feelings too much. I didn't want to get involved with him or any man, after Robbie. I still love Robbie. I'll always love him. He's the father of my child. How could I ever stop loving him?

Just then, Louise appeared. She looked wild, her hair stuck out like a clowns and her lipstick was smudged.

'Where have you been?' I asked.

She winked. 'Outside with a few blokes.'

'Come back to our place,' Jim said, 'for a smoke.'

I felt cheered up around Jim and hoped we could just be good friends. I wasn't interested in having girlfriends. I'd had enough of females.

When we got back to the house it was quiet and dark. The others were still out. Jim lit some candles and put on a record – he liked Jimi Hendrix, Bob Dylan and Janis Joplin. He handed me some album covers to read.

Louise kicked off her shoes and flounced on the couch like a Hollywood starlet, with her long, fringed dress draped across her slim legs. I noticed three mottled, blue love-bites on her neck.

For a while Jim sat between us. Later he knelt on the floor at one end of the glass coffee table. He took a plastic bag from his pocket. It was full of crackly brown leaves. I didn't ask what it was; I didn't want him to think I was ignorant. I thought maybe it was some kind of herbal tea. Louise perked up and watched him intently. I was dying of curiosity.

He took out a thimbleful of leaves and teezed it between his fingers on top of a magazine. He broke a Marlboro in half and shook out some tobacco, mixing it with the leaves. Finally, he picked the mixture up and placed it carefully on a giant cigarette paper and rolled it up. I could feel myself staring, so I pretended to look at the wall-hangings.

'Ganja,' he said, licking the paper and smoothing it down with his fingers.

He placed the cigarette in his mouth and lit the end with a lighter. He sat back on his haunches and took a long, deep draw on it, closing his eyes. I was relaxed by then, though still a bit confused, because the ganja Robbie smoked was a small brown, hard lump, like a stone. He used to heat it with a match, then crumble it into the tobacco.

Jim held the smoke in his lungs for ages, and when he exhaled enough smoke to fill a car filtered out and settled under the ceiling. Then, without a word, he passed it to Louise. She sucked hard, then passed it to me. The end was wet where they'd slobbered on it. I inhaled slowly, trying not to touch it with my lips, in case I caught something. The smoke snagged in my throat, it felt harsh and hot, and made me hack uncontrollably.

'Don't worry, it always does that if you're not used to

it,' Louise laughed. She whacked me on the back a few times, but that made it worse.

She went out to the kitchen to get me a glass of water. I sipped it thankfully, then took another drag. This time it felt smoother. I held it in my lungs till I thought they'd rupture. Jim took the cigarette from me. I was in a numb trance. My head felt weightless. I leaned on the sofa and closed my eyes. It was as if all the torture of losing Alicia was fusing into the furniture.

'That's nothing,' Louise said, giggling, 'wait till we get some acid into you.'

'Where do you think you've been?' Mum said. It was the next morning. She looked as though she'd been up all night, like me. Her hair was a fright and her eyes puffy. I knew I probably looked worse, but I didn't care.

'Out,' I said. 'And I'll be going out again, and again, and again.'

'Oh, you will, will you?' she said. She was standing at the front door with one arm against the wall so that I couldn't get through.

'Yes, I will. This is a free country, and I'm going out whenever I want.' My face almost touched hers. She smelt of cigarettes, luckily, so I knew she wouldn't notice it on me.

'Not while you live under this roof you're not,' she said sharply.

'We'll see about that,' I said, glaring at her.

'Your grandmother would turn in her grave if she could see you,' she breathed, shaking her head despondently.

'Yeah, well she can't, so who gives a fuck.' Then I ducked beneath her arm and locked myself in my room.

The drugs take away a lot of the ache.

We have some wild nights, me, Jim and Louise, listening to music, dancing, talking, gorging on food in the grotty kitchen and bingeing on a smorgasbord of drugs – acid pot, pills. Jim supplies everything, his family sends him a cheque every month.

He pays me a compliment every time I see him: 'You're looking gorgeous today,' or 'I love your hair that way.' Once, he told me I had the most incredible green eyes he'd ever seen. And he told me I was very intelligent.

He asked me to roll a joint. It was the first time I'd ever done it, and my fingers felt clumsy. I tore the papers and had to start again three times. I could feel him looking at my chewed nails. After that, I started to grow them. It was hard at first, but whenever I forgot and gnawed them, I remembered Jim's dark eyes resting on them and stopped.

Acid is my favourite drug. Sometimes the trips last three nights because of the speed in it. I don't like pot much, it makes me feel too giggly. It's good for numbing the hurt, but the next day the aching is there again anyway, only much, much worse. Acid makes me elated and aware, without the pain, and it's scary sometimes, but I like seeing things like that – crystal-clear.

It's four months now since I had Alicia. I still look at other mothers when I'm out, and I'm tempted to look inside prams, but I don't see many because most days I'm asleep.

At night, when I take the ferry across the harbour to meet Louise in the city, that's the worst time. I sit on the top deck – outside if it's not raining, which it rarely is – and I hang my head over the railing to watch the water boil against the sides of the boat. When the ferry swings out backwards into the harbour, slowly turns, then rolls for a few minutes, as though the engine is catching its breath, that's when I begin to think of Alicia most. When the ferry reaches the middle of the black harbour, and the lights along the hills blink like a tangled necklace, that's when I think of her. I imagine her being tucked up in her cot with a teddy, a full tummy and the warmth of some strange woman's hand on her head as she drifts off to sleep. Sometimes, when I think of that, I dig my nails into the back of my hand and draw blood. Then I close my eyes so that I can't even see the lights of all those bloody red-brick houses.

Later, when we come back from the city with a few drinks inside us and we're laughing about some awful bloke we teased at a bar, Jim gets out of bed to roll joints and by then the pain begins to fade. That's the best time of day, when I'm deadened to it all.

One night Jim gave me this new acid: white lightning.

'This'll blow your head off,' he said, grinning.

'My periods started a few days ago,' I said, blushing. 'I don't know if I should, it might be too scary.'

'This'll take your mind off everything, honey,' he said seriously.

But I wasn't sure, because the bleeding was so bad – I had to wear three large-size Kotex at once, but still I leaked on to my panties and all over the sheets. Mum went nuts the first time it happened, so now I put my red-and-black beach towel underneath me, so she doesn't know.

'Come on, don't be feeble,' Jim said. 'It's good for you, this is the real world, man.'

He looked at me critically. I took the tab and swallowed it without water.

Two hours later I was soaring. Jim was right, it blew my head off, all right, except that the pain was worse, and my skin felt as though it was stretched.

Jim decided to light a fire, even though it was a stinking-hot night. Then he threw plastic bottles and bowls from the kitchen into the flames. We sat there cross-legged, mesmerised by the dripping, waxy shapes folding into the blue-and-silver embers.

'You're crazy,' Louise said.

'I know,' he said.

A sour smell filled the house. February is the stickiest summer month. The fire and the hot weather made the house seem molten.

In the old-fashioned kitchen with its red linoleum floor and green-painted cupboards we stuffed ourselves with fruit, enthralled by the colours and textures and honey smells of the pineapples and pawpaws, the juices dribbling down our arms, and we laughed at nothing. Even the wholemeal bread and the tomatoes and lettuce that Jim dragged from the back of the fridge were alive: everything breathed and moved and we gasped in disbelief, marvelling at the intricate patterns and colours, as though we'd discovered something rare.

Late on the fourth night, when the music was grinding my nerve-ends to a raw pulp, and my skin felt like sandpaper and my eyes like hot pokers, the pains in my tummy became terrible.

Jim and Louise were naked on his bed with the door wide open. Janis Joplin was shredding her lungs on the stereo.

As I tiptoed past on my way to the toilet, Jim sat bolt upright on the bed. He was holding his hard red thingy and staring straight at me with black, bullety eyes. For a moment I stared back, wondering if he was actually asleep sitting up, then he beckoned with a jerk of his head. With a firm grip he began to rub his thingy vigorously. I lowered my eyes and slipped away.

In the bathroom I locked the door. My heart was speeding and my skin crawling with a sweaty tingling. When I stood naked under the shower the blood poured out between my legs like a flash-flood.

I think I was haemorrhaging. I learnt about it from Mrs McGrath when I did the Nurse's Entrance Exam. She said some women haemorrhage after abdominal surgery. I couldn't figure out why it was happening to me, but put it down to the strychnine in the acid and not sleeping. Then I began to think it might be something to do with the birth, but the Nurse's Entrance course didn't cover pregnancy, so I wasn't sure.

Later, on the bus, I sat right at the back so the driver couldn't see me. My panties were stained and soaked, and the pains were getting unbearably fierce.

The bus to Coolamon seemed to take for ever. I could

see the driver glancing at me anxiously in his mirror. I lay down, lifting my head now and then to make sure I didn't miss my stop. When I finally got up to pull the bell, the brown plastic seat was streaked with red.

The walk from the bus stop to Mum's was agony – every step on the pitted roadside triggered sharp pains and the blood trickled down my thighs.

The front verandah was bathed in moonlight. I slipped off my shoes and sneaked into the house. In my room I switched on the bedside lamp, my eyes smarting at the glare.

I stood in front of the full-length mirror. In it was reflected a grotesque sight – a figure with scruffy, matted hair, smudged black eyes and crumpled, dirty clothes.

The scars bearing Alicia's name were swollen and alive, like red worms under the skin. My eyes were bloodshot, and there was a dark vein in the corner of one that made me look cross-eyed and crazy.

I stood there gawping at myself, hypnotised by the horror of my own flesh. My silhouette suddenly expanded, then contracted, then reappeared. My eyes traced it and came to rest on my mother's ashen face.

When I turned around she wasn't there.

All morning I thrashed about in bed, rubbing my tummy. By mid-afternoon I had run out of pads. I had no money – I never have any money, only the coins I take from my mother's purse for the fare into Manly; otherwise, if I'm completely broke, I hitchhike. I found an old bath towel in the linen cupboard and rolled it up between my legs under my dressing gown. Within half an hour it was soaked through and I had to replace it. I didn't know what to do with the stained one, and I was frightened my mother would see it and panic; I didn't want to go to hospital. So I filled the bath with water and threw in the towel to soak. The water turned a deep purple.

I lay on my bed, staring at the patterns before my eyes. I must've fallen asleep, because the next thing I knew my mother was cradling my head in her lap. She was stroking my head and crying.

'What's wrong?' I muttered.

'Oh, Ellen, what have you done, what have you done?' she cried. 'You can't go on like this.'

I was lying in a pool of blood.

Fourteen

Grief smothers – but not fatally,
The wide wind dries my tears.
                    ANNA AKHMATOVA

Mum looks flustered. Not like my mother at all. At least, not like the mother I'm used to, with her teased and lacquered hair, her sharp suits and stilettoes.

She has closed the gift shop to stay home with me. Berenice quit, so there was no one to take over.

'She was running you down and I told her to please be quiet, so she left,' Mum said. I looked at her, and felt a stirring in my heart.

'Please don't take me to hospital,' I pleaded.

'I'll look after you,' she said, and in those few words she seemed to be saying – I could tell by the tone – *I should've been looking after you all along, then none of this would ever have happened.*

Three times a day she brings me a tray with a little bunch of lavender in an egg cup and healthy meals – cereal and fruit for breakfast, salad for lunch, fish and veggies for dinner.

'I don't care about the business any more,' she said the first day. 'I just want you to get better and make a new life.'

'It's too late,' I said. 'Alicia's gone. I haven't got a clue where she is. They won't tell me.'

'They won't tell me, either,' she said. I looked at her, puzzled.

'You mean . . .?'

'I spoke to the hospital, and to Sister Dawson. They said they were sorry, but it was the agency's policy not to give details. They said if adopted children decide to locate their real mothers when they grow up, then sometimes, in exceptional circumstances, access to files is given. But it's a long, drawn-out process.'

I sat up. 'You mean, if Alicia wants to find me one day, she might be able to?'

'Maybe. If she's anything near as stubborn and hot-headed as her mother, she'll find you.'

I smiled.

Because I was stuck in bed and too tired to read, when Mum came into my room I was glad of the company. I began to notice things about her that I hadn't before. When she was straightening my ornaments and chatting, and when she settled the tray across a flattened pillow on my lap at meal times, I saw in her strained face all the things that Frank and Vera mentioned.

Her dark-circled eyes told me she wasn't sleeping. Her flat hair made her head seem shrunken. Her chipped nails told me she was busying herself with chores, to keep her mind off things – I could hear her banging around the house endlessly, cleaning. You'd think I was an invalid the way she fussed. She tucked me in and plumped up the pillows. She bought me magazines and books from the local library. And lots of fresh fruit, because she said it helped heal your insides. She bought me a set of new undies to replace the stained ones, but they were those baggy ones that are the sort you wouldn't want even your best friend to see you wearing.

I could tell by the look on her face that she loved me. I could tell she was equally suffering the separation from Alicia, and even though she hadn't come to my aid when I wanted her to, even though this mess was partly her doing, she was here now, trying to make up for it, mopping up my blood.

'When you're all better you can start going to Fellowship again,' she said, 'and maybe we can get you into dance classes.'

I pulled a face, but not so she'd see. I didn't want her to think I was ungrateful. But I hated Fellowship, and dance classes – here she goes again, I thought, trying to mould me for polite society. She'll probably make me wear gloves and pink lipstick as soon as I'm better.

The smell of my mother was wonderful, sweet and clean. After she came into my room her scent lingered as though it would never leave.

The first day I was asleep mostly, except when I got up to go to the toilet and change my pads. The sheets had to be changed five times. I sat in my cane chair watching her every move. She stripped the bed bare and tucked a towel across the middle of the mattress where I kept leaking.

'Sorry, but I can't help it, Mum,' I said, several times.

'That's all right, pet,' she replied, 'you just sit there and rest for now.'

I was dying to ask her why she'd arranged the adoption behind my back, but I was too exhausted to talk about anything unpleasant. As I watched her capable hands de-wrinkle the bed sheets, I thought: I won't ask because it will just cause a fight. I didn't want to fight with her any more. I wanted her back to normal.

The doctor came that afternoon. I'd never seen him before in my life. He was old and grey with gnarled fingers, and he wore a dark-grey suit that had stains down the front.

'I won't do an internal examination because the bleeding is too heavy,' he said to Mum, as though it was *her* he was here to see. 'I think your daughter just needs to rest for now. When the bleeding stops you can bring her in for a proper medical.' I breathed a sigh of relief as he packed up his stethoscope into a black leather bag and shuffled off.

Mum saw him out, then came back in and sat on my bed, wringing her hands. Then she said, 'It was Pam's doing, you know.' She looked at her lap and chewed her bottom lip. After a while she slowly raised her face to look at me. Her eyes were moist and her lips seemed blue without her lipstick. 'I never would have bothered,' she went on, in a cracked voice.

'What do you mean?' I said.

'You know the day you broke your window?'

I nodded.

'Mr Mac phoned me at the shop to say he'd seen you here and he'd heard a window being broken. I never would've bothered. It was her idea to nail up the windows. When Mr Mac phoned, she was in the shop buying a present for one of her boys. She talked me into it.'

'Into what, calling the police?'

She nodded. 'And packing your bags. She said it was the only way to teach you a lesson. She said you have to be cruel to be kind in this world.'

I shook my head in disbelief. 'Why didn't you stick up for me?'

'Pam won't put up with any rot.' Mum's mouth twisted into a tormented smile, a look that said: I didn't mean to, please don't be angry. 'I'm sorry, Ellen,' she said. She put her hand on mine, but I jerked it away.

'Just leave me alone, will you,' I said.

She shut the door behind her. I fell into a deep sleep that was littered with babies and hard-eyed women, and my mother looking worried in an ocean of leering men.

The following day the bleeding began to ease off. I felt brighter and was glad when Mum came in. She only had to change the sheets once all day. She sat on the chair yacking about fashion and hairdos, but we didn't agree on much. She wanted to see me in shifts and Bermuda shorts, slacks and neat blouses, but I wanted to live in jeans or long, loose dresses.

'I think I've always had very good taste, Ellen,' she said, in self-defence.

A couple of times I nearly said: Yeah, your taste, not mine; but I stopped myself, just in time.

The conversation went on for ages, about clothes mostly and other superficial stuff like that, and what she thought was good and bad fashion. Then out of nowhere she said, 'A lot of girls your age would feel lucky to be taken out on a boat every weekend, you know. But you seemed to think it was one of the reasons to hate your stepfather. He was only doing his best.' She shook her head and sighed. 'Oh well. It's over now.'

'What about the time he tried to teach me to waterski along the Hawkesbury, and he laughed when I couldn't get up?'

'Oh, Ellen, honestly! We were laughing at something else, pet. Married people have jokes with one another all the time – *private* jokes.'

'What about the sharks? Why couldn't he teach me on the lake?'

'Because the boat's moored at Pittwater. Besides, he made sure we were right away from the Heads, where he knows it's safe.' She stood up and leant down to kiss my forehead, but I turned my head away. "I have to go out for a while to the bank,' she said coolly.

She was out for hours and when she did come home I vaguely heard her crashing around in the kitchen, but she didn't come in to me straight away. I drifted in and out of a deep sleep again, my dreams dark with blood and screaming faces, scarred skin and a naked man with black eyes. Then I woke up and forced myself to think of my island.

On the third morning, while eating breakfast, I reached out to touch Mum's hand. Her skin felt rough, like crêpe paper. It shocked me that, because I hadn't noticed before that my mother was getting older. Her bottom was jammed against my legs on the bed. I dipped the butter-logged soldiers into the centre of the boiled egg she'd made me and took a mouthful. While my other hand was still cupped over hers, she said, 'I love you, Ellen.' I squeezed her hand. Our eyes met as the egg dissolved on my tongue.

My heart was pounding.

'Why did you burn all my things?'

She looked embarrassed, but she tipped her head back and jerked it defensively.

'Because they *smelt*.'

'What do you mean?'

'Of *sex*.'

Later Mum was out shopping and I had to get up to go to the toilet. On the way I stopped in the kitchen to get a drink of water. There, next to the sink in a little dish, were Mum's rings – her wedding and engagement rings. They looked tarnished, as though they'd been there for ages. The house was so quiet. From the window I could see the brick barbecue that Jack built, the vegetable patch he dug, overgrown with blackberries. I sat on one of the kitchen stools and read a magazine.

'What are you doing up?' Mum asked when she came in half an hour later.

'I have to tell you something,' I said gravely.

'You'd better get back to bed, young lady, or you'll be sick again.'

'I'm all right. It's nearly stopped now.'

She dumped the groceries on the floor and sat opposite me at the kitchen bar.

'Mind if I smoke?' she said, looking nervous.

'Course not.'

She couldn't look at me. I knew she was expecting me to say something about Alicia. I could tell she thought I was going to launch into some long-winded accusation. I took a deep breath.

'It's about that man, Cliff, what's-his-name?'

She exhaled. A current of white smoke escaped like a jet-stream into the still air. It billowed under the ceiling, taunting us.

She looked at me and one eyebrow shot up. 'You mean, Clifford Malone, the floor sander?'

'Yeah, Mr Baloney. *Him*.'

'I haven't seen him for years. You were only a little girl.'

'*He* didn't think so.'

'What . . . what do you mean?' She took another long draw on her cigarette. The ridge above her nose was creased in a deep frown.

'That's why I was scared of Jack.'

'What on earth are you talking about, Ellen?'

'I thought Jack might do the same thing as Cliff.'

'Are you trying to tell me . . .' Her voice trailed off and gathered with the haze above our heads. I waited patiently for it all to sink in.

After a while she looked at me; her eyes were dark and she stubbed out her half-smoked cigarette angrily. She pushed her stool back. It almost toppled over. She opened the fridge for some ice. Into a heavy-bottomed glass she poured some whiskey. The ice crackled loudly. She took a gulp and stood by the kitchen window staring out at the bald lawn, as though looking at me would make it too painful. Her voice sounded frail, as if she'd suddenly aged thirty years.

'Did he . . . did he, do it properly, you know?' she rasped.

'No, Mum. He just . . . touched me. But still . . . Then, when I saw him twisting your arm, I couldn't stand it. I thought Jack would do the same. I didn't like him being here.'

'But Jack wouldn't – he's a decent man, Ellen. I knew Clifford was a bit funny after he did that to my arm. But I had no idea he . . . Oh, *God*, why didn't you tell me?'

'I thought you'd get angry—'

'I'm angry with *Cliff*, the bastard.'

'He said if I told there'd be trouble. When he went away I thought it didn't matter any more.' I straightened and moved my bottom a bit. The seat felt hard and unyielding.

'Oh, Ellen,' Mum cried.

She buried her face in her hands and began to sob. I slid off the stool and padded across to her. I put my arm around her shoulders and squeezed her, then let my arm drop again. But I stayed next to her, really close, while she cried. She reached for a hanky inside her bra, blew her nose and dried her eyes.

'All men are bastards,' she whispered hoarsely.

I thought I'd done the right thing, telling her, but she seemed more upset than ever. I didn't know what to do.

The following day I couldn't stop thinking about when Jack was here, and Mum's face then, compared to now.

When he first came she smiled a lot, but then I got difficult. Especially after the day I caught sight of his balls protruding from the inside leg of his shorts. He was sitting on the couch. I was lying on the floor watching TV. He said something and I turned around and copped an eyeful. I thought I'd be sick. I went down to the lake for a swim and stayed there for hours. He came looking for me at sunset because dinner was ready. I waved at him from my rusty drum out in the middle of the lake and shouted, 'I'll be there in a minute!' When he'd gone, I swam ashore under the marbled sky and trudged home barefoot, shivering under my wet towel.

After that I avoided him. That's when Mum's face started to change. Then the fights started. I wanted to go out, just to get away from him, but he wouldn't give me any money and he told Mum not to.

'She's too young to go out on her own,' he'd say.

He came home with a puppy for me once, a wire-haired terrier, but a week later the poor thing died from a bluebottle tick. Then he bought a second-hand poker machine and set it up in the shed. You could open it up with a key and get all your money back if you ran out of coins. I got bored with it after the first day, and I was afraid Jack might try and corner me in the shed.

I thought, too, about the holiday we had once, up the coast at a pretty place called Port Mitchell. We took a boat trip to a flower-specked island across from the town. My island. The place I dreamt of taking Alicia. The sun beat down on the wooden deck that day, and Jack, Mum and I stared into the clear water at our reflections. 'Look, the three stooges!' I cried, and we all laughed. When the ferry bumped against the island's jetty, I leapt ashore and ran along the strip of white beach to explore. That's when I found my dream-cave.

We got on all right that holiday, me and Jack, but at night he seemed to get angry and his face went red. We were all sharing a room in a guest house, because it was cheaper. I lay in my single bed rigid as a post till I could hear Jack snoring and Mum's soft, even breathing.

Our house is silent with him gone. It used to feel crowded when he was here. The smell of his sweat was in every room except mine; even though he showered twice a day and was clean-shaven, I could still smell that man-smell.

About a week after I came home bleeding, Jim phoned up. It was a Saturday afternoon. Luckily I answered. Mum was hanging out some washing in the yard.

'Can you come over tonight?' he said. 'I miss you.'

'No, thanks anyway, but I'm not well,' I said. My hands were trembling. I thought of him holding his red thingy, his bullet-eyed look as I walked past his room, the heat in their shabby bungalow, Louise's crazy laugh. He almost shrugged down the phone, as if to say it was my lookout, that I was missing something wild – which I was, but thank God I was. I wanted to say: Don't phone up again; but the words got stuck somewhere and I just said a squeaky 'See ya'.

That night it started to rain. The wind tore at the trees in our garden. The rain on the tin roof sounded like a million horses. After three days it stopped as suddenly as it began. I pulled back my curtains to let the hot dazzle pour in, then crawled back into bed to read. I could hear Mum clattering dishes in the kitchen. A kookaburra laughed raucously in the distance, and next door on old Mr Mac's roof the currawongs were already sliding down the corrugated iron. They were singing like crystal flutes to one another, and I knew that if Mr Mac wasn't out there soon they'd be raiding his fruit trees. I closed my eyes tight for a few seconds (I've been doing it every morning since I came home) and said to myself – not to God, I never ask God for anything any more, ever – *Please let Mum and me be friends.*

I decided to get up pretty soon, because the sun was making my room too hot, and I felt like sitting out the front on the steps to watch the ants and birds and to stare up at the endless blue. I'd just finished dressing – it felt strange to put shorts on – when Mum came in.

She had a stricken expression, and the colour had drained from her face. I could tell straight away something was wrong, because her eyes went this way and that instead of fixing on me. I thought: Here we go, back to normal. Now I'm better, the nagging will start all over. I sat on my bed, and the air felt thick . . . I don't know, I had this feeling that a shadow had passed over me.

'Miss Riley's here,' Mum said. She shut the door and sat next to me. My body went cold and rigid and I felt a strong urge to run to my cave.

'Why?' I demanded, looking at Mum. '*Why?*'

Mum cleared her throat. I could feel her shaking. We both were.

'Apparently you were seen going into a house in Manly. The police have been watching it for weeks. There's someone living there who's involved in drugs. Oh, Ellen, you didn't . . .'

I hung my head. 'It won't happen again, Mum,' I whispered. 'I'm sorry. I think that's why I was bleeding so much. I took LSD and it kept me awake for days. Jim said it had strychnine in it, to make the trip last longer.'

'Oh, my good God,' she said and clamped her hands over her mouth.

'It's all right, Mum. I'm okay now. I won't do it again, I promise. Please don't tell her. Please don't let her send me back to Gunyah.'

'But, Ellen, I can't lie to the police.'

'*Please*, Mum.' She stared at the floor for a few moments, shaking her head. Pellets of sweat had broken out on both our foreheads. A broad white escalator of sunlight streamed through the window on to the floor by the end of my bed. The room felt airless, as if we were trapped in a plastic bag. I leapt to my feet and pulled off my T-shirt.

'Look!' I cried. I stretched one arm over my shoulder and beat at my back with my hand. 'Look, this is what they did in there. They belted me! Look at the marks, they're still there.'

My mother stared, open-mouthed, at my scarred back. Her eyes were full of moisture. Then her expression began to change. Her jaw set hard and her lips quivered violently. The tears spilled out, but she brushed them away with the palms of her hands, took some deep gulps of air and stretched her face as though she were trying to compose herself. She stood up and straightened her spine.

'Wait here,' she said.

As she left the room I was tempted to turn the key, or run out the door around the house to the steps up the back, then on to Snail Rock, but I didn't. I pulled my top back on and I just sat, listening. I could hear them talking, but I couldn't make out the words, and several times Miss Riley's voice rose angrily, then my mother's. My body went cold, then hot, and a sticky sweat poured down my back. I stood up to turn the key in the door, then noticed they'd stopped talking. I was just about to lock the door, my fingers poised on the key, when I felt a deep anger like boiling mud in the pit of my stomach.

Instead of locking the door, I opened it and walked across the verandah, through the front door into the lounge where they were standing. Miss Riley was writing in a little book and my mother had her arms crossed, a look of disgust on her face. When I walked in they both looked at me, startled.

'Hello,' I said. I stared at Miss Riley defiantly.

She tucked her notebook and pencil in her top pocket and clasped her hands in front of her, then parted her feet a little. Her head dipped forward and she looked at me from under the hoods of her eyes, like a bull at the charge.

'Well, young lady, there you are.'

'Yes, here I am,' I said, not flinching. 'And here I'm staying.'

'Hmmph! That's what you think,' she said maliciously.

'I had a baby, you know,' I said. 'I'm staying here with Mum and getting a job. So why don't you just leave me alone.' I gave her the dirtiest look I could muster, but my lips were quivering and my eyes were awash with tears.

'Well, I hope you've learnt your lesson,' she said, with a look of satisfaction.

'My baby's been adopted,' I said. '*Stolen.*'

Riley puckered her mouth like a fish.

'Are *you* happy to have the girl at home with you, Mrs Russell, knowing she's been frequenting a suspected drug dealer's abode?'

'Yes,' Mum said, tilting her head back haughtily, '*Ellen* has promised she is going to be good from now on. *Ellen* will be fine, with my help.' I smiled at Mum for emphasising my name, then looked at Miss Riley again.

'Well, if I hear you've been at that place again you'll have the magistrate to answer to. You've got to learn to keep out of trouble or be put inside for your own protection.'

'You must be joking,' I sniggered.

She gave me a long, hard stare with narrowed eyes, and I knew she was thinking: You *rude* girl.

She turned to my mother. 'Don't forget, Mrs Russell, your daughter is still under-age.'

'Thank you, Miss Riley,' Mum said, in a tone that meant: Thanks for nothing, now go. They walked to the front door and Mum opened it. Then Miss Riley was gone, a strong whiff of body odour lingering behind her.

When her footsteps faded at the bottom of the drive, Mum turned to me and said, 'She stinks!' and we both roared with laughter.

All night I couldn't sleep. A mosquito kept dive-bombing my face just as I drifted off, and when I tried to swot it blindly in the dark, I imagined it flattened somewhere on my bare skin with its insides spilling out. I didn't want to switch on the light because then I'd be wide awake. Even so, I tossed and turned till the sun strapped its dawn heat over the house and the birdsong cut through the hush.

At breakfast, which I was having in the kitchen with Mum, I asked for some money.

She said, 'You're up bright and early,' in a tone that meant it's high time I was up and about and getting *stuck in*.

'I want to take the bus out to Palm Beach for the day,' I said.

'Whatever for?' She eyed me suspiciously.

'Something to do. I like it out there. I might walk to the lighthouse.'

'Are you sure you're well enough, dear?'

'I'm fine, Mum. Honestly.'

'How about if I drive you to the bus stop? Then I could call in at the shop to pick up any mail and make sure everything's all right. I'll have to open up again on Monday, or we'll end up being hoboes!' she laughed. 'I don't think you should walk too far, though, Ellen,' she said more seriously. 'That path up to the lighthouse is a long way and it's very steep. Why don't you just stay in the picnic area, where you used to sit in that mulberry tree getting stains all over your clothes? Or go for a short walk along the beach?'

'Okay,' I shrugged. Secretly I was bristling at the way she was bossing me about again, but I didn't let it show – at least, I tried not to. She didn't seem to notice, anyway, and that's the main thing. I didn't want to be bad friends again.

The bus journey brought back all sorts of memories, because it went past the places I hated as a kid – the riding school at Warriewood with its dusty arena and tired ponies, the basketball courts where I played on Thursday nights till I got too embarrassed about my periods – the skirts were so short I was afraid my pad might show. And the hall where I went to Brownies and got caught bunking off to the beach, because Brown Owl was vicious. Mum pushed me into all these things, but all I wanted to do was swim or explore in the bush.

At Mona Vale the bus went the back way and we passed the little sandstone church where I was christened. I imagined standing by the font with Alicia in my arms while the minister sprinkled her forehead with cool water, all eyes on her. Then I thought: By the time we get round to it, she'll be as tall as me and able to bend over the font herself.

When the driver put his blinkers on to turn right at the golf course, I noticed him glancing nervously in the rear-vision mirror, then he stretched his neck to peer at the outside mirror.

'What's *he* up to?' he said loudly.

The bus was only half full, but everyone on board twisted around. A police car was nuzzling the back of the bus, as though it wanted us to pull over. My heart almost ground to a halt. Was it Miss Riley? No, it couldn't be, surely she wouldn't follow me in the middle of the day, in broad daylight. Would she?

I glanced over my shoulder again, and saw that the police driver had switched on the right-hand blinker and was trying to overtake. For a moment I thought they were going to turn on their siren and blue light, and wave the bus down, but then with a screech of tyres they overtook. Their vehicle curled in front of the bus before accelerating around a bend and vanishing.

I settled against the back of the seat once again and took a few slow, deep breaths to calm my nerves. So this is how it will be, I thought glumly. Like a hunted animal, forever looking over my shoulder in case Miss Riley is after me. I sighed. I thought of Sister Agnes at the hostel, and what she said about clichés. That's what I'd be, like an escaped convict, a cliché in an episode of *Perry Mason* or *Homicide*.

At Newport the bus took another detour, around the edge of Pittwater. Robbie's parents' house is somewhere along here, at the bottom of a bush-clad hill, set in an acre of gardens. I peered at every house faintly resembling his description, and even thought I might see his panel-van parked on one of the long driveways, but some of the houses were too far from the road, hidden by trees. I'd be lucky to find it.

Perhaps he was home with them right now, in the kitchen, with Lizzie. Always in the kitchen, so cosy and friendly. A real family. He wouldn't mention me, of course, or the fact I'd had a baby. *Our* baby. Oh, no. He'd skirt round that, all right, the way he weaves in and out of the waves on his surfboard, like a desert snake slithering at top speed across the burning sand. Alicia and me, we'd be the last thing on his mind.

When the bus rumbled up the hill along The Parade, I

could see my stop through the stand of red gums on a hairpin bend. I tugged the bell cord and the driver changed gear and pulled over.

'Thanks,' I said and stepped out on to the gravelled roadside.

I stood there for a long time, staring beyond the trees at the water and the boats in regimented rows. Jack's boat was there, smaller than most, but gleaming and proud all the same.

I looked at my watch. Just gone twelve o'clock. Would he be there? Scrubbing the decks? Fishing somewhere along the network of jetties? In the bar of the club, more likely, swigging on a schooner of beer with his mates. *Hail-fellow-well-met.* That's what they said about him in the District Officer's Home Report. I read it over Miss Riley's shoulder while standing in the court room.

When Mrs Russell remarried there was friction between girl and the stepfather, a bachelor, superficially jovial and hail-fellow-well-met, but immature and quick-tempered.

Quick-tempered. I screwed up my eyes and shaded them with one hand, trying to see if I could spot him, but I was too far away and the sun too bright. I turned to re-focus on the shaded stretch of road behind me, and when my eyes felt normal again I set off down the steep drive to the car park on the hill behind the clubhouse.

His ute was there in its usual place, in the top car park, outside the main entrance. I couldn't go inside the building – you have to be with a grown-up who's a member – so I continued down the steps at the side, past the children's play area. I knew every inch of the club grounds, because

I used to spend ages wandering around while Mum and Jack were upstairs in the bar playing the pokies. Every hour or so one of them would come looking for me with a pink lemonade and a bag of Smith's crisps.

Jack's small cruiser, nicknamed *Banjo Paterson*, was empty. It rocked and bobbed on the green water, and to anyone else it might have held the promise of a great day out. I stood staring down at the deck. There was the battered Esky that Jack stored his bait in, the sun-bleached deckchairs and the tackle box. All I remembered were long, dull Sundays watching the beer inflate Jack's stomach. Now and then he would haul a fish up and there'd be a minor rumpus, but Pittwater was chock-a-block with fish, so fishing wasn't exactly a challenge. Once I asked if Louise could come with us for the day, but he said no, the boat was too small for any more than three, and he was too tired after a hard week at his engineering factory designing tools. I was cursed with *fishing*.

I sat down on the edge of the jetty and let my legs dangle over the water. The smell of stale fish and dead crabs rose up from the sun-warmed timber. Seagulls circled overhead and one or two landed on the creaking masts.

I must've been sitting there for, oh, a good half an hour, idly watching the schools of yellow-striped fish, when his voice startled me. I spun round and there he was, all six foot four of him, walking towards me in shorts and brown sandals. If it wasn't for his deep, contagious laugh, I wouldn't have known him. He'd lost a lot of weight, his tummy was flat and the double chin that wobbled when he laughed had completely disappeared. He looked ten years younger. I had a good look, then stared at the water again. My heart was hammering. He was with another bloke who wore white trousers and a navy-blue captain's cap. They were almost right behind me and still Jack didn't notice me. I suppose I was the last person on earth he expected to see.

Then he saw me, because I could feel his eyes on my back. A silence fell, and after a while he said grimly to his friend, 'Excuse me, will you, Hugh, I'll see you upstairs later.'

'Sure, Jack. Catch up with you at the meeting,' the other man said, and he walked off towards the far end of the wharf.

For a minute I thought Jack was just going to ignore me, get on the boat and speed off. He stood behind me and I glanced round nervously and said, 'Hello.'

'What are you doing here?' he said gruffly. 'Haven't you done enough damage?'

'Yes,' I said. 'I have.' I thought: *So have you*, but I didn't say it, though I was tempted.

I swung my legs back and forth, wildly.

He clambered down on to the deck of *Banjo*, then reached up to load a new Esky aboard. I grabbed the handle before he could and lifted it down to him under lowered eyes. He inched his way along the starboard ledge to haul up the anchor and untie the bow ropes. When he glanced back at me, I looked away.

Back at the wheel he turned the ignition key and the inboard motor churned and boiled under the boat's belly.

My heart was pounding, because I knew in a minute or two he'd be chugging out of the harbour and it'd be too late.

'Untie that rope, will you,' he shouted just then, 'and get in.'

I did as he said, fast, and before I knew it I was sitting right next to him, because he patted the seat with his hand, indicating that he wanted me to. I peered through the windshield. I thought: This feels weird, because usually I perch on the bow with my legs over the side and my face in the wind, as far away as possible from Jack. As we nosed out into the sun-filled bay it felt like the first time I'd ever been on board his boat.

He tucked the boat in the shelter of a small cove on the south side of Lion Island, where the Pacific rolls in between the Heads. While I dropped the bow anchor and watched it hurtle into the depths, Jack disappeared inside the cabin.

When I clambered back along the narrow ridge, he was bent over on the deck peering inside a large sack. He tipped it upside-down and out tumbled snorkels, flippers and face-masks.

'Where'd you get those?' I said, stepping on to the deck.

'I've had them a while,' he said, matter-of-factly. He handed me the smaller pair of flippers.

'But I haven't got my swimsuit.' I felt disappointed, because the water might do me good, especially now the bleeding had stopped. And I wanted to stay close to Jack, now I'd come this far. But there was one thing worrying me.

'There's an old one of your mother's in the cabin,' he said. 'It might be a bit old-fashioned, but out here no one except me will see you.'

'But . . . aren't there a lot of sharks round the island?'

He grinned and snorted, as if I was talking complete rubbish.

'A few,' he said, 'but I've got a spear-gun. You'll be safe with me.'

He undid the buttons on his blue shirt and took it off. Now that his stomach had gone his chest seemed bigger, as though that part of his body had been inverted.

I slipped into the cabin to change. My mother's cossie was there in a basket, and an old towel. At the bottom of the basket were a pair of sunglasses, a bottle of tanning lotion, a lipstick and a faded black-and-white photograph of me and Mum. I was aged about eight. I looked stiff and unhappy, because she'd put me in tight black ski pants, a white polo-neck sweater and a red waistcoat. We were standing on a beach, posing for God-knows-who.

I went back on deck, self-consciously adjusting Mum's cossie. Jack must have noticed my tattoos and the marks on my back, but he didn't say a word. I tensed, because I wasn't ready to explain everything just yet.

We were in the water for two hours and didn't see one shark. I was aware of my heart thumping beneath Mum's black one-piece. There was so much I wanted to say to Jack.

It was hard to keep up with him, because he was a strong swimmer and dead-accurate with his spear-gun – he shot three big bream, one after the other, and stuffed them in a net bag. Blood seeped out of their wounds and clouded the water pink. He surfaced and threw them on to the boat. I was right next to him, treading water.

'Blood attracts sharks,' he said. 'Never leave a dying fish in the water.'

We climbed aboard and dried off, then spread our towels on the scorched deck. The Esky was full of soft drinks and fruit, not a can of beer in sight. Jack handed me a paper bag of sandwiches. We sat munching, and when I finished he offered me a peach.

'My favourite,' I said. I leant over the side and plunged it in the sea. The boat was rolling and dipping, but not uncomfortably. I sat down again and rubbed the peach gently with a corner of my towel. When all the fur had disappeared I took a bite. It tasted sweet and salty.

'I had a baby,' I said at last. I watched Jack's response. 'A baby girl. I called her Alicia. It means *noble*. I looked it up.'

He stopped chewing. The sea had dulled his silver hair. He smoothed it off his forehead with the palm of his hand. His blue eyes looked sad.

He gestured at my scars. 'That her?'

'She's been adopted,' I said.

'Geeze,' he breathed. 'How's your mother?'

'Upset.'

'She's not the only one.' He sighed.

'I think she misses you.'

He raised his eyebrows. We put our peaches down, as though they were weapons, or as if it was rude to keep eating. Like when someone dies and everyone's embarrassed to come right out with things, to say: *Sorry*, or *Isn't death terrible.* Instead there's a hush and you can hear the rumble of tummies.

'I've never had children,' he said. He looked at me. 'I didn't know what to do.'

'I don't know how to look after a baby. But I would have learnt, given the chance,' I said.

'Will you ever see the baby?'

I shrugged. 'One day I'll find her. I *hope*.'

Our fruit was toasting in the sun. I scraped the soles of my feet along the ruts of the deck. A wasp buzzed near my peach. I shooed it away, but it hovered stubbornly. I stood up, finished the peach, then rinsed my hands in the sea. The wasp had jetted across to Jack's peach, but before it had a chance to land, Jack smashed it between his hands.

'Time we both grew up,' he said. The wasp fell to the floor, kicking its legs.

I nodded. 'Yep.'

There was a long pause. I was trying to avoid a fight, but it wasn't easy. I watched him as he sat opposite me, absorbing my news. His face showed a mixture of amazement and sadness.

Then I said, 'They put me away, you know. In Gunyah.'

He shook his head in disbelief. 'Christ!' he said, 'I'm sorry, Ellen. I didn't think they'd do that. I thought they'd just give you a fright – you know, give you a good talking to.'

I felt as if my head might explode when he said that, because for a grown-up he seemed so clueless. But I took a deep breath and waited till the words on my tongue thawed.

'I never meant to hurt you,' he said. He looked at me. His eyes were a clear blue, ringed by a crisp white border.

'Why don't you ring Mum up?' I said in a choked voice. His face brightened.

'I've had plenty of time to think these past six months. I want to be friends with you,' he said.

'Me too.'

'Do you think there's much point phoning? She might slam the phone down.'

'Mum would never do that. She's too polite.'

'You think she'd want to see me?'

'I don't know,' I said. I thought: You dummy, Ellen, why didn't you say: Yes, ring her up, make friends and *come home.* 'Why don't you try?' I said. 'That's what I've been doing.'

There was another long pause. He ran his hand through his hair in an exasperated way, like it was all too much to take in.

'Let's get back in the water,' he said. He shaded his eyes with one hand and looked up at the sky. 'It's too hot sitting here.'

Fifteen

May 1971

The view from the cliff is perfect this morning.

The lake is a clear cobalt blue. I can see the sand bars beneath the water, spread like ribs across the breadth of it. If I screw up my eyes and concentrate hard enough, I can almost see the crabs scuttling along the strip of beach on the far side, making the most of their freedom before the skiers arrive when the water has warmed. A mob of cockatoos are screeching in the valley, trying to win some attention and tit-bits from the neighbours. Just beneath me, on the top of a tree, a solitary magpie is dissecting a lizard with its beak. I was the only kid in the neighbourhood who was ever game enough to jump off this cliff and land on the mattress of vines on the tree-tops – even the Foote kids, who were used to pain, wouldn't try it.

I'm sitting under my favourite umbrella tree. It hasn't

changed much, except that the roots, which grip the scorched rocks, are healed over now – I used to carve messages and my name on them with a stick or sharp stones. It's a stubborn tree, because it never bled sap; it was bone-dry.

My mother is hanging out her aqua-blue trousersuit on the Hills Hoist; she was squeezing it in the concrete tub in the laundry when I set off, said she wanted to get it dry for her last dinner out with Jack tonight. They're going to their favourite restaurant to say goodbye. When she turns to go back into the house, she stops to look up at the cliff. I think she can't see me, because the sun is too savage and she's way down in the shadows. She lifts her arm to wave. For a few seconds I don't do a thing. Then I raise my hand and wave back; she catches sight of me and waves frantically, as though she hasn't seen me for years.

I used to spend hours sitting here, just looking at the view. Once, on a hot summer's day, when my mother and Jack were in the bedroom with the door locked, I sat here staring into the leafy back yards of the houses up the hill. In one a man was mowing grass; in another a woman was hanging out washing; next door to her a group of kids from my school splashed in a pool.

The sun was boiling that day. I wiped the sweat from my forehead and felt the streaks of sticky dirt on my face. I inched along the cliff edge to the shade of the umbrella tree and settled in between its roots with the dust and the ants. Now and then I glanced up at the whorls of glossy leaves that drooped around me in graceful circles, like the folds of a Victorian parasol. After gazing into the back yards for a while, I clambered down the rock to a ledge below. I knew I wouldn't be able to get up again. There were no footholds and the moss crumbled underfoot.

For a moment I hesitated, my pulse racing, then I opened my mouth and yelled 'Help' at the top of my lungs.

They all stopped dead, as though in a game of statues, then turned their faces up at me, squinting at the blinding blue. One kid pointed and yelled, but the words bounced off the rock-face and fell back on them in a dull echo.

Then the pool lady disappeared into the house and popped out of the front door a few minutes later on to the street. She was dragging a thick rope.

She charged up the hill, then shot into a thicket of bush at the top of the road, where I knew that a path led to the cliff top.

A while later – it felt like for ever at the time – she appeared on the ridge above me, pouring sweat and swearing between tight lips. She threw down the end of the rope and hauled me up.

I stood in front of her, blinking. She was panting loudly. She smelt of chlorine and her hot breath was tainted with pineapple juice.

'Thank you,' I said, beaming.

I waited, hoping she'd say: Want to come for a swim? But she just said, 'You should be at home with your parents.' She gave me a withering look and stomped off through the bush, tutting like a cranky bird.

I've come up here for a different reason today. I've come to have one last look at the place where I grew up. Because tomorrow we're going away.

Jim keeps ringing me up, and Mum said if I don't make a new life she'll get Miss Riley to put me away again, for my own good. I don't really believe her, but if Gunyah did anything it made me scared to go back there, and that in itself has a pretty strong effect on a person's behaviour. Some of those girls, they'll be back and forth for years, then they'll be sent to the women's prison when they turn eighteen. Not me.

Robbie's dumped me and gone off with Lizzie; I'm frightened of Jim; Louise is a dead loss; Mary's locked up; and the Foote kids have moved out west. And I'm scared of Miss Riley hassling me. So we decided it'd be best to go away. Even though I don't want to be too far away from where Alicia was born, it doesn't matter now that she's adopted, because she could be anywhere. So we're going to Port Mitchell, with Jack.

It was Jack's decision to go there.

'We got on all right that time, don't you reckon?' he said one morning at breakfast. He'd been back about three weeks. Things were going okay, I thought, but I could tell the small house was getting on his nerves.

'Up there we could get a decent-sized place with some land,' he said. 'Might take your mind off things,' he went on, looking at me.

I was making a big effort, helping round the house, being polite, not answering back, and I even managed to make him laugh sometimes. Once he was snoring on the couch and I recorded it on a cassette. When I played it back he chased me out the back door and up the yard, laughing his head off.

There was another reason he wanted to go. To do with his factory. 'Can't get any half-decent blokes on board any more,' he complained. 'Nothing but long-haired surfies applying. Bludgers,' he sniffed hatefully. So he decided to put the factory up for sale, along with his boat and the ute.

'Berenice will take the gift shop, she's had her eye on it for a while,' Mum said enthusiastically. 'She might take my car, too.'

'Let's do something different,' Jack said, wiping the toast crumbs off his stubbly chin.

'Sounds fishy,' Mum said warily.

'*Exactly*. That's it!' Jack exclaimed. 'Deep-sea fishing for serious fishermen. With the money from the factory and the boat, we could get a catamaran or a clipper.'

'I'll help,' Mum said. 'I could pack a picnic for everyone, charge extra. And while you're off at sea I can make a bit extra doing dressmaking.'

I said I still wasn't sure what I wanted to do for a career, but I'd do waitressing, or nursing with geriatrics, just till I decided. Mum said we can go to a careers advisor. I might even go to college and get some more qualifications.

'But till I decide, I could help with the boat, maybe,' I said.

'Course you can,' Jack said. 'Strong girl like you. You could take people snorkelling if they want to get in the water. You're a terrific swimmer.'

I beamed.

We're going to rent a house first, with three bedrooms, so there'll be no problem with Jack's snoring, like there was on holiday up there. And they even said I can have friends to stay, when I make some, which I've never done before because this place is too small. I'll never barge into Mum's bedroom again, either. I'll make sure they get their privacy.

When Jack said we were going I knew straight away I'd like it there. Because wherever you are in Port Mitchell you can see my island in the distance, out in the middle of the bay, like a green jewel. I'll be able to look at it whenever I like and imagine I'm there with Alicia. In the isolation cell at Gunyah, I imagined her sleeping in a cot by my bed here at home, and I even pictured us crammed into the room at Searles Court with Robbie. But those mirages always faded and my island kept popping into my mind instead.

I know it's silly to think I could live on an island with a tiny baby and be all right, but because it's only in my head it doesn't matter, because I know now that until I find her, or she finds me, it's the closest I'll ever get to real happiness. I still don't know what I want to do for a job, but I do know this. If Alicia wants to find me one day, I want to be ready for that day. I want to be someone. Not a drug addict, not a hippie, not a gaol-bird or a slut. I'll make something of myself, then one day I'll come back to Sydney, to try and track her down. I want her to meet a good mother, a mother who is healthy and sensible, and boring probably, but a mother she can rely on if she needs me. Because one day she might. You never know.

Mum took me shopping for new clothes when the decision

to go was final. She even let me choose; said I could have a pair of jeans and one long dress, so I made an effort to pick things she approved of. I decided to wear the jeans on the train, and a plain white T-shirt. My hair's been cut in a modern style, too, and earlier this morning Mum gave me an opal necklace.

'Your father gave me this,' she said, solemnly. She was bleary-eyed from their night out. Jack was grumpy at the kitchen table, eating the fruit Mum forced on him. We'd left him to it and gone out to the quiet of the back verandah. Mum clasped the necklace at the nape of my neck. The feel of her fingers on my skin made me cranky, but I breathed in and waited until she'd finished.

'It's the only thing he ever gave me, apart from my wedding ring,' she said. 'Look after it.' I touched it and held it up to the light. It was green and blue, mostly, but in the centre it had a golden glow, like an eye.

Later, when the last few things had been packed into boxes, the removal men came and went, and we swooped through the house for anything that had been forgotten. It felt odd in the empty rooms, as though no one had ever lived there; and as Jack closed the front door for the last time, I didn't feel upset or sad at all. In fact I was glad to be going, because Alicia was all around me here, and I felt like screaming sometimes, or punching myself. I wanted to stop all that nonsense and feel normal again.

Mum sat in the back of the taxi with me. She kept twisting her white gloves, and now and then she squeezed my hand. We sat in silence, listening to Jack and the Yugoslavian driver yack on about rugby and fishing. I wound down the window and put my face to the wind, but after a while Mum said, 'Wind that window up, Ellen, it's blowing my hair to billyo.' I did as I was told, even though it went against the grain; after a few minutes the rage inside me went away. But I couldn't help wondering how long I could keep this up, being good, being nice.

The opal looks beautiful against the white of my top, here in the cool, dim light of Central Station; it has more depth in the shadows than it does in the blazing sun.

After collecting our tickets, we find a bench and watch the hordes of restless travellers decked in cameras and bags. Some are shoving swollen trolleys along, and now and then a worried mother rattles past gripping a pram or a buggy. When I see them my heart skips a few beats. But I turn my face away and think of Port Mitchell.

There is an announcement over the Tannoy. It is muffled and the voice bounces around the high ceiling like a steel-winged bird. It's a strain to hear the words properly, but I just manage to catch them.

'Platform Three to Grafton! That's us,' I cry. I gather up my shoulder bag and jacket. 'Come on, let's go. I can't wait!'

'Are you ready, Gracie?' Jack says. He looks into my mother's eyes. Their arms are linked. She nods and smiles. They stand together in one smooth movement, as though they are one. As they turn to follow me across the main thoroughfare, they are left behind for a few moments, and Mum seems hesitant. Jack leaves her side to position himself behind the trolley loaded with our suitcases. Mum is looking this way and that, for the right platform number.

But I know exactly which way to go, because I made a point of reading the signs when we arrived, and I asked at the ticket counter, just to be absolutely sure. Right down the far end, the lady said, near the main entrance.

When I'm a few feet away I call over my shoulder, 'This way, Mum.'

'You go with Ellen, I'll catch up,' I can hear Jack saying. He begins to coax the trolley around the outside edge of the throng, where there's more room. Other passengers, too, are struggling with pigheaded trolleys; business types rush to catch their trains; nervous tourists are gathered in loose bunches inspecting their luggage and tickets for the umpteenth time.

Without hesitating, I slice a path through the crowd towards Platform Three. So Mum does.

Acknowledgements

There are many people to thank for believing in this book. Firstly, you, the reader, for reading it. My husband, Jaime Gilbert, for his inspiring editorial advice and encouragement. My daughter, Lucille Bethell, for the perfect title. My son, David Bethell, and Lucille, for their patient understanding with my frequent trips to Australia. My mother, Gloria Entwistle, for accepting my motives for writing the book. She would not have wanted me committed to Parramatta had she known the truth. My friends in the UK, Australia and France for their loyalty. Bonnie Djuric, for her hard work to preserve the Parramatta Female Factory Precinct, (which includes Parramatta Girls' Home) as an International Site of Conscience.

Thanks to my publisher at Hachette Australia, Vanessa Radnidge, for her high-octane energy and competence. Little, Brown, London for backing me in the first place. Fiona Hazard at Hachette Australia for identifying the significance of the book. The team at Hachette Australia for getting behind it and making some fast decisions. The Arvon Foundation, U.K. *SHE*

Magazine, London. A.M. Heath, London, for their unwavering support. Lily Arthur at Origins Australia, for her help with adoption research.

And last but not least, my original publisher and dear friend at Little, Brown, London, Barbara Daniel, who has been loyal and tenacious throughout.

I am forever grateful to all of you.

Maree Giles, 2014
www.mareegiles.com